AMISH SWEETHEARTS

"Those are good trees," she told him. "Now, whenever I see them, I'll think of us." She tilted her head and squinted. "But tell, which one is me?"

He chuckled. "The prettiest one."

"Now I know you're just courting me." Essie had never considered herself to be a beauty. With glossy brown hair the color of caramel and eyes just a bit darker, she knew that she fit into Gott's world just fine, but she didn't spend too much time looking in the mirror or fussing over her hair. During her rumspringa, when other girls snuck out of the house in English clothes and lipstick, Essie had stuck with her clean-scrubbed face, simple dresses, and kapp. There was too much to do in the course of a day to waste time painting faces and shopping for tight, impractical clothes.

"I *am* courting you. So I guess it's working." Harlan shifted toward her until their knees were touching and his face was just inches away. "It's not every girl who sees the beauty in two trees, in the song of the river on the rocks, in a simple carved flower. I love you, Essie. I hope you'll have me as a husband just as soon as I can get enough money squared away."

"You know I will." Her heart seemed to grow in her chest as he leaned closer and pressed his lips to hers . . .

BOOK YOUR PLACE ON OUR WEBSITE AND MAKE THE READING CONNECTION!

We've created a customized website just for our very special readers, where you can get the inside scoop on everything that's going on with Zebra, Pinnacle and Kensington books.

When you come online, you'll have the exciting opportunity to:
- View covers of upcoming books
- Read sample chapters
- Learn about our future publishing schedule (listed by publication month and author)
- Find out when your favorite authors will be visiting a city near you
- Search for and order backlist books from our online catalog
- Check out author bios and background information
- Send e-mail to your favorite authors
- Meet the Kensington staff online
- Join us in weekly chats with authors, readers and other guests
- Get writing guidelines
- AND MUCH MORE!

Visit our website at
http://www.kensingtonbooks.com

An AMISH HOMECOMING

Rosalind Lauer

ZEBRA BOOKS
KENSINGTON PUBLISHING CORP.
www.kensingtonbooks.com

Acknowledgments

My time in the fictitious town of Joyful River has provided a delightful escape from some difficult realities, and I am grateful to have the opportunity to start a new series featuring the Amish of Lancaster County. As with any novel, it takes a team of dedicated individuals to make an idea fly, and I am blessed to have many talented individuals working with me. My editor John Scognamiglio always leads with an interest in new things and a strong sense of what people like to read; he's the best! I'm grateful to copy editor Debbie Kane for saving me from my own mistakes and understanding how a story should flow and make sense. Robin Rue is a dream agent with vision, enthusiasm, and a great sense of what matters in life. I'm so fortunate that she makes things good happen all around her.

While I was writing this book I was reminded how blessed I was to have the guidance of Dr. Violet Dutcher at an important juncture in my life. With generosity and vivid detail, Vi shared how it felt to have parents who had been raised Amish and what it was like to step into Amish life on occasion. Her experiences of summers and reunions with her Amish family inspired me to write about the bridges that can be built between cultures, the connections that all folks share, and the power of love.

As I write this bit of a thank you, I'm deep into the tale of Sadie and Sam, the main characters in Joyful River #2. For now, it's a wonderful good place to be!

Chapter One

With fields of green and the sun setting pink and orange against the rolling hills, the yard was pretty as a summer page from a calendar. In the distance, the twins were playing cornhole with Lizzie, while little Sarah Rose pushed herself on the tire swing, chattering to no one in particular. A perfect day for daughter Essie's celebration. Miriam Lapp let her eyes roam the yard and imagined how it might be transformed for the event that was bound to happen once wedding season rolled around in October.

They would put a new coat of paint on the barn door, and trim back the bushes along the fence line to make space for the wedding tent. They would bring in the rented wagons with benches and china for dining, as well as ovens, sinks, and stoves for food preparation. Inside the house, they would scrub the walls, wash the windows, and wax the floors. An Amish home had best be clean and shiny when hosting a wedding.

Their oldest daughter's wedding! Joy danced in Miriam's heart, making her giggle.

She hadn't dared mention it to Alvin, who would have reminded her to keep patient. Essie and Harlan weren't even engaged yet, but anyone could see the spark in their daughter's eyes whenever Harlan was near. Their Essie was in love, and Harlan had it bad as well. The boy melted like ice cream when Essie spoke. He'd been invited today to celebrate Essie's eighteenth birthday, and Miriam wouldn't be surprised if those two got engaged before the sun went down.

Miriam let the screen door close behind her and squinted against the lemony sun of the late afternoon. The picnic tables were set for dinner, the mouthwatering aroma of grilled chicken filled the air, and wisps of smoke rose from the charcoal grill where her team of cooks was finishing the last of the roasting for Essie's special dinner.

"How do you know when they're done?" Annie asked her grandmother.

"The kabobs need to soften a bit," Esther said. "We want a little black around the edges. A few more minutes, and we'll have a fine meal without heating up the kitchen on this hot August day."

That had been Miriam's plan. This week the thermometer in this part of Lancaster County had been soaring to the nineties. They needed to do what they could to keep the house cool. "You know, most of the vegetables came right from our garden. The tomatoes are sweet as candy, and the zucchini seems to grow bigger overnight. Alvin will be happy for zucchini bread."

"Yes, Gott is good to provide such a bountiful garden for us," Esther said as she supervised the grilling process. Since it was the eldest daughter's birthday, cooking duties had fallen on sixteen-year-old Annie, who kept offering the tongs to her grandmother. Annie preferred stable duty to kitchen tasks.

"Do you want to take over, Mammi?" Annie asked. "You're such a good cook. You make everything taste better."

"You'll learn with time and practice." With ten grown children of her own, Esther was too wise to fall for Annie's flattery. "Keep going until you finish."

"You're doing a great job, Annie," Miriam said, moving the platters of roasted chicken over to the picnic tables, which had been set with checkered tablecloths and enough plates and flatware for eleven people. A warm breeze shimmered through the trees on the fence line, filling the air with the scent of lilac. The clip-clop of horses' hooves drew her attention to the driveway, where the family buggy had turned in from the main road. "Looks like our men are back from their errands," Miriam said.

"My sons are never late for dinner." Esther's tone was flat, but Miriam knew she was joking. Under that stoic façade lay a heart of gold and a fine sense of humor.

"Can I be done now?" Annie asked. She lifted a kabob with the tongs, nodded, and placed it on the platter.

"I'd say so," Miriam said. "Looks like everything's ready. Everything but the birthday girl. Where's Essie? And Harlan's supposed to be here."

"He got here half an hour ago," Annie reported. "Essie went for a walk with him. And she's wearing her Sunday dress."

"They went down to the river," Esther said, untying her cooking apron.

Miriam couldn't help but smile at the sweet notion of the two of them dipping their toes in the cool, clear waters. Those two might be engaged by the time they made it to the supper table! She took the platter of kabobs from

Annie. "Go get your brothers and sisters to wash their hands. And send one of the twins down to the river to fetch Essie and Harlan."

"Which one?"

"Let them go together. They can make it a race." As Miriam placed the platter on the table, her husband lumbered toward her with only a slight hitch in his gait. You'd never know that he'd suffered a torn ligament recently when a cow had knocked into him in the milking barn. Gott had blessed him with quick healing. "You're back, in the nick of time."

"The smell of chicken guided us home." He patted her shoulder, lifted his hat, and wiped his brow with a handkerchief. The outer edges of his eyes had laugh lines that were permanent now, and it delighted her to know that this man always had a smile in his heart, always had a hug for his children or a kind word for folks who needed it. Ah, when there was true love in a man's heart, it shone in his eyes. She always told her girls that; she hoped that it helped them find happiness with their husbands.

"Can we eat now?" Lizzie asked as she skipped toward the table and noticed the chicken and kabobs piled high.

"Go wash your hands; take Sarah Rose, too."

"I can take myself, Mem," the little girl said as she trudged past the tables toward the house. Her dress was smudged with a grass stain, her kapp slightly askew.

"Our bundle of energy," Alvin observed. "One of the first up in the morning, and she's still going strong. I don't know how she does it."

"She's got your energy, Alvie. Did you find the mason jars in town?"

"We did," he said. "Three dozen of them. That should be enough for Essie's jam."

"With the strawberries ripening so fast in our garden, and all those wild blackberries along the road, you never know."

"If we need more, we'll go back to Melvin's dry goods store," Sam said as he approached from the lane, where he'd tied Brownie to the post, planning to unhitch the buggy after dinner. Sam was twenty, their oldest son, and a big help around the dairy farm since Alvin's injury. "Why did you need so many?"

"Essie's having a jamming frolic with her friends. Many hands make quick work, and it's a blessing that she's taken over that task for me," Miriam said.

The children were filing out of the house, taking their seats at the table as Alvin's mother poured lemonade and water. Paul and Peter came running around the side of the house.

"They're coming," Peter called as he whipped open the screen door and disappeared inside to wash up. Paul caught the door before it closed and sent it flying open again.

"Boys." Alvin sighed. "They're hard on a house."

"They'll learn," Esther said. "Boys don't know their own might."

Smiling, Miriam waited for her husband to take a seat on the bench. It was a slower process since the injury, but like most men, Alvin didn't want any more assistance than was absolutely necessary.

This was one of the finest hours, their family assembling for a meal at the end of the day, about to share the bounty of Gott's blessing. They had much to be grateful for here in Joyful River. Miriam breathed in the scents of their dinner, the flowers, the grass, and the summer evening as her gaze swept over the broad lawn.

The flash of something metallic in the distance caught her eye. A car on the road. A Jeep coming down their lane. Visitors? Or some English folk who'd taken a wrong turn?

The vehicle pressed on with determination, convincing her that it was someone they knew. "Looks like we have visitors."

All eyes turned toward the lane, where tires crunched on gravel as the car drew closer. The vehicle made a wide sweep around the tethered horse and buggy and pulled up to the stretch of green lawn.

"Who is it?" Lizzie asked, putting down her lemonade.

It was hard to tell, with the windows shaded to the color of ash, but the mystery was soon solved when one door opened and a tall, lanky man emerged from the driver seat.

"It's your Uncle Sully," Miriam told the children. "Looks like the girls, too."

"Did they drive over all the way from Philadelphia?" asked Alvin.

Miriam shrugged. "I haven't heard from them since . . . since Sarah's passing." It had been a rainy week in May, more than a year ago, when Miriam had gotten word that her sister had passed. Ovarian cancer had struck hard, and Gott had taken her swiftly, leaving behind her loving husband and three daughters.

Miriam had told the children to dress in their church clothes, and Alvin had hired a van to drive them to Philly for the English funeral. It had been a strange sensation, going into Sarah's house, sitting in her kitchen at a shiny marble counter and looking out into the garden plot, trees dripping overhead. It was a gift to see Sarah's world just one time, a picture of how her older sister had lived in the two decades since she'd left her family and her Amish community behind.

Sully raised his hand in a greeting, but as he approached his shoulders sagged and hc seemed weary. Gray, as if age had been sapping the color from him. The man her sister Sarah had once fallen in love with, fallen so hard that she up and left their family, left the plain way of living, was in a bad way. He almost looked worse than he had the last time she'd seen him, over a year ago at Sarah's funeral.

He paused, turned back, motioned toward the vehicle. "Come on out, girls," he called. "Time to face the music."

The Lapp family was unusually silent as the other doors opened, and one by one Sully's daughters, Miriam's own nieces emerged. First came Serena, one of the twins, her toffee brown hair falling like a shiny curtain over her shoulders. Always the social butterfly, she gave a nervous smile as she walked toward the family.

Miriam didn't recognize the next girl who stepped out, a cute thing with pink hair and a ring in her nose. Could it be Grace, the youngest one? She was probably fifteen or sixteen by now, and, from the way she stared down at the ground as she followed Serena, it was clear she was not happy. Both girls wore little denim shorts and tops that seemed to be barely more than an undergarment adorned with thin ribbons and lace.

Then came Megan, quite similar to her twin, except her hair had been cut short and she dressed like an athlete in baggy shorts and an oversized T-shirt. She slammed the door of the Jeep, leaned against it, and folded her arms, clearly not eager to budge from her place.

Miriam asked Annie to go inside to fetch more plates

and utensils, then hurried over to greet their visitors on the path.

"Well, isn't this a nice surprise! When I saw that car coming down the road, I'd have never guessed it was you."

"Miriam." Sully took her hand between his and gave a warm squeeze. "Sorry to descend on you without notice."

"Family is always welcome." Alvin paused at Miriam's side. "It's good you're here, just in time for supper." His attempt at lightening things up was lost on Sully.

"I didn't know where else to turn." From this close, Miriam could see how worn-out Sully looked. "I've been up all night and all day, trying to think of a solution, a way to keep them safe." He shook his head. "And you're my only hope."

Miriam pursed her lips, her heart aching for Sully and his family. "Tell us, what's the problem?"

"The girls are a mess," Sully said, his low voice raspy with misery. "I can't think of any other way to save them. I need you to take my girls."

Chapter Two

Essie Lapp had noticed the visitors and their vehicle as soon as she and Harlan had rounded the corner of the house. As she'd drawn closer, she'd recognized her uncle and cousins, the English relatives who lived in the big city of Philadelphia. The dark, sad look in the girls' eyes made it clear that they hadn't driven out to be a part of Essie's birthday celebration.

"Looks like some English visitors," Harlan said.

"My uncle and cousins. You've met the girls. They used to visit with their mem."

"The girls who lost their mem," he said, sympathy glimmering in his amber eyes.

"That's them." As Harlan and Essie walked, her fingers traced the small, mounded petals of the flower Harlan had carved for her on a block of wood. A bookend, made by his very own hands. The weighted block could be used to keep her books in order, lined up on the dresser in the bedroom.

The carved flower was the most special gift she had ever received. It warmed her heart that Harlan had given her a practical gift that would complement the books that had entertained her over the years. But mostly, it was the hours he had spent carving and chiseling wood that made her smile. Whenever she saw the bookend, she would think of Harlan carving by the light of the kerosene lamp to make sure the flower was symmetrical, the wood smooth to the touch.

Her fingertips curved over the smooth ridges of the flower now, but it could not stop the storm looming ahead. Something was very wrong. Essie's pulse quickened in that nervous way of an animal on alert as she and Harlan hurried toward Mem and Dat.

"Now, Sully, I'm sure you don't mean this," Mem said in a soothing voice.

"I do," her uncle insisted. "It's the only way."

"I'm out." Over on the gravel stone drive, cousin Megan pushed away from the car and started heading down the path that cut past the barn.

"Megan!" her twin sister hollered. "Where are you going? Come back here!"

Without turning back, Megan kept stalking off in the other direction.

"Where is she going?" Uncle Sully raked a hand back through his graying hair. "She shouldn't be alone. She could be a danger to herself."

A danger to herself? Wondering what that meant, Essie turned to Harlan, but there was only confusion in his warm amber eyes.

"Megan!" Sully shouted after her. "Come back!"

But Megan kept walking, prompting her sisters to call after her. Sarah Rose and Lizzie, the littlest Lapp children, chimed in, but Megan pretended not to hear anyone.

"Follow her," Miriam told Essie.

Essie nodded, handing her carved bookend to Harlan for safekeeping. "What do I say?"

"Comfort her. I don't know what's going on, but Sully and all his girls seem out of sorts."

Essie obeyed her mother, motioning to Harlan to stay put before she started off after her cousin. Such an unexpected twist in the celebration, like a sudden shift in the weather, but Essie couldn't let it dampen her good mood.

The joy of Harlan's special gift.

The wonder of his kiss.

"Your birthday is like a holiday," he had teased, taking her hand in his as they sat on the rock ledge, overlooking the gurgling water. "Zed let me off work early so I could be here for your birthday dinner."

"Don't go getting in trouble with Zed on account of me," she said, knowing how much Harlan needed the job at the furniture factory.

"You are the last girl who could be trouble," he said, pressing his fingertips to the side of her face. The line he drew along her jawline sent little sparks of sensation down her neck. "That's one of the things I love about you. Serious, practical Essie. You've got your feet on the ground, firmly planted."

"Just like you."

"Like me. The two of us are two strong trees, standing on solid ground, reaching for the sky." He nodded toward the far riverbank, where two oaks stood side by side. "Like those trees there."

With their straight trunks and upturned branches capped by fat green leaves, the trees seemed to be shouting: "Hooray!" The light breeze flickered through the round, green treetops, like a thousand glimmering fish in the pond.

"Those are good trees," she told him. "Now, whenever I see them, I'll think of us." She tilted her head and squinted. "But tell, which one is me?"

He chuckled. "The prettiest one."

"Now I know you're just courting me." Essie had never considered herself to be a beauty. With glossy brown hair the color of caramel and eyes just a bit darker, she knew that she fit into Gott's world just fine, but she didn't spend too much time looking in the mirror or fussing over her hair. During her rumspringa, when other girls snuck out of the house in English clothes and lipstick, Essie had stuck with her clean-scrubbed face, simple dresses, and kapp. There was too much to do in the course of a day to waste time painting faces and shopping for tight, impractical clothes.

"I *am* courting you. So I guess it's working." Harlan shifted toward her until their knees were touching and his face was just inches away. "It's not every girl who sees the beauty in two trees, in the song of the river on the rocks, in a simple carved flower. I love you, Essie, and now that you're eighteen, I hope you'll have me as a husband just as soon as I can get enough money squared away."

"You know I will." Her heart seemed to grow in her chest as he leaned closer and pressed his lips to hers. The kiss that swept over the sensitive nub at the center of her lips was both gentle and bold.

A whisper of love on the wind.

A searing brand, marking her as his one and only love.

She touched one fingertip to her lips now, wishing she could bring back the wondrous moment of their kiss, as well as the hopeful conversation about the future—their future. Although Harlan sometimes made decisions with the slowness of a man whose boots were stuck in the mud, he had mentioned once again that he hoped they could get engaged soon. Just as soon as he had saved enough money for them to build a place of their own. Harlan was so responsible that way. He didn't want a repeat of what had happened to him, with his father leaving the family, and them losing their house. Although Mem said there was nothing shameful about living in an apartment, Harlan felt bad about it. Not that he would talk much about those very difficult years he'd gone through with his mem and sister, but Essie could tell.

When you loved someone, you got a little peek inside his heart.

After their sweet time together by the river, Essie hadn't expected to be pulled away from Harlan at the sight of the English visitors. But here she was, trying to catch the girl, who seemed nimble as a deer.

"Megan!" she called. "Wait for me." She hoped that her cousin would stop or slow down a bit so that she could catch up without running in her special church dress. But Megan kept streaking ahead at a swift pace.

With a huffing sigh, Essie broke into a run. Once she caught up, she wasn't quite sure what she'd say to her cousin, besides asking what was wrong. Since Mem's sister Sarah had jumped the fence, leaving Joyful River when she was eighteen and giving up the plain life, Mem and Aunt Sarah had drifted apart. But Mem always said that sisters are sisters for life, and Essie couldn't imagine losing one of her own sisters to the English world.

Aunt Sarah had brought her girls around each summer,

and all the cousins had made memories picking berries, yanking weeds in Mem's garden, and swimming in the river. Over the years Essie and her siblings had enjoyed having her cousins around. Since Aunt Sarah had chosen not to be baptized, her exit from the community hadn't been punished by a ban. There was no shunning, no sitting at separate tables or refusing to look her in the eye, as had happened with another couple in their community.

The evening heat was getting to Essie, and she could feel the perspiration on her forehead as she caught up to her cousin. "You're moving fast for a hot day," she said.

"I couldn't stand to hang around there and listen to him tell the story again. I'm so sick of hearing how we all let him down. How disappointed he is that his daughters turned out to be an addict, a party girl, and a goth."

Essie couldn't quite digest these words, but she figured it was good to have her cousin talking. "He was worried about you going off on your own. Everyone was. Didn't you hear them calling? Your dat said you could be in danger."

"He has no idea." Megan stared ahead, walking on.

"We should go back. Dinner is ready. Grilled chicken. Are you hungry?"

Megan shook her head. "Is this the way to the river?"

Essie glanced over her shoulder. "We usually cut down the path behind the house, but this will take you there eventually."

"I'm going to jump in and float away and never come back."

In all her life, Essie had never wished to float away from her family. Yah, she'd been annoyed with her brothers and sisters plenty of times, but in her heart, she always knew she belonged here. "I'm sure your family would miss you."

"Not Dad. Didn't you hear him? He doesn't trust us to be alone, so he brought us here to dump us on your parents. As if we're five-year-olds."

"And why doesn't he trust you?"

Megan pressed her hands to her cheeks and groaned. "So many reasons. It's super complicated and super simple at the same time."

"I'm all ears."

"So, he's mad at Serena because she sneaks out with boys and parties all night with her friends. Actually, there's not much sneaking around, since Dad is almost never home at night. He's a cop, and he works four to midnight. A lot of damage can be done during those hours," Megan said. "Dad thinks she's got a drinking problem, and Serena says no, but there's always booze around when Serena's with her friends."

Essie kept silent. This was something she didn't do, though she knew plenty of teenagers who went off to drink beer and whiskey. It was forbidden in their church, but teenagers on rumspringa often bent the rules, and most parents looked the other way.

"Dad's been relying on Serena and me to be at home for Grace, but really? We're only eighteen, and we have lives. Grace is still a kid. She needs to have someone around, especially with Dad working five nights a week. But Serena is always out with her friends, and I have my own things going on."

"Like what?" Essie wondered what Megan's days were like, living in a big city. "What do you do each day? Do you go to school?"

"I'm about to start senior year of high school, and I'm definitely going to college. Besides that I used to have soccer. I was going to go pro. I was training with the US Olympic Team. But I blew my knee out, and now it's gone." Her pace slowed. "Everything I loved is gone. And now I . . ." She turned to Essie, tears in her eyes. "I never signed up for any of this. I don't want to be an addict and a broken soccer player. I can't—" Her words were cut off by a sob. A moment later, she covered her face in her hands and cried.

So sad and alone.

Essie's annoyance vanished as she put an arm around her cousin's shoulder and tenderly smoothed back her short wisps of hair. "So much pain inside you," Essie said. "I can feel it, and I hurt for you."

Megan sobbed again. "I don't know what to do anymore."

Essie considered this as her cousin cried quietly. "Isn't it a relief that you don't need to make a choice right now? You're to live here. You'll be with your sisters and your Amish family. This will give you time to make this choice, to choose a path."

Megan sniffed and wiped her eyes with the backs of her hands. "I just feel the pressure to do everything right now. It's too much. Sometimes it's hard to breathe."

Essie stroked her hair, waiting as Megan calmed a bit. "You know, I have a special place I go to. It's very easy to breathe there. Come."

She got her cousin walking again, and soon they were under the cover of dark leaves, the thick trees that lined the riverside. In a few minutes they had reached the rise that overlooked the river. Essie pointed out the water below.

"I've always loved the way it courses over the rocks and pebbles. It moves so fast that it churns into a white froth around the big rocks. There's power and peace in the river." As she spoke, the breeze off the water seemed to gurgle up over Essie's skin, cool and effervescent. "Do you feel that?"

"I do." Megan closed her eyes, spread her arms wide, and lifted her face to the sky. "It's good to breathe again."

Essie nodded. "It's important to breathe."

"Well, yeah." Megan laughed, putting her arms around Essie. "Thank you. Thanks for sharing your secret place."

Essie squeezed her, trying to fill the hug with love. "It's yours, anytime."

Chapter Three

"Dinner's just off the grill and ready to go," Miriam said, turning back to the table. "Best take a seat and get started."

Serena and Grace looked at their father. "Go ahead," Sully said. "I need a minute to talk with your aunt and uncle."

"Sit by me," Annie told Grace, and the two squeezed in together on a bench.

"Sometimes we eat in shifts," Esther explained, pushing a platter of chicken toward Serena. "But don't worry. We have plenty."

Miriam poured her brother-in-law a glass of lemonade and followed the men around to the side porch, where a rocker and a swing faced out to the garden and trees that provided a natural border to their property.

"Now, Sully, we're sorry to see you and the girls in such a state," Alvin said, his bad leg propped on a stool. "But it wouldn't be right to leave the girls here. Much as they've visited, it's not their home, and, after growing up English in the city, they wouldn't be happy here."

Sully accepted the glass of lemonade, but simply stared

down at it. "Right now happiness is too high a goal. Safety is what matters most, and they'd be safe here."

"Yah, they'd be safe," Miriam said, "but safe from what? You'd better tell us what's been going on."

"They're beyond my control, and I'm afraid the twins might end up dead or in jail or both."

Miriam pinched her chin as she listened. Was this an exaggeration?

"Last night, when I was at work, I got another one of those phone calls that stops you dead in your tracks. Megan was in the hospital, suffering from a drug overdose."

"The hospital . . ." Miriam realized this was indeed serious.

"I left work and rushed to the hospital. Megan lay there, hooked up to monitors, brought back from death. I'm so grateful Grace found her sister and called an ambulance. Not the first time for Megan. She's been taking pain killers ever since she had knee surgery for a soccer injury. I've been working with the doctors to wean her off, but she keeps going around us. She's developed an addiction."

Miriam turned to Alvin, who nodded. "We've heard about these addictions," she said. "It's happened to some Amish youth, too. Such a problem for everyone."

"It doesn't help that I have to work night shifts. It's a bad time to let teens loose on their own. After Sarah died I took three months off to be with the girls and try to provide some stability. It wasn't enough, but I'm out of vacation time, and I can't afford to quit the job."

"A man must work," Alvin agreed.

"But Megan isn't the only problem. Grace was hunched

up in a chair beside Megan's bed at the hospital, but Serena was nowhere in sight. When I got home, pillows were propped up on Serena's bed to make it look like she was asleep. Again, not the first time. She goes out drinking and socializing. Our resident party girl."

Like her mother, Miriam thought. Sarah had possessed a wild streak, a contagious laugh, and a desire to escape the traditional ways of her family.

"I can't rely on Serena for anything, and the older two are no help to Grace, who's only fifteen and hates being alone in the house at night. Grace is basically a good kid, but she's not as independent as her sisters. She needs people around her. Lately she seems to be afraid of everything. I worry that one of these days she'll be afraid to step off the curb and cross the street."

"Children need to know they're loved," Miriam said. "Family is important."

Sully nodded. "When she was little, I used to tell her she needed to be brave like the Irish warrior princess she was named after, Grace O'Malley." The tension left his face for a moment. "Those were good years, when the girls were little and Sarah was there to guide and inspire them. Sarah filled our days and nights with so much love and laughter. I didn't realize how precious those days were until they were gone. But now, I can barely stand to look at my girls. Not because I'm angry with them, but because I know I've failed them. I can't provide the home they need. That's why we need you. The twins are of legal age, but neither of them is ready to face the world alone. If you will have them, maybe for just a year, I'm sure they'll abide by your rules."

Oh, dear Gott in heaven, what to do? Miriam wanted

to help her nieces. Those three were not the best behaved of children, but years spent corralling her own brood had taught her that a little discipline and a lot of love could go a long way.

But to bring in three teenage girls. And here their youngest, Sarah Rose, would be going off to school next year, not to mention the good prospect of Essie's getting married and moving to a home with her husband.

So many changes on the horizon. Were she and Alvin prepared to take on Sarah's girls? Miriam believed that true challenges came from Gott, and this one would bring her closer to the memory of the sister who had filled her childhood with laughter and joy. But how did her husband feel about taking this on?

She turned to Alvin. Those tiny crinkle lines at the edge of his eyes made him look weary but wise. "What do you say, Alvie?"

He took a deep breath and rubbed his injured leg. "We can't turn away family. The girls can stay with us, but they'll pitch in like all of our children. That's all."

Looking at her dear husband, Miriam found it hard to contain the swell of love she felt for him at that moment. In Alvie's heart, there was always room for one more.

Miriam insisted that Sully stay and eat, despite his claim that he had no appetite due to the heartbreak of saying good-bye to his girls. Mammi served up a right good plate of chicken and vegetables, corn bread and butter, and Miriam was satisfied to see her brother-in-law bite into a drumstick. By the time Miriam and Alvin sat down, the little ones were finishing up, and Essie and Megan were in sight.

Harlan left his half-eaten dinner to get up and go meet Essie.

"Where are you going? Was it something I said?" Serena called after him, her brows lifting in merriment. From what Miriam had seen, Serena had said plenty, all right. That one had always been a chatterbox, but at least, tonight, she seemed more upbeat than her sisters.

The youngest one, Grace, was more of a concern. Her eyes were red, her face puffy, and she seemed on the verge of tears as she chewed a chunk of zucchini. Miriam knew it was hard to handle so much raw emotion, but life's sorrows were really a matter of perspective. Miriam wished Grace could see how blessed she was to have a father who loved her and a family in the country that was happy to take her in.

It made Miriam smile to see her youngest one, Sarah Rose, watching Grace with curiosity and awe. She kept patting Grace's hand like a doting grandmother, and, at one point, she climbed onto the bench to get a closer look at Grace's pink hair, finally nodding in approval.

"There's plenty of food left," Miriam told Essie and Megan when they arrived at the table. "Help yourself." Peter and Paul got up to give them a place to sit, reminding the others that they would be back for dessert—German chocolate cake, Essie's favorite for her birthday cake.

"It's Essie's birthday?" Serena leaned past Harlan to get a peek at Essie. "Happy birthday! This will be one for the record books, the day your cousins crashed your party."

"I'm sure I won't forget it," Essie said in a voice that seemed both sweet and sour.

Maybe Essie was disappointed that her celebration didn't turn out as planned, but when life gave you lemons, lemonade was the best you could do.

Instead of bringing out dessert, Miriam saw that all the dinner dishes were cleared from the tables and brought inside. She set up her girls in the kitchen to wash dishes, then had Paul and Peter scrub the vinyl tablecloths. Mammi wanted to head home to her small house down the road at the larger farm of Alvin's brother Lloyd. Miriam asked Harlan and Sam to take her in Harlan's buggy, then come right back for cake.

Again, Miriam and Alvin summoned Sully to the side porch, this time with his daughters. The twins sat together on the swing, while Grace took a seat next to her father on the glider.

"So I've talked with your aunt and uncle," Sully began, "and they've generously agreed to the plan. They're going to take care of you here for the next year or so. You can finish high school. You'll be safe, and surrounded by family."

"What high school?" Serena asked. "I just asked Annie about it, and she doesn't go to school and she's only sixteen."

Miriam noted the quickness of Serena's objection. The clever girl had been doing some investigating, and she'd uncovered the truth. Annie had finished eighth grade, as was traditional with Amish youth, who then went on to jobs at home or in the community.

"Annie looks after the animals here on the farm," Alvin explained. "The horses and the chickens need tending, and the vet thinks she's got good instincts when it comes to taking care of the dairy cows. Are you good with animals, Serena? Was it you helping us milk the cows last time you visited?"

"Probably not," Megan said. "The closest she's been to a cow is drinking a vanilla latte at Starbucks."

"Then it's settled," Miriam said. "The county high school will do just fine for the three of you. There's a bus to take you there. An English girl down the road goes there. Jenny is her name. I'm sure she'll tell us all about how to do it."

"Figuring out the school system is not the issue," Megan said. "The problem is that we all want to go back to Philadelphia."

"That's not an option," Sully said. "Look, we went over this on the ride here. I need to work to support you girls, at least for the next four years, until I can vest out. And you need a stable, steady environment. A more positive environment, away from the temptations that have gotten you in trouble."

"I'm not in trouble, Dad." Grace's hand slid down his arm as she looked up at him. "I didn't do anything wrong. Why can't I just come home with you?"

"Because I can't be there when you need me, Gracie-girl. You know you get lonely, being alone in the apartment, and you deserve to be surrounded by people who love and support you. Besides, your sisters will be here. Don't you want to be with them?"

"I want us all to be together at home," Grace pleaded, tears shining in her eyes.

Sully shook his head. "I'm sorry, kiddo. This will be your home for now."

"Actually, you can't force Megan and me." Serena folded her arms across her chest. "We're both eighteen now. Legally we're adults, and we can do what we want. Maybe we'll just run away."

Sully seemed crestfallen as he faced Serena. "It would destroy me to know you're not in a safe place."

"Stop! Just stop, Serena." Megan gave her sister a stern look. "Can't you see he's trying his best?"

"It's not my fault that you landed in the hospital again last night," Serena said.

"Nice." Megan scowled. "Way to be sympathetic."

"Girls . . ." Sully warned.

"We're not here to argue or lay blame," Miriam said. "Better to look ahead and agree on the best solution, which is truly to have you girls stay here with us. I know you two are eighteen, and that makes you legal adults. You're not prisoners here, of course, but won't you agree to give it a try? If it turns out you want to leave, we won't stop you. We just ask that you let us know you're going."

"That sounds fair," Sully said. "Would you agree to that, girls?"

"Only if they're staying," Grace said.

"I guess," Serena said. Megan gave a nod.

"Okay." Sully clasped his hands together. "Progress. I'll let you keep your cell phones, but you'll have to find someplace in town to charge them. Same with the laptop."

"Some folks use the library," said Alvin. "But I hear that cell phones don't work too well out in these parts."

"No service," Serena said. "I've been having trouble

since we got here. You people need to have some antennas installed."

"All right, then. Let's go get your stuff from the car." Sully turned to Miriam and Alvin and shrugged. "I had them pack clothes and toiletries. Is that okay? They can wear their regular clothes here?"

"Hold on, Dad," Megan said. "You can dump us here, and we'll try to bloom where we're planted and all that," she said, "but you can't make us be Amish."

Miriam had to bite back a smile. As if you could make a person accept a way of life, as well as the Anabaptist faith.

"What? We have to be Amish?" the youngest one asked, her eyes shiny with yet more tears. "This is worse than death. I'm not taking out my piercing. You can't make me."

"And I'm not going to wear a saggy dress and a bonnet," Serena said. "No offense, but there's no way I'd let anyone see me that way."

Megan held up her hands. "Same."

"Girls, please . . ." Sully scraped his hair back. "Show a little respect."

"Come on, now." Miriam held back a smile. "In all the times you visited, did you ever dress like us?"

The girls looked at one another and shook their heads.

Miriam went on. "We wear plain clothing because this is what the scriptures in the Bible tell us. But you weren't raised Amish; we know that, and no one expects you to dress like us. You can wear your clothes, and we won't force you to church."

"See, girls?" Sully said. "I told you they weren't a cult."

"But if you were to live here, we ask that you live by our most important rule," Alvin said.

"Here we go," Megan muttered.

"We ask that you love your neighbor and treat others as you would want them to treat you," Miriam said.

"Oh my gosh!" Serena's eyes were wide with wonder as she stared at Miriam. "When you said that just now, you reminded me so much of our mom." She touched her twin's arm. "Did you see that?"

Megan nodded. "So, what other rules?"

"That's the important one."

Alvin smiled. "We can make up the others as we go along."

The girls seemed horrified, but Sully laughed at that, and Miriam chuckled, too. "It was a joke," she said.

"Right." Megan arose from the bench. "If the touchy-feely session is over, let's get a move on. We're not getting any younger here."

"This is true," said Alvin. His face was neutral, but Miriam thought she noticed a twinkle in his eyes as Megan rallied the group to move. Sarah's daughters were feisty, stubborn, and still grieving their mother's death. They were going to be a handful, but, oh, what an interesting year they would have together!

Chapter Four

Later that night, Serena lay on the mattress, staring at the bunk overhead and listening to the soft sounds of breathing all around her. Even with Sarah Rose sleeping in the nursery, this room was chockful of people. The large girls' room in the Lapp house had always been very much like a dormitory, with three bunk beds and two mismatched dressers. But unlike a dormitory, storage space was limited. The Amish cousins hung dresses, nightgowns and bonnets on hooks, and the single closet was packed with blankets and quilts. Cousin Annie had moved her clothes to offer Serena two empty hooks, which was a start. Serena had pushed aside the few books on the dresser top to install her perfumes and hair products, bottles that might otherwise spill into her luggage. Still, there was no way she and her sisters could unpack. Consequently, two suitcases and a duffel bag lay on the floor against the wall.

Wide awake, she rolled over and tried to slow the thoughts whirring in her head. What was she doing here? Why was she even in bed so early? How could anyone expect her to fall asleep at nine o'clock? The grandfather clock in the living area had just struck nine when the younger Lapp kids headed up the stairs, yawning, and Aunt Miriam reminded the rest of them that they'd be up with the crowing roosters in the morning.

Seriously? Serena doubted that Dad's plan was going to last a month. She was going to miss her friends way too much, Grace was going to fall apart without Dad, and Megan . . . Well, Megan might be the exception.

Although Serena gave her twin a hard time, she worried about her a lot now. Everyone knew that Megan's addiction had been accidental, but Megan had almost died twice, overdosing on drugs she had bought from friends when she couldn't get her prescription refilled anymore. Dad said the addiction had broken Megan's strong will, but Serena refused to believe her sister was broken. Megan was the toughest person she knew; it might take time, but she believed her sister would get her bold, fearless life-force back. Amish life would be good for Megan—being here, away from the city and stuck on this pokey old farm. Serena hoped this would keep her sister out of trouble.

The steady breathing of the girls around her was reassuring, sweet in its way, but it also made Serena that much more annoyed that she couldn't fall asleep. She threw off the bedsheet and sat up, careful not to bump her head on the bunk where Grace was sleeping. The curtains on the windows lifted and fell back with the gentle breeze. It would be cooler outside. Maybe some fresh air would help. Not wanting to wake anyone, she grabbed her cell phone and Ugg slippers and tiptoed to the door. Out in the hall, she put her slippers on, smoothed down her favorite cotton nightgown with little hearts embroidered on the white bodice, and headed down the stairs.

The main room downstairs was dark, and she paused, her hand against the wall, until her eyes adjusted to the bit of moonlight coming in through the windows. Although it was unfamiliar, there was nothing creepy about crossing the large room, its wood floors smelling of lemon wax, the kitchen sweet, probably from years and years of baking delicious pies and cookies. Serena had lots of memories of visits here. Decorating Christmas cookies with colored sugars. Spreading the filling between the two cookies of a whoopie pie. Dipping lard cakes in sugar. And standing on a stool so that Aunt Miriam could teach her how to make the gravy "nice and smooth" without lumps.

When their family came to Joyful River, it was the one time when Serena's mom seemed younger, in the presence of her sister Miriam. Serena's Amish grandparents had moved to another Amish settlement in Michigan a few years after Sarah left home. Serena had never met Mom's parents, but she didn't think it was any great loss. Although she was curious, any parents who would cut their daughter off for rejecting their lifestyle were way too strict in Serena's book.

The kitchen door had been left open so that a breeze could come in through the screen door. Dad would have freaked if they left a door unlocked in the city, but here, things were probably different.

Her slippers made a shuffling sound on the porch, where it had to be at least ten degrees cooler. Much better. She took a seat on a rocker and looked up at the starry indigo sky. The coolness seemed to tamp down the farm smell, a mixture of hay and manure that Serena had noticed the minute she'd stepped out of the car. She checked her cell phone for service, but still, no luck. Frowning, she placed it on the little table. When she finally got to a place with service, she knew she'd have a gajillion messages. Probably dozens just from Jigger, her boyfriend, who had texted that he was going to miss her like crazy, that his heart was broken, that he'd be lost without his angel. They hadn't even had a chance to say good-bye in person, since Dad had been so frantic to get them out of town. Fix things. Save their lives.

He could be so dramatic.

Maybe Megan needed saving, but Serena had been going along just fine. Just because Dad didn't like her grades or her talent for having a good time, it didn't mean there was anything wrong with her. He didn't understand how important it was to live for the moment. He didn't get that her friends were *everything*.

She slid out of her slippers and put her feet up. The state of her toenails was a concern, and she was wishing that she'd gotten a pedicure before coming out here when a low rumbling sound came from the other side of the house.

In the country quiet of gentle wind and crickets, the noise sounded like an approaching monster.

And it was getting louder.

Maybe it was just a passing truck on the main road. She popped her slippers back on and went along the porch to take a look toward the barn and the front of the house.

A truck trudged down the lane, its bright headlights like two eyes, staring her down. What in the world?

Gripping a fence post, she considered bolting upstairs to wake her aunt and uncle. The truck groaned, gears downshifting as it slowed and then turned right, grumbling along the stone drive to the milking barn.

Was someone coming to steal the cows?

She hurried back inside, up the stairs. In the darkened hallway she wasn't even sure which door led to her aunt and uncle's room, so she went back to the girls' room and put one foot on the ladder so she could peek up to Essie's bunk.

"Essie!" she hissed, touching Essie's shoulder. "Wake up. Something major is about to go down. A truck just pulled up to the barn, and I think they're about to steal all the cows."

"Nay." Essie brushed a braid from her neck and sighed. "The cows are out to pasture. It's just the milk truck, come to pick up the milk."

"The milk truck," Serena whispered. Of course, it wasn't a major heist. Good thing she hadn't bothered Miriam and Alvin.

But now that she knew the truth, she wanted to check it out. After all, it would be someone else to talk to at nine o'clock at night.

She dug a sapphire-blue bolero jacket from her suitcase and put it on over her nightgown. The short jacket made her nightgown look like a summer dress. Perfect.

Outside, she crept toward the barn, the soles of her slippers crunching on gravel. The rumbling beast had been pulled up to one of the barn doors, and a fat blue hose stretched from the barn to the back of the truck. Interesting? No. But at this rate, watching paint dry would be better than tossing and turning in bed.

"Hello?" she called. "You have a visitor, Mister Milk Truck Man."

A shadow moved inside the barn, and a lean figure in jeans, black T-shirt, and a trucker's hat appeared in the doorway.

"Is that Essie there? Or Annie."

"No. Neither." Hands on hips, she struck a pose. "Do I look like an Amish girl to you?"

He tilted his head and squinted at her. "Actually, no."

Although she couldn't see a lot, he had the agile movements and bright smile of a young man. Maybe even her age. What a relief!

"I'm their cousin, from Philly. My name's Serena."

He nodded. "Scout Tanner. I'm just here to pick up the milk. I hope the noise of the truck didn't bother you."

"I was awake. Who can sleep at nine o'clock at night?"

"A lot of farm folk," he said. From closer up, she could make out his handsome face and golden blond hair that hung in a fringe beneath his cap. "That's why I come through at night. I can zip in and out without getting in the way of the workers or animals."

Serena walked along the shiny truck that was shaped like a silver flask on its side. "So this is your big ol' truck?"

"The tanker belongs to the company I work for. I collect milk and deliver it to the factory for processing."

"So you're the driver?"

"I am. And an accredited milk grader. We grade the milk before we pump it onto the truck."

"Really? So what kind of grade does Aunt Miriam and Uncle Alvin's milk get? An A plus, I hope. Or are you a tough grader?"

"I have my standards," he said. "But it's not like school. We see how it looks, check the temperature and smell.

If it's all good, I pump it into the truck and take it to the processing plant."

"But you drive the truck, so that means you're normal, right? You're not Amish."

"Normal?" He tipped his hat back, and she could see a flash of blue eyes. "I don't know about that. But I'm definitely not Amish."

"So we've got that in common," she said with a smile.

"That we do. I was just about to start pumping. I'm done with the testing." When he moved from the doorway into the light from the back of the truck, she saw that he had a nice face—friendly and open—with those gorgeous cornflower-blue eyes. He was so close she could have reached out and touched him, which might have been nice, except he was focused on something over her shoulder.

"Excuse me," he said. "I need to get to the truck."

"Oh, sorry. Do whatever it is you do." She stepped aside so that Scout could lean into the back of his truck, where there was an illuminated bay full of screens and dials, plastic boxes, and other gadgets. He worked there for a minute, then the truck gave a new groan, and the blue hose inflated, filling with milk.

Okay, maybe it was a little more interesting than Serena had anticipated. She stood back and watched as Scout went into the barn for a quick check, then returned.

"It only takes a few minutes. I'll be out of your hair soon."

"Are you kidding me? This is the most exciting thing that's happened all day."

He chuckled. "So how long are you visiting for?"

"Not sure." She flipped one side of her hair back and shifted toward the back of the truck, hoping that the light would catch the highlights and make them shine like spun gold. "I might be staying for a few months, maybe a year. My sister needs the peace and quiet of a farm right now." She gave a smirk, amazed at how quickly she'd concocted the half-truth. "It's sort of her therapy."

"And you came along to be with her? That's great. I'm sure she appreciates your love and support."

"I can't even tell you," she said, waving off the topic. "So Scout. Is that your real name?"

"It is. My mother's a big fan of *To Kill a Mockingbird*. You know the book?"

The book read by every other student in Serena's ninth-grade glass. She'd gotten bogged down in the section about the town of Mayberry or Maywood or whatever. Everyone had said she should see the movie, at least, but black-and-white movies were so depressing. "Everyone loves that story," she said. "So you got a very special name out of it. I'll bet your girlfriend appreciates that."

"Most girls liked Scout in the story. And I don't have a girlfriend right now, if that was the question. I'm too busy with college. Classes start in two weeks. I also work as a volunteer firefighter, so yeah, I've got a lot going on."

"Fighting fires? That's cool. And then you do this job at night? I'm honored that you have time to talk to me."

"There's always time to talk to a nice person."

"Aw. You think I'm nice." She gave his arm a playful nudge. "I got you fooled."

"I'm a pretty good judge of character."

"I bet you are." Serena smiled up at him, so glad she'd been outside to see his truck roll in. Mom used to say that every raincloud had a silver lining. Maybe she'd found her silver lining.

They chatted for a few more minutes, but all too soon the timer on the truck went off, and Scout had to disconnect the hose and pack up. The machine on his truck printed a receipt for Uncle Alvin, which he left tacked to a board in the barn.

"I'd better get going. Need to stay on schedule, but it was nice to meet you, Serena."

"Same. So drive safe, and I'll see you around. You said you come by every night?"

"Every day or two."

"So maybe I'll catch you next time."

He nodded. "Hope so."

"Later." She smiled, and then turned away, pulling the lapels of the bolero jacket close against the night air. So, bad news? She was stuck here for who knew how long. Good news? She'd get to visit with this Scout guy just about every night. A new friend.

Her silver lining. Her lifeline to the real world.

Chapter Five

Late Friday morning Essie was in the kitchen sterilizing her jars for when her friends and sisters would gather for the canning bee this afternoon. Two large pots were boiling half of the jars, while she washed the remainder in hot, soapy water, preparing them for their turn in boiling water. Steam rose from the sink, leaving a tinge of moisture on her face. Hot work, but better to get it done in the cooler time of day. Since she'd been a girl, Essie had found comfort in canning, capturing Gott's summer bounty to enjoy throughout the year. Humming a tune, she had begun to place the rinsed jars on a clean tea towel when Serena appeared.

"Good morning." Still wearing her pretty white nightgown, Serena stretched and yawned. "Those bunk beds are pretty comfortable, but I had so much trouble falling asleep. I guess I'm just a night owl."

"I noticed," Essie said. Last night when Serena woke her about someone stealing the cows, she'd been too tired to make much sense of it. But this morning, it had made her chuckle. How would a thief load cows into a milk truck? Serena had an active imagination.

"Where is everyone?"

"The boys are helping Dat make hay, and the girls are doing chores. Your sisters are out in the barn, mucking stalls with Annie."

"Aw. Am I missing something fun?"

"Mucking a stall?" It wasn't Essie's favorite chore, by far. She always preferred to be in the house, cooking or baking. "You'll get your chance," Essie said, wiping her brow with the back of one hand. The boiling pots of water were creating a steam cloud, but the first batch of jars was almost done.

"Before we leave, I want to learn how to milk a cow, too."

"No more hand milking, like when we were little. We use diesel-powered milking machines."

"Way to take the fun out of it," Serena said, taking a seat at the table. "So what's for breakfast? Do you have any eggs?"

"We do, but the rest of us had breakfast hours ago."

"I'm so hungry. Could you make two, sunny-side up, please? With toast. And do you have coffee? I need my morning caffeine. Unless you have a yerba mate in the fridge. It's so much healthier."

With pursed lips, Essie turned the fire off under the pots and scanned the countertop covered with glass jars and lids. Couldn't Serena see that there was not a single inch of space on the kitchen counter or stove? "There's no room to cook eggs right now. I'm sterilizing jars for the jamming bee this afternoon. Remember I mentioned it? We're counting on your help."

"But I'm so hungry," Serena whimpered, thrusting out her lower lip.

Essie removed the coffeepot from the back burner and poured the dark liquid into a cup. "There's cream in the fridge if you want, and sugar on the table. I'll make eggs for you once I'm done, but it'll be close to lunchtime."

Just then the screen door creaked, and Miriam entered carrying a zucchini that had grown as big as a cat. "Look at this!" She held it up with a chuckle. "Everything in the garden is growing so fast. I've got a bin of vegetables on the porch, but I'll leave them outside until you're done with the jamming, Essie."

"That is so cool. Wait. Let me get a picture." Serena tapped her cell phone a few times and then pointed it toward Miriam.

"Just the zucchini," Mem said. "We don't want to be in photos. Don't want to encourage self-pride or vanity."

"No photos! That would kill me," Serena said, snapping the picture.

"Do you think it will be too dry to eat?" Essie asked, nodding at the huge vegetable.

"It will be fine if we shred it into muffins or bread." She smiled at Serena. "You missed the morning, sleepy-head."

"I was tired, but now I'm starving. Would you make me eggs, Aunt Miriam? Please?"

"I will show you how to make your own breakfast when you've slept late." Miriam opened a cupboard and tapped one finger against the clear plastic bins. "This one is granola, and this is cornflakes, I think. The milk is in the refrigerator, and the bowls are over on those shelves."

"What? No. I hate cereal."

"We'll be eating lunch in an hour or so. Ham salad sandwiches and fruit salad."

Serena got up with a sigh. "I guess I'll wait. But wow. I'm probably going to lose a zillion pounds while I'm here." She added some milk to her coffee and went out the door to the porch.

Essie felt relieved to see her go. It wasn't easy having the three cousins arrive out of nowhere, making more mouths to feed, more laundry, more work. Not to mention Serena's manners, sweet-talking Harlan for much of last night, and eating the last piece of cake when it was Essie's birthday.

As Mem tidied the kitchen, Essie longed to share her concerns. The cousins were already straining Essie's patience. Instead of enjoying carefree conversation and laughter with her friends at today's jamming bee, Essie would need to include the three English girls. And Mem had asked that the three girls be included in an upcoming youth outing. Essie wished the best for her cousins, who had suffered, losing their mother. She wanted them to be healthy and happy. But why did they have to search for happiness and a stable life here in Joyful River?

They needed to find their own joy back in Philadelphia, where they fit in with the city and the people. That would be the perfect fix.

Hours later, the outdoor picnic tables were covered in buckets of bright red berries soaking in water. The girls were gathered round to pull the little green crown off each strawberry fresh picked from the berry patch.

It was the first time Essie had been able to invite her friends over to help, and their light conversation and amusing stories had made the berry picking seem like a party. Annie and Lizzie seemed to know the sweetest spots of the berry patch, and Megan and Grace quietly followed instructions. Serena had a lot to say about everything, and though her voice was beginning to wear on Essie like a tree branch tap-tap-tapping against a window in a storm, Essie could tell that she was trying to be nice.

They had already cleaned gallons of berries—enough to start two pots on the stove—and Essie made sure to measure out four cups of sugar and the right amount of fresh lemon juice for every four cups of mashed berries. Now that she had two pots going, she had to flit inside and out like a butterfly in springtime. It was up to her to keep the girls hulling the berries, up to her to make sure the preserves didn't boil over. She had to stay on her toes, but she was happiest that way.

"Where are all the boys?" Serena asked. "Why aren't they helping us?"

"They've been helping Dat make hay," Lizzie said. "It's hot work, but I like to ride the cart when they let me. At the end of the day, you get to cool off in the river."

"So the boys do men's work and the girls do the cooking," Grace said. "It's kind of sexist."

"What is sexist?" Lizzie asked as she deftly used one finger to poke and pull the stem and greens out of one strawberry after another.

"When boys have to do one thing and girls have to do something else," Grace explained.

Lizzie's mouth twisted around in confusion as she gave a shrug.

She doesn't understand, thought Essie, annoyed that

her cousins were trying to fill the heads of her family and friends with things that just didn't make sense. Essie was happy to be a woman and leave certain tasks to the men. It had always been that way, and it was a comfortable part of her world.

"Never mind that," Essie told her little sister. "We're almost finished hulling the berries. Why don't you go inside and get our snack? The Rice Krispies treats on the counter."

Lizzie nodded eagerly and jumped off the picnic table bench.

"We're getting to the end of the buckets," Laura said, pushing the last of the berries out to be hulled.

"So many hands make quick work," Essie said. "As soon as these are done, we'll take a little break. The jam on the stove should be about done. I'll check it one last time."

Inside the kitchen, Lizzie smiled over the plate of marshmallow treats.

"Take them outside," Essie said. "And I'll bring the lemonade."

Leaning over the stove, she moved a spoon through the liquid, which looked about right. She took a frozen dinner plate from the freezer, spread some jam on the center, and ran a spoon through it. The indentation remained. It was ready to set up.

She removed the two pots from the stove, set them aside to let them cool, and brought the lemonade outside. As she poured drinks for everyone and passed around the treats, the conversation was about boyfriends.

"My boyfriend was heartbroken that I had to come here," Serena said. "He'll be lost without me."

"He's sort of lost with you," Megan said.

"You're always so mean to Jigger," Serena said. "Sometimes I think you're jealous."

"Not I. You can keep that bad boy to yourself."

"So what's dating like when you're Amish?" Serena asked. "Are you girls hooked up?"

The stone-cold response from Laura, Sadie, and Essie prompted Megan to smack her sister in the arm. "They don't know what you're talking about," Megan said. "What she means is, do you have a boyfriend? A special guy."

"I've been courting Mark Miller for three years now," Sadie said.

"What's Mark like?" Serena asked. "Is he a strapping, strong young man?"

"He's . . ." At a loss for words, Sadie turned to Essie. "He's handsome."

"He works at the auction house," Essie said. "And they've known each other forever."

"Childhood sweetheart." Serena nodded. "That's sweet. How about you, Laura? You got a guy?"

"I don't have a special friend," Laura said, "but during rumspringa, some girls go with many different guys. Better to sample all the ice cream flavors before you decide," she said with a teasing smile.

"Well, look at you, playing the field," Serena said.

"What's rumspringa?" Grace asked.

"It means running around," Essie said. "It's a thing that happens when most kids turn sixteen. The parents give teens freedom so they can try different things. This way, the teen learns whether he or she wants to get baptized and live Amish."

"Cool." Grace lifted her lemonade glass with a grin. "I'm almost old enough for rumspringa. I'm ready."

"Running around is overrated," Megan said. "Take it from your older sisters, who did more than our fair share. That's why we're here, to straighten up and fly right."

"Speak for yourself," Serena said. "I'm just here to keep the sisterhood together."

"Denial." Megan shook her head. "It's a family thing."

"Anyone want another Rice Krispies treat?" offered Essie. Her friends seemed to be amused by her cousins, but Essie didn't appreciate such frank talk. She believed that matters of love were personal, to be cherished in the heart, not tossed about like a lunch salad.

"You haven't told us about your relationship with Harlan, Essie." Serena popped a berry in her mouth and smiled. "You guys seem pretty serious. Have you been together long?"

"Two years. He's been my, my boyfriend for two years."

"But Essie has had her eye on Harlan since we were girls in school," Laura said.

"We were friends, and he was around our house, helping Dat with the farm," Essie said, not wanting anyone to take away the innocence of those times. How she'd admired him so, always positive, always offering a helping hand or a smile, despite the sorrow nipping at his heels. Harlan had been working odd jobs from the age of eleven, when his father Jed had up and left home, leaving Harlan and his mem and sister with nothing more than Collette Yoder's wage from Smitty's Pretzel Factory. Harlan had still been in school, but he'd been put to work weekends and afternoons in nearby farms. At the Lapp dairy farm, Dat had appreciated Harlan's hard work.

Countless times when Harlan had helped her carry a bucket or basket or hitch up a horse and buggy, Essie had seen something in Harlan that wasn't apparent in other boys their age. A good and true heart. Most of his days now were spent working at the Amish furniture factory, where he built things like bed frames and desks, hoping to be taken under the wing of one of the experienced carpenters. In his spare time, he was a reliable hired hand for farmers. He wasn't one to monkey around in the haymow or wrestle other boys to the ground to prove his might. He was a hardworking fellow who did the right thing.

"That Harlan is always working," Laura said. "Sometimes I wish he'd slack off a little and have some fun with the rest of us."

"You know Harlan doesn't have two parents to give him a roof over his head," Essie said. "If you had to support your mem and sister, you'd be having a lot less fun, too."

"What happened to his father?" Serena asked.

"He's been gone since Harlan was eleven. He moved away." Essie hoped it was answer enough for Serena, who didn't have to know all the details, the sad history that had hurt Harlan and shamed his family.

"Yeah," Serena said. "Divorce is always hard on the kids. I have some friends who went through that."

"But divorce isn't allowed by our bishop," Sadie said. "Amish folk don't get divorced. It's not permitted."

"Really?" Serena tilted her head. "So what happens?"

"Nothing," Essie said. "Folks go on living."

"Has Harlan ever tried to find his father?" Serena asked. "You know, just out of curiosity."

In fact, Harlan had written letters to some Amish settlements in search of Jed Yoder, but it was not something

Essie could share. "It's a matter of shame. Not to be talked about." Eager to change the subject, Essie asked Laura about the blackberry brambles near her farm on Foster Road. "Do you think we could pick enough blackberries to put up some jam?"

Essie was so upset by the talk of divorce and Harlan's parents that Laura's answer might as well have been soap bubbles popping silently in the air. Why did Serena have to question everything, probing at secret things and private pain, picking away at wounds? Even five-year-old Sarah Rose was more adept at sensing people's feelings.

Essie tamped her annoyance down, as there was still much work to do. She started her sisters mashing the second batch of strawberries, then directed the older girls into the kitchen, where it was time to pour the jam into jars.

"It's cooled a bit, but mind that you don't burn yourself," Essie said.

"I'll get the funnels," Sadie offered. Essie's childhood friend Sadie knew the Lapp kitchen as well as her own.

"It smells *won-der-ful* in here," Serena said, drawing out the word.

"Wunderbar," Laura added.

Serena closed her eyes and let her head roll back. "I want to take a bath in a vat of strawberry jam."

The laughter that followed tugged at Essie's irritation, but she chuckled along.

Serena meant well.

Essie shouldn't let it get to her.

Chapter Six

As the strawberry jam party wrapped up, Serena walked off with her cell phone in hand, hoping to get a signal.

"Serena!" Grace called after her, running to catch up. "Where are you going?"

"Toward the closest cell phone tower, I hope. I'm beginning to get antsy without being able to talk to my friends. This is ridiculous. I'm going to see if we can get a ride into town tomorrow. They said we can charge our batteries at the library, and there's got to be cell service there."

"Probably." Grace's voice seemed glum.

"What's the matter?"

"I want to go home." Her voice trembled on the last word.

Serena slung an arm around her sister's slender shoulders and swayed back and forth with her as they walked. "Home? No way. We just got here."

"I know." Grace sounded forlorn. "Everyone is really nice, and the farm is green and beautiful, and the food is delicious. But it's not home. I keep thinking about Dad all alone."

Serena had had the same thought, but she dismissed it. "Don't you worry about him. He's probably working tonight, anyway. And if not, it would be his first night to himself in years. He'll probably go to a baseball game or out with one of his cop buddies."

"I bet he misses us. Being alone will give him a chance to think about Mom and miss her more."

"That's true," Serena said. Sometimes Grace had flashes of wisdom like an old Yoda. "We all miss Mom. I don't think that will ever go away. It just hurts a little bit less as time goes on. Right?" She gave Grace's shoulders a squeeze.

"If you say so."

At that moment Serena realized there were more important things than finding cell service. "Come on, Gracie. Let's find something fun to do here. We haven't milked the cows yet, and tomorrow we can go into town and get ice cream and fudge. And then there's swimming in the river. Trust me, this is going to be great."

"If you say so," Grace repeated, with a note of doubt that Serena dismissed. Was this going to be a time to remember? Yes, yes, yes! It would go down in family history as the summer of sisterhood. Serena was going to make that happen. Yes! Step aside, pessimists. Hope was about to spring forth in Joyful River.

"We're here to help with the milking," Serena said as she and Grace strode into the outbuilding next to the barn that Aunt Miriam had told them was the milking parlor.

"Milking starts at five a.m. and p.m., twice a day, seven days a week," Aunt Miriam had told them earlier. "Once a cow is producing, she can't be kept waiting."

Serena and Grace had tried to find Megan to come along, but Aunt Miriam had explained that she was off walking, which seemed to be her way of blowing off steam. "A good, long walk in the fresh air can clear the mind," Aunt Miriam had said with that sureness that Serena admired.

The milking parlor was a hub of activity, with Uncle Alvin and Sam working the milking machines, while Annie, Paul, and Peter guided a line of cows in from the paddock. With the cows bustling in through the opening, no one seemed to hear Serena's sunny announcement.

"Hello?" she said as a black-and-white beast came charging her way. She had to jump to the left to dodge him. Annie and Peter giggled at the girls' wariness as they somehow managed to get the giant cows into place.

"They know where to go," Peter said, "but you need to stay out of their way."

Grace stood off to the side, shaking her head. "I don't think anyone needs our help in here."

"Stick around if you want to pitch in," Sam called over the groan of a cow. "You can help wash the equipment down."

It wasn't nearly as exciting as Serena had hoped. She was sent around with a brush and a bucket of soapy water to scrub all the milking suction tubes, while Grace followed her, hosing them off.

"Hey!" Serena shouted when Grace spritzed her.

Grace shook her head. "'Let's milk the cows,' you said. 'It'll be fun,' you said."

"I didn't know they'd put us on cleanup duty." Serena slopped a dollop of soapy water over the ends of the tubing, which resembled jump rope handles. Annie had helped Grace and her find black muck boots that came up to their knees, so their feet were sweaty and dry, but their arms were speckled with water. Serena pretended to slip, slopping some water onto Grace.

"I can't believe you. . . ." Grace's mouth opened wide. And then she held up the hose and gave Serena a healthy spray. "Gotcha."

Serena let out a squeal as cold water drenched her clothes. And then they were laughing together, splashing each other with cold water, which was a shocking but welcome relief from the heat of the day.

"What's going on here?" Sam asked as he approached, and Grace quickly whipped around and shot him in the shoulder with water.

"Oops!" Grace shrugged, still chuckling. "Sorry, I guess."

He pulled his wet shirt away from his chest. "I've done worse. You know, if you like getting wet, we can set you up to wash down the cows tomorrow."

Serena liked the idea of washing a cow, the way she used to bathe her poodle. "We'll see about that."

"But for now, you'd better get back to cleaning the equipment if you want to get to dinner."

Since Serena had missed breakfast, the promise of Aunt Miriam's home cooking sounded good. "We've got this," Serena told Sam, turning to her sister. "Time to power wash, Grace."

"I'm right behind you."

By the time they left the barn, they were both in a better

mood, despite the fact that Serena sensed herself beginning to smell like that odd combination of earthy grain and manure. They both took quick showers and hurried outside to where Essie and Aunt Miriam were setting up dinner.

"Tomato sandwiches?" Serena was dubious. That didn't seem to make a meal at all. But the garden tomatoes were delicious on homemade bread, along with grilled sausage, corn on the cob, crudités, and rhubarb juice.

As they ate, she asked Megan where she kept disappearing to, and Megan explained that she'd walked the four corners of the farm. "Just to get my bearings," Megan said, "and it's a good way to condition my knee."

After Megan's ACL injury, doctors had been skeptical that she would ever play soccer again, which had been one of the things that had thrown Megan into depression. Was Megan thinking soccer would be in her future? Serena hated to see her twin disappointed again. "So how's your knee feeling?"

"Fine." Megan's friends used to call her "brevity girl." Everyone in the family totally understood why.

"Did you find anyplace on the farm that gets cell phone service?" Grace asked.

Megan shook her head no.

"What good are your phones if they never work?" Lizzie asked.

"Good question," Megan said, picking up a sandwich half. "You want to field that one, Serena?"

"When they work, they're awesome," she said. "We need to go into town. There's got to be some service there." She turned toward the head of the table. "Aunt Miriam, can we pretty please get a ride to town tomorrow?"

"Saturday. Hmm. Alvin might take you along when he does errands."

Alvin's beard bobbed as he chewed. "I reckon I could."

"Yay," Serena said as quietly as she could. "At last . . . civilization."

Most of the family at the table didn't seem to hear her, though Essie's lips tightened into a frown.

"I'm kidding," Serena said, though everyone's attention turned to Aunt Miriam when she mentioned that it was time to bring out dessert, bumbleberry pie.

While the table was being cleared, Serena checked her cell phone again. Nothing. Why did she torture herself?

"Did you get enough to eat, girls?" Aunt Miriam asked, leaning in to remove an empty pitcher.

They all agreed that they had.

"Now that you're done, you need to clear your plates and go into the kitchen to help. Essie will show you what needs to be done."

Serena exchanged looks with her sisters. Should she be embarrassed for not offering to help, or annoyed at being put to work?

"We're stuck now," Grace muttered on the way into the house. "Now they'll expect us to pitch in all the time."

"It's not that bad," Megan said. "When you have something to do, it makes the time fly by."

"Fast-forward one year," Grace said. "That's all I'm asking for."

In the kitchen Essie was at the sink washing, Annie was drying, and Lizzie was putting things away in the cupboard. When Serena said they had come to help, Essie acted like it was a wonderful thing. So like her mother.

Serena and Megan could take over the washing and drying so that the other girls could move on to other chores.

"And you can help me put things away," Lizzie told Grace. "Sometimes it's hard for me to reach the top shelf."

"What are the other chores?" Serena asked as she grabbed a rag and submerged her hands in warm, soapy water. At this rate, she'd have the cleanest hands in the county. "Just wondering."

"Annie needs to make sure the chickens are in their coop for the night," Essie answered, "and I'll take the slop bucket out and wipe down the tables outside and prepare to mop in here."

Slop bucket? Gross. Serena would stick with the dishes. She felt a tinge of self-pity, stuck here with her hands in hot water, but then, she wasn't alone. Her sisters and cousins were all doing chores, too.

As they worked, Lizzie taught them a song about how Gott made the stars shine and the ivy grow because of love. Essie returned with bucket and mop and began singing harmonies, and, for a moment, Serena felt as if they were all different flowers wrapped together in a sweet bouquet.

When the dishes were done and the countertops wiped clean, they went outside to enjoy the cooler air and waning light. Sitting at the picnic table, Serena and Grace hatched their plan to go into town in the morning.

"I hope I can talk to Dad," Grace said, her voice a little wobbly.

"Me too," Serena said, though her first call would be to Jigger. What would she say? He would get a large charge out of the selfie she'd taken with the black cow in the milking parlor. But after that . . . What would there be to say beyond words of regret that she'd been whisked away to a Lancaster County farm to live with her Amish family? Suddenly, she was feeling a little blue, too.

The littlest one, Sarah Rose, tapped Grace on the shoulder and held a cardboard box out to her.

"She wants you to play a game," Lizzie said. "That's her favorite."

Serena looked down at the box. "Trouble. I remember that game. It's got dice in a plastic bubble."

"Sorry, little rug rat," Grace said. "I don't know how to play."

"It's okay." Sarah Rose pushed the box onto the table and climbed onto the bench beside Grace. "I'll teach you."

Megan and Grace took lessons from the tiny girl in the white kapp. So cute! She reminded Serena of a little doll.

They played the game together until it was too dark to see and Aunt Miriam called them in. Sarah Rose, kneeling on the bench, was good at counting out the spaces, but mostly she liked popping the plastic bubble that held the dice on the game board.

Although it was barely nine o'clock, Serena felt tired. Aunt Miriam had lit a kerosene lamp inside the house, enough for her to read by, and she went upstairs to change into her nightgown. By the time Serena washed up, the other girls were already in bed, yawning and making up bedtime stories. Serena tossed her cell phone on the bed and turned toward the door, planning to read one of the family's books until Scout rolled in on the milk truck. As she passed by one set of bunk beds, Grace scooched over to the side and patted the mattress.

"Snuggle with me?" Grace asked, turning the sheet down. "Just for a few minutes."

How could she say no? Neither of her sisters had asked Serena to get close like that since . . . well, since they were little kids. She slid out of her slippers and wiggled into the narrow bed. "Cozy."

"I'm sorry I'm such a pain." Grace turned toward the wall, giving Serena more room to nestle in behind her.

"You're not," Serena insisted, though it was clear that Grace was in pain.

"I just feel kind of lost here. Like I'm drifting on the current." Grace's voice was low, a dull whisper. "But you and Megan are my anchor. You keep me from drifting away."

"Okay, then." Serena put her hand on her sister's shoulder and rested her chin against Grace's hair. "I'm holding on tight."

"Don't let go."

"I won't. I promise."

They fell asleep that way.

Sometime in the early morning, Serena woke up and returned to her bunk. When she pressed the button on her cell phone and saw that it was after three a.m., she realized she'd slept through Scout's visit. She was too tired to feel sad.

There would be plenty more chances. She would catch him next time.

Chapter Seven

The next day, Serena and Grace waited on the front porch as Sam brought a gray buggy around from the stables. The horse pulling the rig was a chocolate brown, and, watching it trot along, Serena imagined herself as some kind of royalty awaiting her carriage. Uncle Alvin came out the door behind them and told them to come along if they wanted to go into town.

In Serena's memory, the carriage had seemed bigger, as she remembered times when the whole family had piled in. She and Grace sat on the bench in the back, while Alvin sat in front beside his son. The carriage bounced over a rut in the lane, and then they were on the paved highway, the horse's hooves settling into a steady clip-clop rhythm.

"When I was a boy, we went to the library to borrow books," Uncle Alvin said. "Now even plain folk go to use the computers for all manner of business."

"I thought the Amish couldn't use electricity," Serena said.

"We can't have it in our homes. We can't own the electric machines. But we can use them. Though I don't. And

I don't need a phone to carry round in my pocket. If I need to make a call, there's the phone shack."

"But you're missing the beauty of a cell phone," Grace explained. "It's more than a phone. Really, it's a tiny computer with a camera and access to the Internet and games and stuff. There's even a calculator that you could use for business."

"I do calculations with paper and pencil and the brain Gott gave me," he said.

Sam shook his head, avoiding the conversation.

"But cell phones help bring people together," Serena explained. "When we get to the library, we can send a message to our dad, and send photos to all our friends."

"When I was a boy, we sent messages. Wrote them on a piece of paper and left them on a person's doorstep." Uncle Alvin's voice seemed gruff, but when he turned back to face the girls, there was a twinkle in his eyes. "That's how I courted your aunt."

"Aw." Serena smiled. "That's so sweet."

"It's just the way of the Amish," said Alvin. "And we live plain to keep distractions and temptations away. It's those things that threaten to take family members away and lead congregants away. We choose to live without them."

Serena didn't believe that cell phones led people away from you, but she respected her uncle's opinion and realized this wasn't a matter up for debate. "Well, thanks for the lift to the library," she said. "I'm kind of excited to be in town."

Sam gave them the farm's address, which they would need to get library cards. As the buggy clopped along the highway, two cars passed them, one honking so loudly that it made all the passengers flinch. The horse let out a cry, but Sam managed to keep it under control.

"That's so obnoxious," Serena hissed under her breath.

"Seriously?" Grace turned to her. "You're the most impatient driver I know."

"But I would never do that to a horse," Serena insisted.

Soon they reached an area where the houses and buildings were set closer together, and they had to line up and wait their turn with cars and a few other buggies at stop signs. The edge of town. Serena looked down at her cell phone as it started to buzz. Messages were coming in! They had cell service, at last.

Serena's heart nearly burst with joy when she saw that she had twenty-three text messages. Her friends had missed her!

But before she read anything, she wanted to send out the photo of her with Daisy the cow. People would get such a laugh out of that. She sent it in a group text, and then posted it to her social media accounts.

Once in town, their progress was further slowed by traffic. "What are all these people doing here?" Serena asked.

"It's Saturday. Lots of tourists come to Amish country on the weekends."

"It's really hopping," Grace said. "What do these people come all the way out to the country for?"

"Good food. Handmade items." Alvin nodded at a group of little kids waving from the sidewalk. "And some just come to look."

"That sounds annoying."

"It's good for local businesses," Sam answered. "Though we usually don't come into town on the weekend. Too much traffic."

"They're all staring at us," Serena said.

"We don't mind," said Alvin, "as long as they don't take pictures of us."

Serena's phone was down to seven percent battery, dangerously low, when they arrived at a low-slung brick building with darkened slats for windows—Joyful River's library. Sam stopped the horse, and the girls climbed down from the buggy. Agreeing to meet their uncle and cousin in an hour or so, Serena and Grace went inside and quickly found side-by-side cubbies with outlets to plug in their chargers.

Right away, Serena started reading her text messages. Jigger saying he missed her already. When was she coming back? Thinking of her. What would he do without her? Could he visit?

She took a breath and sighed. It was so nice to know she was missed.

Next she went through text messages from her friends. All of them were in disbelief that she had been dropped onto an Amish farm without warning. Stella said she was freaking out without her bestie, and Hallie teased that she was going to drive out and rescue her. A few of them suggested her story would make a great reality show. That was sort of true, except she knew the Amish didn't want to be photographed. It was too much of a vanity thing for them.

After she read through her messages and emails, she went to her other social media accounts, the ones with photos and quick, fun captions of what people were doing. She already had thirty-two stars for her photo with Daisy the cow!

Grace tapped her arm. "My phone is recharged," she

said, standing up. "I'm going to go outside and see if Dad can talk to me."

Serena gave her a quick nod. Scrolling through her feed, she saw photos posted from last night's party. Already she was missing out. Hallie and Stella posed together, looking tough. There was a picture of Hallie falling into her boyfriend's arms, and another of Stella holding a shot of tequila in one hand and a lime in the other.

Seeing her friends, Serena felt a twinge of sorrow. She didn't miss partying as much as she had thought she would, but she missed her friends. It bothered her that they'd had a party so soon after she'd left, but then, what did she expect? There was nothing else to do on a Friday night. She scrolled down and saw more photos of the party. Kids doing shots. Jigger toasting with two other girls. Hmm. The photos seemed to get sloppier as the night went on. Peoples' eyes drooped, and their faces lacked animation.

She kept scrolling until she came to a photo that made her jaw drop. A couple embracing, and the guy with his arms wrapped around Kylie Jessup was Jigger.

Serena bit her bottom lip. Maybe it was a joke.

The caption read: Does it count if you're too drunk to remember?

She felt a stab of pain deep in her chest as she closed the app and stared down at the desk in the cubicle. She didn't want anyone in this library to see her cry. Even if they were strangers, it was embarrassing. She could only swipe at her tears with the backs of her hands and hope that no one noticed.

After a few minutes, she pulled herself together, raked back her hair, and went over to the main desk. "My sister and I need to apply for library cards," she told the woman with short gray hair and a flowing pink top anchored on one shoulder with a dragonfly pin.

"All right, then." The woman gave Serena two short, paper applications and found an extra pen for her to use.

Serena felt responsible, setting up the cards and thinking ahead. The Lapps didn't have much of a book collection, and she was going to need something to pass the time.

The clerk, who introduced herself as Mavis, told Serena to go on and pick some books. "By the time you're done, I'll have your cards ready for you."

Roving through the aisles, Serena found the mystery section and picked up a book on display. For years, the only books she'd read were those assigned by teachers. She decided on a mystery about a young Japanese American detective. Then she went to the main fiction section. A book about a woman named Eleanor Oliphant spoke to her, and she picked up a copy. Finally, she thought about Scout, and the book he'd mentioned. She knew the title, but how was she supposed to find it? She went back to Mavis to ask for help. "I'm looking for a book called *To Kill a Mockingbird*," she said. "Have you ever heard of it?"

"Absolutely. It's one of my favorites." Mavis showed Serena how to look it up on the computer, then follow the number code to the shelves of books.

When Grace returned, Serena was sitting at the cubicle, reading one of her new books.

"I talked to Dad." Grace's face beamed with joy. "He's good. He sounded pretty happy, and he wanted to hear what we've been doing. Everything's good. He's going to come out for a visit soon. In a week or so." She shrugged.

"I feel better about things." She tilted her head at Serena. "Are you okay?"

"Sure." Serena wasn't ready to talk about her friends in Philly; it was still all too tender. "I got us library cards, and I already checked out some books. Here's your card."

"Cool."

As Grace browsed the stacks, Serena closed her book and tried to rationalize the information she'd gotten on her cell. Somehow, she hadn't expected all her friends back in Philly to be able to survive without her. Instead, they'd had a party without her. Well, sure they did. She had expected that to happen. She just didn't think they'd be so . . . so happy without her. And she hadn't been in love with Jigger, not really, not at all, but still. She hadn't expected her boyfriend to chase another girl so soon after she'd left.

She'd been wrong about them, all of them.

And it hurt to realize that she was . . . dispensable. Replaceable.

Chapter Eight

"I can't believe you've walked this far from our farm," Essie said, following Megan down a sun-dappled path that cut between two farms that had to be miles from home. "You know, you can use one of the scooters or get a ride if you want to go into town."

"Nah. Walking is my therapy. And Sam offered to take me into Joyful River in the buggy, but I'm definitely not trying to get into town."

"Where is it you want to go?"

"It's not really about the destination. It's more a journey of the mind," Megan said.

Essie let her cousin's words lie between them as they walked along. How could the mind take a journey without the body? It was impossible. But Essie didn't want to argue with Megan, who seemed to be driven by restlessness. "Is it peace you're looking for?"

"Maybe." Megan stared off in the distance. "Peace would be great. But mostly I'm trying to stay ahead of the pack of wild horses nipping at my heels."

Wild horses? Essie looked behind them.

"You're so literal!" Megan said. "But you keep your

feet on the ground, and you're a team player. I like that about you. Anyway, after we put up that jam yesterday, I thought you might be interested in the wild blackberries that I found here. There's a patch growing along that ridge. See that tangle of green in the sun?"

Essie shielded her eyes from the sun and saw a stretch where the wild berries had taken over an old fence, almost using it as a trellis to climb and expand. "I see what you mean." She moved closer for a look at the berries—plump and dark, undiscovered because of their distant location. "This is truly a gold mine that you've found."

"I thought so." Megan plucked a fat blackberry and popped it in her mouth. "That one's sweet, but some of them are on the tart side."

"Wild berries can be sour, though that makes them good for canning." Essie started picking. The ripe berries made a thumping sound as they dropped into her tin bucket. "We can fill our buckets now, then come back for more another day. And we'll need to buy more mason jars if we're going to put up everything from this summer."

"I'm glad you like making jam, but how many jars of preserves does one family need?"

"We use it all year," Essie explained, "and we give it to friends and family. It's good to have some in the cold cellar."

"If you say so."

With so many berries dangling from the brambles, they had filled their two pails in no time, and turned to head back to the farm. After a time, Essie admitted, "This is a lot of walking."

"Yeah. Right now I need to use up my energy so I can sleep at night."

"We'll both sleep well tonight," Essie said, though sleep wasn't what she longed for.

Saturday night was courtship night, when Harlan came over after everyone was asleep and they got to be together, alone, in the quiet house. For the past year Harlan had made it to Essie's house nearly every Saturday night, traveling in his buggy through rain and sleet and snow. Only once, when the spring rains had swollen the river, making it rise to the bridge, Harlan had wisely stayed on the town side, missing one courtship night. But every other Saturday, he'd come round and met her downstairs, his amber eyes so bright at the sight of her.

A few times he had brought Sadie and Mark, and the four of them had played a few games and talked a bit. But mostly, Harlan and Essie wanted to be alone, just the two of them. There was so little time for couples to talk in the busy day of plain folk.

Those were precious moments when they sat together on the glider. Sometimes they held hands, twining their fingers together, and she was sure she felt the tingling warmth of love passing between them. Sometimes he let his face drop to the side of her head, nuzzling her hair with his nose and whispering "My Essie" in her ear. And sometimes, when they kissed, she felt like a tender flower in his arms, a rosebud ready to open in the warm sun.

Their marriage would be blessed by Gott. If only Harlan would pop the question!

Not that they hadn't talked about getting married. It was something they both wanted, but Harlan wanted to be ready. He wanted to be sure his mother and sister would be able to live without him, or else find a place where all four of them could live together. Essie would be happy to live with Collette and Susan Yoder. Suzie was already like a sister to her, and it would be a blessing to make Harlan's family her own. But whenever Essie tried to nudge him along, Harlan worried over the money. How much they'd need to save. How crowded the Lancaster area had become. How hard it was to find property or a suitable home. How important it was for him to do the right thing, after the taint of his dat leaving the family.

His concerns made sense. But as far as Essie was concerned, he kept stoking the fire beneath a pot bubbling over with worry.

Tonight, she would nudge him toward trusting in Gott to provide, and taking a leap of faith.

Tonight . . . if she could stay awake. Over the past year there'd been many a Saturday night when she and Harlan had worked so hard during the day that they'd both fallen asleep, leaning against each other on the glider. At first he had apologized, but she had assured him that it didn't matter. They didn't have to be playing a game, sharing hot cocoa or talking. As long as she was with him, she felt happy.

The rest of the day was as bumpy as a buggy on a rutted road, but Essie set her sights on the joy of seeing Harlan after all the busy Saturday activities. When she'd been sweeping the upstairs room, she'd had a bit of an argument with Serena, who wanted to put all of Essie's books on the floor so she could use the dresser top for her bottles and tiny tubes of makeup. The last straw had been when Serena had knocked the carved flower bookend to the floor. Essie had gasped as she bent down to retrieve it.

"It's just a block of wood," Serena said.

Essie held it against her chest. "It's a bookend. Harlan made it for me."

"Well, sorry. I didn't know. But it can stay on the floor, right? I mean, we're living out of suitcases on the floor. But I need a place to set up my stuff, and the books can go anywhere."

Essie had looked around the room, realizing that Serena was right. The suitcases had seemed an annoyance to be tolerated, but if the three girls were staying, they would need a place for their clothes. "We need to talk to Mem about finding a dresser for the three of you."

"That'd be great." Serena added two perfume bottles to the dresser top. "In the meantime, I'll set up here."

Essie was glad to escape the upstairs and seek the comfort of the kitchen. There were gmay cookies to be baked for church, which would be held the following day at the home of Joe Byler. But as Essie began to gather the ingredients for baking, Mem came into the kitchen and asked for Essie's help on an important task. "We need to help the English cousins get into the swing of things on the farm."

"I've been trying," Essie said, setting the canister of flour on the table. "Yesterday I showed them how to put up jam, and just now I went a long way with Megan to pick some berries."

"You're a big help," Mem said.

"And I told Serena I'd talk to you about getting another dresser." Essie explained about the incident upstairs.

"I'm sure we can find another dresser for them." Mem nodded. "And I'm happy you're helping them adjust. You know most of my tricks in the kitchen now, but I'm not sure these girls know how to cook an egg. They're still sticking out like sore thumbs, and I know Gott has given them talents that are yet undiscovered. They've taken to you, Essie. All the girls enjoyed your frolic yesterday. Won't you teach them the basics of cooking and baking and tidying up the house?"

Although Essie agreed, she tried to hide the disappointment that swept over her like a sudden downpour of rain. She always intended to be kind to her English cousins, but this would mean corralling them every day and watching over them like a shepherd chasing stray lambs. This on top of her daily chores, which would take extra time with her cousins tagging along. And at the end of the day, would there be an ounce of free time left for Essie and Harlan?

She would have to hope and pray that the cousins caught on to the work quickly and found some chores that they wanted to make their own. "Right now, I can show them how to make the cookies for church," she said, fetching the bowls and baking sheets. The last thing she wanted to do was play teacher to three English girls who didn't care about learning how to live Amish. She wanted to tell her mother that Serena was bossy. That Megan was sad in a way Essie didn't understand, and Grace looked as forlorn as a lost kitten. Instead, she said: "I'll do my best, Mem."

"I know you will. I'll go outside and send the girls in."

"And I'll fetch Serena from upstairs." Essie went to the stairs and called up to her cousin, trying to make her voice sound more cheerful than she felt.

Within five minutes, Serena was in the kitchen, staring into the refrigerator. Soon after, Grace and Megan popped in, screen door slamming behind them.

"Do you have lemonade?" Grace asked. "I'm so thirsty."

"I would give anything for an iced mocha latte with whipped," Serena said.

"So Aunt Miriam said you're making cookies?" Megan asked. "I thought you didn't use the ovens on hot days."

"Sometimes we have to bake, like now," Essie said. "If you wash your hands, you can help. It's an old Amish recipe that's been in our family a long time."

"Cool," Grace said, soaping up her hands at the kitchen sink. Today her fingernails were painted a shiny black, like the darkest stones in the river. There was something fascinating about black fingernails that made it hard for Essie to stop staring at them.

"So, is this a cookie emergency, or what?" Megan asked, nudging in next to her sister to wash her hands.

Essie chose a wooden spoon and began pummeling the butter to cream it. "Not an emergency, but we need to have the cookies for church tomorrow. Our church meeting lasts for a long time. Sometimes three or so hours. Everyone gets tired, but it's hard for the little ones to last so long. So we always come with gmay cookies. Gmay is our word for church. We hand out the cookies during church to keep the children from getting too restless."

"Are we going to have to dig our hands in?" Serena asked. "I hate getting butter under my nails."

"We'll use spoons. First we need to soften the butter and mix it with sugar." Essie offered up the spoon. "Who wants to mix?"

For a moment, the girls stood watching with their arms crossed. At last Megan stepped forward. "I'll do it."

"After you get the butter creamy and mixed with the sugar, you add in the eggs and vanilla. While we're waiting for that, Grace and I will do the dry ingredients." Essie moved over to the second bowl and gestured for Grace to come closer. "I'll let you measure. Two and a half cups of flour first. Then we add baking soda and baking powder."

Grace began measuring the flour. "Why don't we add this right into the bowl Megan is stirring?"

"They have to be separate, or else the cookies won't bake right," Essie explained.

"I believe that's called chemistry," Megan said wryly.

"Fascinating." Serena groaned, taking a seat at the kitchen table. The sour look on her face made Essie wonder what had happened to burst her usual bubbly mood.

"What's the matter?" Essie asked.

Serena stared down at her phone.

"She's bent out of shape," Megan said.

"I just don't know what good this cell phone is going to do without service out here." Serena put her cell phone on the table and lay her head down beside it like a dog curling up in pain. "What am I supposed to do?"

"You can help us with the baking," Essie said brightly.

Serena sighed. "No, thanks."

"Trust me, it's no great loss," said Megan. "If you haven't figured it out yet, Serena's kind of a disaster in the kitchen. Your cookies will turn out better if she keeps her distance."

"I don't think so," Essie said as she measured out the buttermilk—the ingredient that made this recipe different from most others. "When I'm baking with Mem and my sisters, I always think that the more loving hands in the kitchen, the better the food tastes."

"That's kind of nice," Grace said.

Megan nodded. "Ess, you could work as a motivational team coach."

Essie wasn't sure what that meant, but it seemed to be

a compliment. "Don't worry, Serena. There's a job for you coming up at the end."

"Oh, goody."

Essie delegated Megan to grease the cookie sheets, and finally the batter was ready to be dropped onto the sheets in heaping teaspoons. "Now we sprinkle the cinnamon sugar." Essie combined them in a small bowl and turned to Serena. "This job is for you."

"Seriously?" Serena lifted her head and gave a sad look.

Megan frowned at her twin. "Get off your duff and sprinkle the cookies."

"Fine." With a dramatic groan, Serena came over to the counter. She listened to Essie's instructions and began to coat the globs of dough with sugar.

"That's it," Essie said, taking the bowls to the sink.

"Ugh. It takes so long." Serena tried to move faster, but ended up flinging the sugar over the counter and onto the floor. "Oh. Sorry. I'll clean it up." When she went for a rag, Essie had to turn off the water and stop her.

"Best try to sweep it up first," Essie said. She went to the broom closet for a dustpan and brush. "When you add water to a clump of sugar, you get a sticky mess."

"That's science," Grace said. "I'm impressed, Essie."

"It's just good common sense," Essie said.

"Proof that I don't belong in a kitchen," Serena said, her arms folded across her chest. "I'm not good at science *or* common sense."

Essie had to press her lips together to keep from agreeing. It would have been the truth, but she knew that sometimes the truth hurt.

Maybe Mem could interest Serena in quilting or knitting. The kitchen was not the place for her.

Chapter Nine

That night, when everyone else had gone to bed, Essie sat on the porch, listening to the crickets' song as she waited for Harlan. It was Saturday—date night! Most times the young man came round to the girl's house after dark, after the family was asleep. He would shine a flashlight on her bedroom window or toss some dried corn kernels up to the glass, the signal for her to come down and let him in.

Tonight, as everyone got ready for bed, Essie didn't want to have to explain all this to her cousins. She just wanted a chance to be alone with Harlan, to hear how his week had gone at the factory, to tell him about the jam she'd put up, to see if he'd come up with any customers for their new business. Mostly, she wanted to lean against him, his arms around her, and listen to the soft notes of his breath in her ear.

She yawned and shifted on the glider, her ears straining for the clip-clop sound of the hooves of Harlan's donkey, Beebee. When everyone had gone upstairs to change into their pajamas, Essie had stayed downstairs in her dress, apron, and kapp. Although she felt a tiny twinge of guilt for ducking into the cellar door when she'd heard Serena head toward the kitchen calling her name, Essie figured it was best this way. She planned to stop Harlan before he flashed the light on the girls' bedroom window. No need to wake her English cousins. And to be honest, right now she wanted to be left alone with her beau.

But what was taking him so long?

She was tired, and it was beginning to cool off out here. She went inside to find a jacket or a blanket. The kerosene lamp on the table had been turned down low. Beside the rocker was a copy of *The Connection*, a magazine with articles written by Amish folk. She sat down for a moment to browse through it. One writer from out west described a yellow-headed blackbird with a striking cap, brighter than a lemon. She was reading about how the female built her nest when her eyelids slid shut.

"Quiet! You're going to wake everyone up!"

"I can't help it. I can't see in the dark."

"None of us can. Do you think I have X-ray vision like Superman?"

"That would be Supergirl."

"Just keep going. There's a light at the bottom of the stairs."

"Thanks, Supergirl."

The voices, interlaced with giggles, tugged Essie awake. She bolted up in the rocking chair and found herself face-to-face with her cousins. The soft glow of the lamplight made their faces look like those of little girls again. Or maybe that was their nightclothes and faces scrubbed of makeup.

"I told you she had to be down here," Megan said. "Annie said she would be here."

"I wanted to make sure she was okay," Serena said. "It's not every night that a strange beam of light flashes in the window and then I find my cousin missing from her bed." She turned to Essie. "I thought maybe you were kidnapped."

"Oh, no. I'm fine."

"You were waiting up for your boyfriend," Grace said. "That's so sweet."

"Yah. Well, I fell asleep waiting, but I guess he's here." Essie was already edging toward the door, trying to think of a way to shoo her cousins back upstairs. "Thanks for waking me," she called back to them. "Good night."

She opened the door to Harlan, his body seeming to fill the frame with his broad shoulders, white shirt, black broadcloth trousers, and black suspenders.

"Essie." His smile lifted her spirits. "Sorry I'm late. I thought I'd never get here." He took her hand to pull her into his arms, but she tugged in the opposite direction, bringing him inside.

"We have company. My cousins saw the flashlight."

He let out a steamy sigh. "All right. I'll say hello. And good night."

Together they crossed to the bottom of the stairs, where the girls watched curiously.

"You remember Harlan," Essie said.

He nodded, and the girls all said hello as they stared. Their eyes were round with interest, as if they were watching an animal in the zoo.

"So Harlan," Serena said. "Do you stop by every night? Or is this just a Saturday thing?"

"Saturday," he said.

"And Aunt Miriam and Uncle Alvin don't mind?" Grace asked.

"We wait until they're asleep," Essie said. "But when you're courting, parents don't fuss with rules about who you can see."

"Wow." Serena nodded. "English parents could learn a thing or two from the Amish. It would be so great to be left alone, without curfew and parental hassles."

Essie nodded, wishing she could be left alone, too. "Sorry if the flashlight bothered you."

"Yah, sorry," Harlan agreed.

"You can go back to sleep now." Essie smoothed down her apron and swayed from one foot to the other. "See you in the morning."

"Wait. No. Hold on," Serena said. "We're not tired, anyway. I mean, I didn't realize that staying up was an option."

"It's still early," Grace said. "We can hang out with you guys."

Essie looked longingly toward the glider by the window where she usually sat with Harlan, then turned to the dining room. "Okay," she said, taking a seat at the big table. "How about a game?"

"A board game would be good," Harlan said.

"Or a game to keep us from being *bored*," Serena said with a grin. "I'm kidding. Count me in."

After looking through all the games on the sideboard, the girls settled on Parcheesi.

"I'm green," Grace called. "It's my lucky color."

"Wait." Megan frowned as the colored pieces were

being set up on the board. "Only four players allowed. We need to pick something else."

"Harlan and I will play together," Essie said, leaning a little closer to him.

"So we roll to see who goes first." Harlan shook the dice in his hands, a smile in his amber eyes. "Watch out, girls. I play to win."

"Same," Megan said.

Serena put her hands on her hips in a serious pose. "Game on!"

Essie kept to herself during much of the game. Although she felt a tinge of annoyance at having her time with Harlan cut short, her cousins' enjoyment softened her mood. How they loved rolling doubles or sending another player's marker back home! They were rarely this merry during the day, though she understood the special feeling of night, when parents and little ones were asleep. It allowed a certain comfort and privacy that wasn't available during the day.

Even Harlan seemed to be enjoying himself. At first she thought he was being patient, but as the game went on, his full-throated laughter joined in with that of the girls. Essie gripped the edge of the table, wondering if this was to be the future. Not a moment to herself. Her days and nights occupied by her cousins.

They were a few rolls into the second game when the familiar rumbling sound came through the open windows. The yard out front was swept by the stark white of headlights.

"The milk truck!" Serena jumped up so suddenly she bumped the table. "Scout's here. Come on, you guys."

"What are we doing?" Grace asked.

"Come on out and meet him. And you can watch while he pumps the milk," Serena said.

With a sigh, Megan put the dice down and arose. "I never thought I'd be spending my Saturday night watching milk go through a hose. What's there to see?"

"Just come on." Serena was already at the front door, holding the screen open. "Come on, come on," she sang, then clapped twice. "Come on, come on. . . ."

"Come on. . . ." Grace sang along as she went to the door.

Megan didn't sing, but she followed along, muttering, "Big excitement."

When they continued the song outside, Essie hurried toward the door to call for quiet. People were sleeping! But the girls were too wrapped up in their song to hear her thin warning as they laughed and skipped across the lawn. Such a commotion!

Essie turned back to find Harlan sprinting toward the door. He leaned close to her and pushed it closed. "Lock the house! Quick, before they come back."

They chuckled as he put his arms around her and she melted against him.

"What are we going to do with them?" she asked. "We'll never have a moment alone."

"How long are they staying?"

"A year, maybe two? They really have nowhere else to turn."

"Then they must be treated like family. Sisters."

"Sisters who sleep the day away and can't find their way around the kitchen."

He leaned back, and she saw a warm light in his amber eyes. "Still . . . sisters. Brothers and sisters annoy us. No one is perfect. You just have to find the good to outweigh the bad."

"You're right." He had such a good heart. She took his hand and led him over to the glider. "I need to be patient with them, but I've been eager to talk to you alone. I talked with Mem and Dat about your idea, and they thought it was a good one."

His face brightened. "That's good news."

She nodded. "If you can find some shops to sell it, they'll let me sell all the extra jam I put up, as long as we pay for the jars and the sugar."

"I already found two places. There's a quilt shop near the furniture factory—Wanda's Quilts—and she sells cheese and honey at the front of the store. She wants a case of your jam, just as soon as it's ready. And remember the place in Crabapple Ridge? The shop owner told us she can sell anything Amish. Once we start asking around, I'm sure we'll find plenty of places to carry it."

"I've got two cases of strawberry ready right now, and at least a case of raspberry left over from last month. We can load up your buggy before you leave tonight."

"Good on you," he said. "Looks like Essie's Amish Jam will be landing on breakfast tables all over Lancaster County."

"Let's hope some of that jam makes it onto the toast," Essie teased. Although she wasn't one to get wrapped up in material things, there was no denying the good feeling at having a small job that would make some money. It would feel good to contribute to the little savings account she and Harlan had started at the bank in town.

Their house fund. Every little bit would help. If sales went well, maybe they'd be able to tie the knot this wedding season. That would be one way of solving the cousin problem.

"It's good to have something to work on," she said, nudging closer to him.

"Yah, it is. That's how I feel at the woodshop, building things. Sometimes the hours fly by, and you're wrapped up in measuring, sawing, and hammering. You lose track of time, and suddenly—there it is. A finished table for a family to sit around." He put his arm around her shoulders, and she rested her face against his chest. Sometimes, if everything was still, she could hear the sound of his breathing, steady and strong.

That was her Harlan, steady and strong. But not too strong to laugh at her cousins' jokes.

Her Harlan.

Chapter Ten

Miriam nuzzled her cheek into her pillow, trying to find her way back to sleep after the bright voices of her nieces had woken her up.

Those three girls were spitfires at night. They hadn't yet adjusted to the early-to-bed, early-to-rise schedule of a dairy farmer, which was no surprise. It would take time. Miriam would speak to them tomorrow about keeping their voices down at night, so as not to wake the rest of the family.

She tried to close her eyes, but her maternal sense wouldn't allow it. She sat up and, moving the sheet as quietly as possible, went to the window. Down by the milking barn sat the milk truck, its red taillights gleaming like two eyes. She assumed the girls were still down there, visiting with the driver.

Gathering her summer nightgown close, she tiptoed across the room, out the door, and down the hall. If she descended the stairs staying close to the railing, the floorboards were less likely to creak. She went down eight, nine, ten stairs until she could get a peek into the main room.

A game board was set up on the dining table, by the

light of the kerosene lamp. There was movement in the sitting area, on the glider. In the dim light she could just make out the two of them cuddled together, Essie and Harlan.

Miriam ducked back behind the wall before they saw her. She hadn't meant to spy, but it was her job to make sure all was right in the house.

Staying close to the handrail, she climbed back up the stairs and moved silently down the hall to the bedroom she'd shared with her husband for more than twenty years. Only a pale light sifted through the window curtain, but she knew the room by heart. Perching on the edge of the bed, she studied the still form of her husband, who faced away from her.

"Alvie?" she whispered. "Are you awake?"

"Who can sleep with the noise of you tiptoeing?"

She muffled a soft laugh. "And here I was trying to be quiet."

"You were. It was the other noise that woke me."

"Sully's girls are lively. I checked, and everything's fine. Go back to sleep. I can't believe you're up."

"I can't believe it, either. Any decent dairy farmer who puts in a full day's work would be asleep right now."

"You're a mighty good dairy farmer, so I suppose you must be talking in your sleep."

"I don't mind the girls talking with Scout when he comes for a pickup, but I'd rather they crossed to the milking barn without a loud yippee and a how-dee-do."

"That's Serena," Miriam said. "She's the spirited one. No slow trot for her. Everything's at a full gallop."

"Megan is just as swift. Have you seen her walking the fences?"

"She's quick on her feet, but not willing to test the waters. I see Serena jumping right into the pond, while her sisters wait on the shore, so afraid that they'll never find anything better than the stubby grass under their feet."

Huddled on the bed, she pondered that image of the girls at the pond. Alvie's breathing slowed again, deep and steady, this man she loved. She thought he had fallen back asleep until he asked: "Are we talking about girls, or ducks?"

With a muffled chuckle, she put a hand on his chest. "Maybe both. I reckon you're too tired for storytelling."

"Never for your stories."

She rubbed his shoulder. "We should sleep. There's church tomorrow at Joe Byler's, and even though it's Sunday, the cows still need a milking." She slipped under the sheet and stretched out beside him, her hand rubbing his shoulder blade. "You're a hard worker, Alvie."

"Not so much anymore. When we were kids and cows were milked by hand, it was a lot of work, a lot of time spent with each cow. Now, with the milking machines, it's easy. The cows line up and pretty much go to the machines. If they had fingers, I think they'd attach the machines to their udders all by themselves."

She giggled. "Cows with fingers. Wouldn't that be a sight? But even with the machines, you have plenty of work to do."

"Yah, and your work just increased by three. Three more mouths to feed, and three more to clean up after. Three more on laundry day."

"Sully's girls will learn to pitch in. I've got Essie trying to teach them a few things in the kitchen."

"Essie's a right good cook, but I don't know about her as a teacher."

"Every parent needs to be a teacher in one way or another. Essie needs to learn for when she gets married and has kids of her own."

"This is true. So the students will teach the teacher?" he asked.

"A little of both. Essie needs to learn patience, and the girls need to learn how to take care of themselves. My sister was a good mother, I think, but the English don't teach some of the important things. Cooking, cleaning, and tending the summer garden. Our nieces have none of these skills, but they're smart girls. They'll come round."

"Bend the branch while it's still young. That's what my dat used to say."

Miriam took a deep breath as she thought about the old saying. Was it about shaping the growth of a tree? Funny, how living things seemed to grow so slowly while you were watching. And then, whammo! The thin sapling you planted ten years ago now towered over the rooftop of the house.

What would Sarah want for her girls? She hadn't been a strict mother, but she'd tried to instill kindness in her daughters. Love of family was important to Sarah, despite the fact that she'd left their family when she turned eighteen. She had told Miriam that she couldn't live in a box, constricted by the rules of a small group of people. At that point, their parents had already received a few visits from the deacon over his concerns about Sarah in her blue jeans wanting to do men's work on the farm and luring other Amish teens off to music festivals and fairs. Other youth in their community had delved into drugs and alcohol— far worse things, in Miriam's eyes. But Sarah had been singled out for her defiance. Come Monday morning, when other young people changed to their daily clothes and got back to work, Sarah kept her jeans and her painted face. The deacons and bishop just couldn't permit a person to keep breaking the Ordnung, the rules of Amish life.

When she closed her eyes Miriam could still see that cherry-red lipstick her older sister favored. Sometimes she'd wished Sarah would put her lipstick away and follow the rules, just so she could stay. But Gott had forged a different path for Sarah.

And so at the age of eighteen, off she went, first to York and then to Philadelphia. Miriam had missed her so much she bore an ache in her chest for years, until at last, after Miriam had given birth to Samuel, Sarah had gotten in touch to say she was married and pregnant and happy with her city life.

And when Sarah had brought her family for visits, she'd seemed to be still juggling that hot potato of joy. Two different paths they'd taken, and yet the sisters had managed to meet down the road.

And now, decades after the split, Sarah's girls had landed here. What would Sarah want for them?

Just love?

Lots of love.

"Has anyone seen my church pants?" Peter called down the hall. "Oh, here."

"No, those are my pants. Mem!" Paul bellowed. "Peter has my pants."

The usual Sunday morning rush to get to church, Miriam thought as she hurried down the hall toward the boys' room.

"You can have them back. They're too small."

"Let me see." Miriam pushed open the door to find Peter in a pair of pants that were far too tight and too short.

"Did you grow a foot while you were sleeping?" she asked. The twelve-year-old twin boys were growing like pole beans.

Peter shrugged. "I can wear them, Mem, but if I sit down I won't be able to breathe."

"If he can't wear them, I can't wear mine," Paul said. "Because we're the same size." He was sitting on the bed in his usual broadcloth pants, the ones with the patch Mammi had sewn into the knee. "I knew my church pants were getting too small."

"Why didn't you tell me?" Miriam asked.

He rubbed at the patch on his knee. "I forgot."

Every church day there seemed to be a new challenge that threatened to make them late. Miriam instructed the boys to wear their everyday pants—a bit embarrassing, but oh, well. She would search for some hand-me-downs from Sam, or else a trip to Walmart would be in order.

In the girls' room Annie and Lizzie got held up explaining about church to their cousins. Miriam popped her head in and told the cousins they didn't have to go, on account of the service being in German, and not really suited for them.

"That's a relief, 'cause church is not my thing," Serena said from her bunk.

Miriam appreciated her honesty. "Just be sure to make your beds, and clean up after yourselves in the kitchen. We'll be back in three or four hours."

"Four hours?" Megan winced. "We could drive to Philadelphia and back."

Miriam chuckled. "Church is closer. But there's always a lot of socializing to be had afterward. We take our time."

* * *

Two hours later, when Miriam noticed the sunlight streaming in through the open doors of the Byler barn, she had to smile. It was Gott's hand casting a golden light on a swath of his congregation. Such a beautiful sight!

Seated on a bench with her daughters in the women's section, she realized the barn was heating up. Inevitable, with a hundred or so warm bodies tucked into one space. An older fellow in the men's section was hunkered over and sleeping, as was someone in the back, whose snore made a nap seem awfully appealing. Granted, the air in the barn was still and hot, and the preacher was covering a lot of scripture that was hard to follow.

She opened a bin of gmay cookies and passed them to Sarah Rose and Lizzie. Essie declined, so Miriam reached down the aisle, offering them to the Hershberger children before taking one herself. Her eyes closed at the sweet, buttery flavor. At eighteen, Essie had mastered most of the family recipes. She was good and ready to be a fine wife. Miriam glanced at the container, longing for another cookie, but held herself back. A healthy diet did not include extra cookies. Besides, soon enough they'd have the lunch spread out, which was sure to include one of Miriam's favorite things: Amish peanut butter. The creamy combination of peanut butter and sweet, smooth marshmallow was like a cross between peanut brittle and marshmallow heaven. Such a treat for young and old.

Later, at a table shared with Alvin, his brother Lloyd, and Lloyd's wife Greta, they munched on sandwiches, carrots, and radishes as they talked about the break in the heat and a problem Lloyd had been having with his harvester. Greta was not only family, she was also Miriam's closest friend. Greta had a gift for spilling the truth, whether it was difficult or not, a quality Miriam appreciated. Plus, she had a sharp sense of humor.

As the men spoke, Greta turned to Miriam and nodded across the lawn toward a group of young folk. "Your Essie has really come into her own."

Miriam looked over and saw Essie handing drinks to her younger sisters. "She's such a help. I don't know what I'll do without her."

"But that time's coming, isn't it?" There was a spark of joy in Greta's eyes. "Have they mentioned anything yet?"

"Not yet," Miriam said. "But I planted plenty of celery this year, just in case."

The two women laughed together, enjoying the little joke. It was a tradition to serve celery at Amish weddings in Lancaster County. Celery was a healthy snack, easy to grow, and the stalks propped in water were so decorative on the wedding tables.

Just then Linda Hostetler stopped by and nudged in to perch between Greta and Miriam. Linda's husband Len owned a harness shop in town, and she had a habit of asking probing questions when Amish customers stopped in for supplies. Linda seemed to enjoy the collection and distribution of local news.

"How are the girls?" she asked Miriam.

"Just fine." It seemed like an odd question, but with Linda, you never knew. "The young ones are playing by the barn."

"Not them. Your *English* girls."

Taken by surprise, Miriam opened her mouth and

closed it. She hadn't expected the question. She hadn't thought anyone knew about her sister's girls.

"I saw them in town with Alvin and Sam," Linda went on. Something about her long nose and pointed chin reminded Miriam of a fox. Not unattractive, but something to be wary of. "I was coming out of the library when they got out of your buggy. Two girls, right?"

"Actually, three. Only two went into town."

"You have visitors then?" Greta asked. Miriam hadn't had a chance to tell her yet.

"My sister's girls." Somehow it seemed wrong to have to explain to Linda that Sarah was dead, that the girls needed family now and, with the work demands on their father, had nowhere else to turn. Besides, it was more than Linda Hostetler deserved to know.

"How long are they staying?" Linda asked.

"We're not sure. Maybe a year. Might be longer."

"Are they going to school?" Linda asked. "You know, the English have to stay in school longer than Amish children. It's the law."

"They'll be going to school," Miriam said, reminding herself to find out the schedule of the county schools. For all she knew, they could be in session now.

"I just had to ask. When I saw them, I knew something was not right." Linda leaned closer to Greta to add: "One of them has *pink hair*."

"That's Grace, the youngest." Miriam's heart sank at the jab. She hoped her nieces wouldn't be picked on while they were here. Especially Grace, who seemed the most tender right now.

"I'm sure you'll be keeping your eyes on them." Linda rose and brushed her dress, as if sitting with them had soiled it. "I'll be praying for you, Miriam. You and those girls. I can't say what would happen if the bishop gets a look at them."

The hint of trouble took Miriam by surprise, robbing her of the chance to reply before Linda moved on. What had Linda meant about the bishop? They'd done nothing wrong. Nothing about taking in family went against the rules of the Ordnung.

Miriam stared down at the table. "That was . . . upsetting." Her throat had grown tight, and her palms were suddenly sweaty. "Though I'm not sure why."

"These are Sarah's girls? Daughters of your sister who passed?"

Miriam nodded. "Their father works late shifts and long hours, and there's no one else in Philadelphia who can take them in. They need a mother's love, Greta. A family."

Greta leaned close, her eyes stern. "Then they've come to the right place."

In her heart, Miriam knew that was true. But Linda's comment about the bishop echoed in her mind like something from a bad dream. Something that would take a while to shake.

She and Alvie were doing the right thing, but some folks got thrown off by the way things looked. Like pink hair and shiny black fingernails.

She would have to trust that Gott would protect them from the likes of Linda Hostetler.

Chapter Eleven

"I can't believe we're doing this," Grace shouted as they zipped down the highway on scooters they'd found in one of the barns.

"Isn't it great?" Serena loved the feeling of the breeze in her hair, and she had gotten into a rhythm, pushing off with one foot to keep moving on the flat parts of the road.

Megan led the way. She was probably the most cautious driver, definitely the most athletic. But she almost hadn't come along because she worried about the three of them being on the road without helmets. Serena had promised that they'd go slow and be extra careful, and just to be sure, Megan had taken the lead.

They crested the top of a slight hill and came to a downhill stretch. "Yahoo!" Serena crowed as she rested both feet on the scooter and coasted. There was something wonderful about sunshine and green fields and open road, something that made her feel like she was leaving her worries miles behind her. Maybe she was getting used to the whole farm thing. Last night had helped. She'd had a blast hanging out with her sisters, Essie, and Harlan. Who knew board games could make them laugh so hard.

And then, there was Scout. It had been the perfect cap on the evening to see him again, to introduce her sisters and chat with him for a while. He seemed to be close to Serena's age, and if they became friends, she figured he would introduce her to his friends and pretty soon she might have friends of her own. If she had to stay here, she would need some normal friends, people to hang out with when she needed to escape the farm.

Serena's sisters weren't quite as ready to dig into their new Amish home, but Serena figured that, in time, they would find their own grooves. For now, she was happy to be the cheerleader. This morning, after the buggies had left, she'd brought her sisters coffee in their bunk beds, and then had dragged them down to the river to splash around in the crazy hot heat. Soaking in the river, they had concocted the idea to ride the family scooters into "civilization."

Now, as they neared town, Serena was glad they were on scooters that could move around some of the sitting traffic. Although there were no Amish people in sight, a good amount of "English" shoppers from the suburbs roamed the streets. Families waited outside restaurants and people of all ages crowded the sidewalks on Main Street.

"How come there are no Amish buggies in town?" Grace asked.

"Remember what Aunt Miriam said? Sunday is a day of rest," Megan explained. "You won't see them running any shops today, but Sam said that some of the bigger businesses hire Sunday help or let their English partners take over on the Sabbath."

"Let's park the scooters over at that rack and walk it," Serena said.

Grace looked around them as she wheeled her scooter over. "But we don't have locks. What if someone jacks them?"

"None of the bikes are locked," Megan observed. "Looks like we have to go with the honor system."

Their first stop was the country diner, where they put their name on the waiting list. They'd decided to treat themselves with some of the cash Dad had left with them, and Megan had been craving a burger, fries, and a milkshake, which sounded pretty good to Serena right about now.

"It's a forty-minute wait," Megan said. "If you guys want to go look around, I'll wait here and text you when they're about to call us."

Grace shrugged. "I've got no money and nothing to buy."

"Come with me," Serena said. "I want to look for a dresser for the three of us to share."

Grace cocked her head, her reaction difficult to read beneath her oversized sunglasses. "Why don't we ask Dad to lug out one of our old dressers from home?"

"Because that's no easy task, and it's time we handled our problems on our own."

"By buying a dresser? Who's paying for that?" Grace probed.

"Just come on." As they headed down Main Street, Serena tried to get a sense of what they had to choose from. "Let's walk down and see what's here." They passed the Country Store, which seemed to feature fabric, yarn, and craft supplies. "You'll never find me in there," Serena said.

A quaint, shingled building called The Amish Wood-shed had a pine scent that seemed inviting. Inside they found small pieces of wood furniture, all of it handcrafted. Most of the stools, cedar chests, and chairs were simple, but some pieces had a design carved into them. The furniture was quaint but woodsy—fine if you lived in a lumberjack camp. There was an entire section of the store devoted to wooden signs, with sayings like "Home Sweet Home" and "Be what you wish others to become."

Next door they walked by the drive-up burger stand, and the smell of charbroiled beef made Serena want to change their plans. "Maybe we should grab Megan and just go in here," she told Grace.

Her younger sister studied the cars pulled up to the parking bays and then peered into the small shop. "Nah. This is just a hangout spot for teens."

As they were checking out the place, Serena caught the eye of a young guy who'd been watching them. Tall and solid, in jeans and a tank top that showed off his well-toned arms and shoulders, he wore a black bandana wrapped around his head to keep unruly dark curls out of his eyes. Back in Philly, he would have been her type—a bad boy. She could tell by the way he swaggered over to them.

"Hey, girls. You've got that lost look. Let Johnny help you out."

"Oh, we're not lost," Serena said, looking him in the eyes. "We're just wondering when was the last time the health inspector checked out this place."

He laughed. "It may not be top-notch, but it's got my seal of approval."

"Good to know. And who are you?"

"Johnny. Johnny Rotten is what I go by now." He was

acting tough, and, although Serena liked playing the game, she wasn't that into him.

"That's original. I'm Serena, and this is my sister Grace." Beside her, she sensed Grace's face icing over. This was not her scene. "We just moved here from Philadelphia."

"Seriously? That's cool."

"Definitely. We've got some errands to do, so see you around, Johnny."

He nodded. "Bye, Queena Serena."

A nickname—how original, she thought as they continued down the street.

"Why do you even bother with guys like that?" Grace asked.

"An old habit."

They passed an ice cream and candy shop with a sign that said FUDGE in the window. The harness shop was closed. Grace wanted to check out the little Christmas shop called Noel, but it was brimming over with people, so crowded that the girls didn't bother to go inside.

"Who needs Christmas stuff in August?" Grace said.

"Some people just can't get enough of Christmas," Serena said, remembering how it used to be a big deal in their house. "Like Mom."

"Dad says Mom did it for us. Christmas wasn't a really big deal when she was a kid, so she went crazy with the decorations. Remember how she would string lights inside our windows?"

"And she let us leave them up until after Valentine's Day."

"When she hung up red lights," Grace added.

"And remember the Christmas snow globes with our

photos inside? We each had one. I wonder if they're still tucked away somewhere in the apartment." Serena hoped so. They were reminders of wonderful holidays with Mom and Dad.

Next they ducked into an antique store that was so full of things, there was barely room to move. Squat tables and desks were covered with platters and doilies that held more bowls and small items like jewelry chests, books, and fake fruit. Most things struck Serena as being dusty and sad, and she wondered what made something truly an antique. Did things qualify just because they were old? Even if the finish was chipping off and the legs were uneven?

The one dresser she could find in the store looked like it had belonged to Benjamin Franklin two hundred years ago. She opened a drawer and crinkled her nose at the dust and dirt accumulated in the corner. No way would she be tucking her clothes away in there.

But this was fun. Walking down Main Street with Grace, popping in and out of stores, Serena felt like her old city-girl self again. It was a beautiful day, not too humid, with a clear blue sky, and she knew she looked good in her thin strapped top, tight black shorts, and strappy sandals. Shopping was right up her alley, a way to chat with people, joke around, and move on before she got bored. If there'd been a shopping class in high school, Serena would have aced it with her hands tied behind her back.

It was after they had crossed Main Street and were wending their way back to the restaurant that she found it. A shop called Joyful Gems, an adorable little boutique that sold everything from soaps to furniture, had a recon-ditioned dresser in a cool shade of turquoise with a dis-tressed finish. The decorative cracks and dents were filled in with metallic silver that made the surface sparkle in certain light. The drawers were lined with pretty flowered paper, and the knobs were cut crystal.

The only thing that wasn't perfect about the dresser was the price.

"Eight hundred?" Serena burst out, maybe a little too loudly. "Does that mean dollars?"

The shopkeeper, a round, middle-aged woman who struggled to move through the store, smiled at Serena's reaction. "Eight hundred is right for that piece. It's green teal, the color of the moment, and the dresser has good bones."

Serena pressed her lips together as she circled the dresser again. She tried to find something wrong with it, but that was impossible. It was perfect, and she wanted it so badly!

But eight hundred dollars was a lot.

"Can we barter?" she asked.

The shop owner straightened and peered at her through violet-tinted glasses. "What price were you thinking of?"

Serena pressed her fingertips to her mouth, wishing she had the credit card Dad had taken away. "I don't know. I really love it, and I'd be giving it a really good home."

The woman nodded sagely. "I'm glad you like it, but it's not a puppy. Honestly, I can afford to let it sit here for the next year until the right buyer comes along."

"No, don't sell it to someone else. I really love it. Can you hold on to it for me until I talk to my aunt and uncle about it?"

"I suppose so." The woman took a notebook and pen from behind the sales counter. "My name is Janice. Write down your name and number, and I'll give you a call if someone else makes an offer."

"Thank you." Serena jotted down her information quickly. "I'll be back soon. I just have to talk to them."

At that point Grace was watching with an astounded expression. Serena handed back the notebook and made a beeline toward the door. Grace hurried out after her.

"What was that about? Have you gone bonkers?"

"It's so beautiful. Maybe Aunt Miriam will agree when she sees it."

"Aunt Miriam doesn't have eight hundred dollars to throw down on a stupid dresser for you."

"It's for all of us."

Grace rolled her eyes. "We need to go. Megan texted, and they're getting close to us."

"Don't tell Megan about the dresser. She'll say I'm materialistic. You know how she loves to tear me down."

"You give her so much ammunition."

"Just let me handle it," Serena said. She was used to getting people to see things her way. "I'll figure it out."

That evening Serena waited and watched for the right time to spring news of the dresser on her aunt and uncle. Dinner was a simple meal—sandwiches, fresh veggies, and leftovers. Serena had expected a big, gut-busting country dinner, but Aunt Miriam explained that the Amish observed Sunday as a day of rest—and that gave her a day off in the kitchen, too. Serena was glad that she and her sisters had splurged on burgers earlier, but she had to admit that the leftover chicken combined with homemade pickles made a delicious sandwich.

After the simple meal, the dinner cleanup took little time. When the kids were out playing kickball and her aunt and uncle moved to the porch glider, Serena knew it was time to strike. She stepped onto the porch and sat down in the swing across from them. "So I may have solved a problem today when we went into town."

Aunt Miriam gave her an encouraging nod.

"Remember we talked about getting a dresser? Well, I found one at a little shop on Main Street. It would be perfect for me to share with Megan and Grace. That way we could get our suitcases off the floor and store them away."

"That would be good," Miriam agreed.

"It's an old dresser that someone restored. It's a beautiful shade of teal, with a silver distressed finish. It's part of that whole reclamation movement in furniture design."

"We wouldn't know anything about that," Miriam said. "I know some women who design quilts, but furniture design, no."

Uncle Alvin put his Amish newspaper down on his lap. "Plain folk don't have fancy furniture."

"It's not too fancy. It's beautiful in a subtle way." Serena explained how amazing it was—crystal knobs, and all— and told them it was expensive, but absolutely worth the price.

"How much?" Alvin asked.

"Eight hundred dollars."

He laughed out loud, exchanging an amused look with Aunt Miriam. "For a used dresser? I think maybe you made a mistake on the price."

"No." A queasy feeling cramped Serena's stomach. Doubt. "I spoke with the saleslady. That's the price."

"That's too much," Miriam said. "And that's for a used dresser? Think of what they would charge for a new one."

"This one was better than new because . . ." Serena had to consider why it mattered. "Because someone put time and creativity into it and made it like a work of art."

"That pretty?" Miriam nodded over her knitting. "There's been many a quilt that's caught my eyes over the years, and the handmade ones are always hundreds of dollars. I know what you mean when you say something is so pleasing to the eye. Too bad it's so expensive."

Serena felt her sweet treasure slipping away. "What if I pay for it? I'll get money from my dad or something." She knew she couldn't ask her dad for that kind of money. "I'll get a job. I'm a hard worker."

"But you're going to be in school soon," Miriam said. "That will take much of your time."

"I'll work after school, and weekends. Please, I have to have this dresser."

Aunt Miriam stopped knitting. "We're not stopping you. You're eighteen years old, and you can buy what you want. But we don't have that kind of money, and I know the same is true of your father. So you can buy it, if you can pay for it."

"I don't have any money right now. But I'll work for it."

"I could probably find you a job," Alvin said. "They need some extra hands at the pretzel factory in town."

"I'll do it," Serena said. "I'll save every penny for the dresser."

"I'll talk to the owner," her uncle said. "But I wonder about the value of a piece of furniture, even one so beautiful, as you say. There's a difference between good sound reasons and reasons that sound good."

Serena squinted at him, wondering if he meant to sound like Yoda from the *Star Wars* movies.

"In the meantime, maybe we can find an old dresser

you can use, so you'll have a place to put your clothes," suggested Aunt Miriam.

The thought of keeping her stuff in a dusty old thing, like the dirty dresser in that antique store, was such a turnoff. "I don't want something old," she said.

"But you said that the expensive one was old," her uncle pointed out.

"Yeah, but it's been fixed up."

"Maybe you can do the fixing," Miriam said. "A little cleanup and some paint might help. The important thing is having a place to put clothes."

"Whatever." Serena didn't know anything about fixing up furniture, but she knew it would be wrong to argue with her aunt and uncle.

She left the porch and went out to the lawn, where Megan was smiling, waiting her turn to kick.

"What's wrong?" Megan asked.

"I might have to work at a pretzel factory," Serena said.

"Pretzels? Cool." Megan nodded, then turned back to the game and faced Sam, who was pitching the ball. "Show me what you got, Sammy."

Annoyed, Serena went back to the picnic table, picked up a cookie, and allowed herself a moment to feel sorry for herself as she polished it off. Living here was going to be harder than she'd thought.

That night, when everyone else went to bed, Serena remained in her shorts and top and sat downstairs with a book she'd gotten from the library. Although most everyone else was in bed, she wasn't tired, and she wanted to wait up for Scout.

Besides, Essie was still out with Harlan, off on a buggy ride. Serena had wanted to come along, just to get away, but Megan had nudged her with a scornful look. "Can't you see? This is the only way those two can be alone."

Duh. How could Serena be so stupid? And usually she was so good at reading people. She was making bad choices right and left.

The rumble of the milk truck sent her out the front door. This time, she closed it quietly behind her, as Aunt Miriam had instructed. As she headed over to the milk barn, her formerly snow-white Vans sneakers crunching over gravel behind the growling truck, Serena hoped she hadn't misread Scout, too. He always seemed happy to see her, and he had laughed along with her sisters last night when they'd joked about city girls stuck on a farm. She hoped his friendship was sincere.

"Hey, city girl," he called as he came around the parked truck.

"Hi. How was your day?"

"Excellent, as always. How about you?"

How could he be so cheerful when he worked two jobs and took classes? "It was fun at first. But I think I'm in a little bit of trouble with my aunt and uncle."

"You, in trouble? You've barely been here three days."

"Right? I guess I'm just like a tornado that sweeps through quickly and leaves a path of destruction."

"I find that hard to believe. What happened?"

As he took test samples of the milk, she explained how she'd tried to solve a big problem by finding the perfect dresser, but instead, she'd made things worse. Now she would have to work for months at some factory and still live out of her suitcase while she saved up money. "I know it might seem petty, but it makes me feel out of place here. Like I'll never fit in."

"I think you're being a little hard on yourself," Scout said. "First, you belong here. God put you and your sisters here, and no one expects you to become Amish while you're here. So you're doing a great job being you. Hang on to that."

"I never thought of it that way." His words filled her with hope and a sense of belonging, especially because he seemed so sincere.

He seemed to consider the situation as he hooked up the hose and started the pump. "And I don't think you should wait to buy that dresser. Get your hands on an old dresser and paint it up the way you like it. There are plenty of antique and used furniture shops around. My mom sells stuff out of our garage in her spare time. I bet she could give you something pretty cheap."

"I'm not good at arts and crafts, and I don't like old stuff."

"You can make something old sparkle. Get out of your comfort zone and find a painting tutorial online. Sometimes, you need to go out on a limb to get the best view."

"I'll think about it," she said. Maybe a dingy dresser would be better than the pretzel factory.

The noise of the pump had them moving away from the truck.

"What a beautiful night," he said with a broad smile. It had cooled down last night, and the day had been warm but pleasant for Pennsylvania summer. He started walking down the lane, toward the house. "Come over here. You've got to see this."

Curious, Serena moved away from the lights of the truck and followed him out onto the bumpy lawn that stretched in front of the house.

"We got a clear night. Check it out," he said, tilting his head back.

Serena lifted her gaze to the sky and gasped. "The stars!" They were everywhere! Even the brightest stars sat in fields of tiny stars that seemed to be so close to her. It was as if someone had tossed buckets of diamonds and sequins into the inky sky. "They're so close! And beautiful. I've never seen a sky like this."

"Funny, but those stars are always there. When it's overcast, we think they've gone away, but no. And when you're back in the city, the light pollution prevents you from seeing most of the stars." He put his hands on his hips and seemed to breathe in the sky. "Yeah, it's pretty amazing. Have you ever studied astronomy?"

"I'm not a science person." To be honest, she didn't like to study *anything*. "But if I lived out here, I'd probably know more. I mean, this sky is amazing."

"Stargazing is kind of a hobby of mine. It fits in well when you drive a milk truck at night. I get to track the stars as they shift in the sky from season to season."

"Do you use a telescope?"

"I've used the one at school—the community college. But most nights I just look up at the sky, and go on the Internet to get information from astronomy sites."

She let her eyes scan the wide expanse, lolling in the joy of a thousand pin dots of light. One star seemed much brighter than the others. She pointed to it. "Do you know the name of that star? The really bright one?"

He moved closer to her, their shoulders touching, so that he could follow the line of her finger. "You're pointing south. That's Sirius, usually the brightest star in the sky. It shines so bright because it's only 8.6 light years away."

"Wow . . . I guess?"

"It disappears in the middle of the summer, but it's back now. Some people call it the Dog Star because it's part of the constellation Canis Major."

"Okay, I'm impressed. But I think Sirius is a much better name than Dog Star."

"Hey, I love my dog, Red."

"Nothing against dogs. Does Red ever come on the truck with you?"

"Sometimes in the winter, when he doesn't get enough outdoor time during the day. Between school and being on duty at the firehouse, I'm not home a lot."

"I wish I could see him. We haven't had a dog in the house since I was in junior high." Back when she had a house, and a mom and a dad, and a happy life.

"Maybe you'll get to meet him sometime."

Serena smiled, still trying to absorb the sparkling sky. "Your Dog Star is actually really pretty. It seems to be kind of bluish or green."

"You're right. The Dog Star flickers in different colors. White, blue, green, purple, and orange. Even pink. Some people call it a rainbow star because of the colors."

"That is so cool. You should teach astronomy. You make it so interesting."

He shrugged. "Maybe someday. Right now, I'm still a student." He looked back toward the milking barn. "And a milk truck driver. The tank's probably empty. I'd better get back to work."

She wished he could stay longer. Her conversations with Scout were easy and bright—an escape from family and farm life. But he had a job to do.

And there was always tomorrow night.

"Thanks for listening," she said.

"Of course. I like talking with you. The pickup at the Lapp farm is now the highlight of my night."

"Aw." She smiled. He was a good friend, maybe her only friend at the moment. "See you tomorrow."

"Same time, same place," he said, a twinkle in his eye as he touched the bill of his cap.

Chapter Twelve

Essie paced the front porch, peering toward the barn, where Harlan was helping her father and brothers unload bales of hay. Staring at them wouldn't make them work any faster. She knew a watched pot never boiled, or so people said. But she was eager for Harlan to be let go for the day so they could get into town before the bank closed.

They had business to attend to in town.

It had been Essie's idea to open a joint account. Her parents had long done business at the local bank, American Heritage Trust, and Essie had thought that if she and Harlan had an account together, they would see progress toward their inevitable marriage. So far they hadn't saved enough to build a home—that was a long way off—but Essie had deposited the money she'd saved in a sock from working two summers on the main road, selling vegetables from Mem's garden. And each month, Harlan put in a portion of his paycheck, usually just two hundred dollars, but Essie knew that his mem needed the rest of his salary to keep food on the table and pay the rent.

When they'd started the account, they'd been saving for a small plot of land to build a house on. Dat had warned that this wouldn't come cheaply, but Harlan was good with carpentry, and, when the time came, they knew men from their church would pitch in to build the house. Harlan and Essie's dreams seemed on the verge of coming true since, recently, the bishop had offered to sell them a parcel of land near town. Heather Denning, the assistant manager at the bank, told them they would need five thousand dollars in their account in order to get the small loan from the bank. Since Bishop Aaron had made the offer, Harlan and Essie had been saving every penny.

Essie turned away from the barn and peeked inside, checking the grandfather clock. It was after 3:30, but the bank was open until 5:30 today, Friday afternoon, so they would have time if Harlan was cut loose soon.

The rumble of a vehicle on the main road caught her attention; a yellow school bus stopped at the top of their lane. The cousins were back from school.

Peter, Paul, and Lizzie had been home for almost an hour, but then the Amish one-room schoolhouse was just up the road a ways. Essie descended the front porch and waved toward her cousins, who walked down the lane, each wearing a knapsack on her back. Essie realized she was happy to see them. After a week of back and forth in the kitchen at night, everyone had eased into a new pattern to get dinner cooked and dishes done. With some of the pressure off Essie, she now had a chance to enjoy the English girls' surprising observations and plans. Sometimes she had to hold her cousins back; it wouldn't do for the bishop to be alerted to English girls swimming in next to nothing at the river with Amish boys. Things like that.

"Hi, Essie," Grace called. "We're hot and tired and glad the school week is over."

"TGIF!" Serena said, scraping her hair up into a pony-tail and letting it fall over her shoulders again.

Essie squinted. "What did you say?"

"TGIF! Thank God it's Friday!" Serena explained. "We didn't even have a full week of school, and I think that was the longest week of my life."

"Remember our deal?" Megan said. "No griping allowed."

"I'm not complaining," Serena said. "Just stating a fact. Schoolwork makes the clock move more slowly."

Essie smiled as she turned round and fell into step with the girls heading toward the house. "And now that the weekend is here, the clock will speed up."

"Exactly!" Serena said.

"Speak for yourself," Grace said. "I kind of like the distraction of school. Food for the brain."

"What about you, Megan? Do you like your new school?" asked Essie.

"It's hardly nonstop fun, but it's my ticket to success, and I'm going to ride that train."

"You sound like the little engine that could!" Grace said. "That's so adorable."

The cousins laughed, and Essie smiled. She wasn't sure just what that meant, but over the past week she had come to enjoy the easy banter among her three cousins. These girls were quick to tease and correct one another, and yet it was clear that there was a strong underpinning of concern and love keeping them together.

"Wassup with you, Essie?" Megan asked.

"I'm waiting for Harlan to get off so we can go into town," she said. "With the break in the weather, Mem and I made whoopie pies this afternoon." She turned to Megan.

"You told me that's been your favorite since you were a kid."

"Tis. Thanks, cuz. I owe you one," Megan said, striding toward the house.

"I love whoopie pies," Grace said. "Don't eat all of them!"

"There's plenty," Essie said as the two girls hurried into the house. "On the kitchen table."

Serena remained in front of the porch.

"Don't you want one?" Essie asked her.

"I'll grab one later," said Serena. "I wanted to tell you what happened last night when Scout came by."

Serena had confided in Essie that her feelings for Scout Tanner seemed to be growing beyond friendship, and Essie was grateful for her cousin's trust. "Tell me everything you know about him," Serena had said a few days ago. Essie had complied, though she didn't have much information. Scout was one of many of the English who worked together to make the Lapp Dairy Farms owned by her dat and his brothers a success.

Now Serena pressed a palm to her chest. "I'm. So. Excited. I might just pop."

Essie blinked, trying to restrain her curiosity. "What happened?"

"Scout offered for me to come by and meet his mother, for real. I mean, it's under the excuse of maybe buying a used dresser for me to fix up, but it's a chance for the two of us to be together, away from here, without a half-hour time limit and a giant pumper truck rumbling in the background."

"That's wonderful. And you said yes?"

"I did. And we're going to do it tomorrow, Saturday,

since I don't have school. He's going to swing by to pick me up." Serena clapped her hands together. "Of course, we'll look at dressers, and I'll meet his mom and everything. But most of all, I'll get to spend some time with him. It'll be like a real date."

"And meeting his mem, that's a big step," Essie said.

"That's what I thought. I can't wait. And maybe I'll find a decent dresser, too. A win-win."

They were still chatting when Harlan's gray buggy emerged from the barn, his donkey Beebee pulling it at a steady gait. A high-pitched squeal came from one of the wheels—the song, they called it, when they joked about the buggy's rundown condition. The rig was on its last legs, but there was no money for a new vehicle. "Here comes Harlan," Essie said. "I have to go."

"We'll talk more later," Serena said. "That's the beauty of having your Philly cousins here. Always someone around to talk to."

"It's a joy and a burden," Essie teased.

Serena's mouth opened in surprise as she pointed at Essie. "You're getting the hang of this witty banter, cuz!" Serena waved to Harlan on her way into the house. "Hi and bye!"

From inside the buggy, Harlan tipped back his straw hat and nodded.

Still chuckling, Essie went up to the porch and lifted a case of jam from the top step. Seeing her, Harlan jumped out of the buggy to help.

"What's all this?" he asked, taking the load from her.

"A case of wild blueberry," she said, pleased with herself. "That gift shop in town, Joyful Gems, already sold out of the strawberry."

"Is that so? Your business is booming, Essie."

"*Our* business," she said as she climbed into the buggy. "I figured we could deliver the jam on the way to the bank." She could tell that Harlan had washed up at the slop sink in the barn. Bringing in the hay could be hot, sweaty work, but he smelled of soap, and his face had that clean, just-washed gleam. His blue shirt-sleeves were rolled up, and he'd gotten most of the dust off his pants. She settled beside him on the bench, and, as he called to Beebee to get going, she reached down and brushed two strands of hay from one leg of his trousers.

"Is that the last of the hay to be brought in?" she asked.

"Looks like it's getting near the end." He swept off his hat and pushed his dark hair from his forehead before replacing the straw hat. "I wasn't sure I'd be able to get away from the woodshop today, not with all the orders that have been coming in. It's a good time to be making furniture. But Zed told me to go. A promise is a promise, and I've been helping your dat bring in the hay for seven years now."

Ever since your dat left town, thought Essie. Back then Harlan had felt so crushed by abandonment and desperate for money to support his family, he had gone round to all the Amish men in the area, looking for work. Alvin Lapp had hired him on as a steady worker, paid him well until Harlan had found a job in carpentry, something he wanted to move on to.

"This time of year, Dat needs every extra hand he can get," Essie said. "But I'm glad you're one of them. My favorite one."

"You know I'd do anything for your dat." Harlan took the lead with his left hand and twined the fingers of his right hand through hers. "He's more of a father to me than my own dat."

She lifted his hand to her lips and kissed it. "I know you still think about your father. Did you ever hear back on any of those letters you sent out?" A few months ago, Harlan had sent letters out to folks in a few Amish settlements, asking if anyone had knowledge of his father. After all these years, Harlan just wanted one more chance to see his dat, to know that he was all right.

"I got a few letters back. Only one person said they'd heard of him. A deacon in Somerset County, near the Maryland border."

"Is that so? Then you made progress in finding him."

"Not really. The deacon said he hasn't heard from Jed Yoder for years. That he really didn't join their church. So it's another dead end."

"That's disappointing. I know you want to see him, but I guess it's not meant to be. But ours is not to cling to what might have been, especially when we have a bright tomorrow."

"You're right, Essie. You're my sunshine, and I thank Gott that we'll be family soon."

She squeezed his hand, loving the strength they could muster together. "You're like family now, Harlan."

"But soon, it'll be real and blessed by Gott. I hope we can marry in November, Essie. There's nothing I want more than to be by your side come winter nights."

This, too, was the ache in her heart, the desire to be by his side always, in his arms at night. His bride, his wife.

She wanted to tell him so, to paint a picture of her love for him, but she couldn't speak of that now. Her longings for him, her hunger for him . . . it bore the heat of a wife's passions for her husband. Those words would have to wait.

"Until then, all we can do is wait," she said quietly.

For a moment, there was only the clop of Beebee's hooves and the squeak of the singing wheel. And then, Harlan added, "Wait, and save our money."

"That's right. Today I'll have a deposit to make. When we drop off the blueberry jam, Janice said she'll pay me for the first case."

"You can keep the money from the jam," Harlan said.

"It's going in the account. Otherwise, we won't be getting married till we're old and gray. And I want to be your bride this wedding season. You're a pretty special fellow, Harlan Yoder. It's time I snatched you up."

His smile beamed bright as he squeezed her hand. "You make me sound like a prize horse at auction."

"So much better than a horse," she teased. "I don't need to groom you, and you won't be coming down with thrush and canker."

He chuckled. "Well, we can be grateful for that. And our bank account is going to start growing faster now that things are changing at the furniture workshop. One of the vendors saw the carving I did for you, and I showed him a few other chunks of wood I was working on. He has a client who wants custom finishes, hand-carved trim pieces for stairways and doorframes, and he'll pay me double to do the carving."

"Double? That's good pay, and fine work for you."

"Carving has never been work to me," he said. "It'll be

a labor of love. Zed is fine with it, as long as I do it on my own time."

"This *is* good news," Essie said. With the extra income, they would have enough saved in the next month or two, and Harlan had found work he enjoyed. "Gott has blessed us for sure."

"We'll be able to tell our parents soon," he said. "Our mothers need some time to get things in order."

Much planning went into an Amish wedding. Besides the celebration, which would probably involve at least a hundred and fifty guests, there were other small traditions, like the quilt the bride's family made for the new couple. Essie smiled at the thought of Mem trying so hard to get her stitches right. Miriam loved to knit, but for her, quilting was a challenge. Oh, it was going to be a wonderful wedding season!

Once in town, they dropped off the case of jam at the boutique on Main Street.

"Bring me more when you have it," Janice said, placing each jar in a prominent place on the counter. The jam gleamed purple inside the ridged glass jar. "Autumn is a busy time for us. Once the weather breaks, people love to make the trip out to Amish country, and this stuff sells like hotcakes."

"And it tastes delicious with hotcakes," Harlan added.

Essie promised to bring more jam in the next week or two, and Janice paid her a hundred and twenty dollars in cash. In Essie's mind, the crisp twenty-dollar bills represented progress. She and Harlan were on their way to building a home.

At the bank, Harlan directed Beebee toward the drive-through line while Essie stared at the cash. "I want to deposit all of it, but I need to pay my parents back for the jars and sugar." She took one twenty from the crisp bills Janice had given them.

"And save some cash for more supplies," Harlan advised.

She took out another twenty. "It doesn't seem like so much now."

"But there's more coming to you, Ess. We haven't been round to collect from the shops outside town yet."

Harlan was right. "If we get a hundred and twenty dollars a case . . ." She gaped at him. "If we sell ten cases, we make more than a thousand dollars!"

He nodded. "It's not a year-round business, but you can do well on it. You've got a good touch in the kitchen."

Essie couldn't help but smile. Right now peaches were ripening faster than they could eat them, and wild berries were free. Time to get picking the last of the season.

Chapter Thirteen

Serena wanted to sleep in Saturday morning, but the prospect of visiting Scout woke her early with a case of nerves—that sensation of butterflies fluttering in her chest. She rolled over in bed and stared at the expanse of tree branches swaying in the breeze beyond the window. In the shimmering mosaic of leaves she saw a happy dog chasing its tail.

She smiled. Scout had a dog named Red.

She hoped she would make a good impression, but when she got nervous she talked fast, yammering on about ridiculous things.

Take a breath. Stay calm. Find a place of peace.

The breeze moved the leaves, and the happy dog disappeared, which she took as her signal to get out of bed.

The smells of bacon and coffee lured her straight to the kitchen, where Aunt Miriam and Essie moved about preparing a meal for the family. "On Saturdays, we have time to eat together after the morning milking," Miriam said. "It's one of my favorite things." Serena realized she had slept through breakfast last Saturday. This time she helped Lizzie set the table, then went upstairs to wake her sisters.

"You don't want to miss this," she said. "There's fresh-baked biscuits and eggs with cheese, and the bacon smells so good."

Megan sat up and threw back the sheet. "You had me at biscuits."

The food was delicious, but Serena's favorite part was the way everyone came together. Sam, Uncle Alvin, Peter, Paul, and Annie traipsed in from the milking barn and washed up. Essie and Miriam brought the food outside to the picnic tables. Lizzie, Sarah Rose, and Serena finished setting out the flatware and took their places at the table. Grace and Megan came out the door with bright eyes, hair still mussed from sleep, and slow smiles. The gathering felt like a family, and Serena felt a new sense of belonging here.

After breakfast Serena took a long, hot shower so that her hair would have plenty of time to air dry. After that, she actually dug into her backpack and did some home-work. Living without a computer or cell service, she'd learned this week that she couldn't leave assignments to the last minute the way she used to.

When it was almost time she went to wait on the porch, where Aunt Miriam was giving Grace a knitting lesson. Both had knitting needles in hand, and Miriam kept hold-ing hers up, trying to show Grace how to loop the yarn around in just the right way. Watching them, it was clear that Aunt Miriam felt at ease with a pair of knitting nee-dles in her hands.

It wasn't long before Scout's red truck came down the

lane. Serena stood up and waved as Sarah Rose and Essie came out to the porch.

"I want to knit too!" Sarah Rose said.

"You can," Miriam said. "Get your needles from the basket."

Grace frowned. "It's a little weird when a five-year-old is more advanced in knitting than I am."

Aunt Miriam chuckled. "Everyone in his or her own time." She looked over toward the truck and smiled. "Scout. We're not used to seeing you before nightfall."

"I was just thinking how your farm looks different during the day," he said. Serena knew that Scout had needed to get the day off from the firehouse to make today work. He hadn't been kidding when he'd said he had a busy schedule. He talked with Aunt Miriam about a small kitchen fire that had occurred in an Amish home the week before, when he'd been on duty, and then he and Serena were off.

There was something comforting about being in a motorized vehicle that wasn't a stodgy school bus. Which was so embarrassing! An eighteen-year-old should never have to ride in a bright yellow bus like a goofy school kid.

Scout's truck was old. The leather of the seats was splitting in the seams and the cab had an oily smell, but for Serena it was like sliding on an old familiar sweater. She loved sitting up high and bouncing over the bumps in the road.

"If it's okay with you, I figured we'd go to my house to work on the dresser thing, and then head into town for a burger." He rested his elbow on the open window of the truck, casual but in control. "I know you don't get sprung from the farm too often."

"I would love that!" She tried not to gush over the plan too much, but she was thrilled that this outing was sounding more and more like a date.

"So how was the first week of school?" he asked.

"Okay," she sighed. "I don't know what it is, but I feel so much older than the other seniors." When Serena watched them talk in the hallways or text one another in class, she wondered what it would have been like to grow up here in their world, surrounded by farmland and Amish communities. She'd already seen posters for homecoming dance, and she cringed at the thought of going to a formal event with any of the boys at this school. Boys, that was all they were. Not men, like Scout.

Even Johnny Rotten, who turned out to be a senior and a football player, seemed immature. He'd flirted with Serena once or twice when his girlfriend wasn't around, but she wanted nothing to do with him. Guys like Johnny were more concerned with petty things like besting their friends and looking cool in fat sneakers. She bet that not one of them knew anything about the stars in the sky.

"I guess things are a little different here from Philly," Scout said.

"That's for sure. So, have you lived here all your life?"

"I was born in Pittsburgh, but I grew up here. I've still got a lot of family in the area, but my grandmother lives in Florida now. My parents have a condo there, and they keep threatening to sell the house and move down there."

"That's awful."

"It's not so bad. They like it down there, and I'm the last kid in the house, so I guess it's about time I got my own place."

"Would you stay here in Joyful River?"

"Probably. It's home for me."

Home . . . She'd always thought Philadelphia was her place to be, but now she wondered. Was home really where your heart was? Where your family was?

They had reached the outskirts of town, and Scout made two turns off the main road to a side street lined with trees and tidy lawns. He pulled into a brown shingled, two-story house and put the truck in park.

"This is it." One of the neighbors was cutting the lawn, and the buzz of the mower and the smell of fresh-cut grass filled the air as they started toward the front door. Scout paused, snapped his fingers, and said: "We should probably go around back."

She followed him around the back of the house to a patio with outdoor furniture and a big, grassy lawn. The noise was coming from a hand mower being pushed by a middle-aged woman with silvery blond hair swept back into a ponytail. "My mom," Scout said, waving at the woman. She nodded at him and cut the engine.

"There's a pitcher of iced tea inside," she called out as she walked toward them. "Why don't you bring it out for us?"

Scout nodded. "This is my mom, Bonnie. And this is Serena." He climbed the steps to the house, leaving Serena to face the mom on her own.

"It's a pleasure to meet you." Bonnie pulled off leather gloves and extended a hand. "Saturday is yard day for me. I do love my garden, but I'm not a fan of spiders and creepy crawly things."

"I hear you," Serena said, surprised by the softness of Bonnie's hand as they shook. "You're talking to a city girl who's still going through culture shock here." They talked about the things that had surprised Serena on the farm. The dust. The fat flies. The smell of manure when you least expected it. "You think you're out in the country, getting fresh air, and then you smell *that*," Serena said, scrunching up her face.

Bonnie laughed. "Everybody wants to get back to nature, but nobody mentions the smells."

"Actually, I didn't choose to come to the farm, but . . ." Serena didn't want to admit that her aunt and uncle were really the only family who could take in her sisters and her. It sounded so desperate, when the last week had seemed more like the extended visits they'd made over the past summers with Mom. "But here I am."

"Living on an Amish farm."

"That's right. But we're going to the normal high school, so we'll be keeping some connection to the real world."

Bonnie smiled. "Actually, the world on your Amish family's farm is just as real as you'll find anywhere else. My family traveled a lot as a kid, and I find that people around the planet have universal wants and needs. Shelter, food, to love and be loved." The lines at the edges of Bonnie's eyes spoke of experience and wisdom.

"What countries did you live in?" Serena asked.

"All over. Belgium. Argentina. Japan . . ."

They were talking about Bonnie's travels when the door opened and a dark red dog darted down the porch steps and blew into the yard at a gallop. Serena missed part of what Bonnie was saying as she watched the dog loop around the lawn mower twice, then double back to the patio and sit in front of Bonnie.

Scout was out the door seconds later, carrying a tray with iced tea.

"This is Red," Bonnie said, turning toward the beautiful rusty-colored dog who looked at her with eager eyes. "She's a sweet dog, but hopelessly afraid of the lawn mower." Bonnie stroked the dog for a minute, and then Red came over and looked up intently at Serena.

"Hi, Red. You're a beauty." She held out her hand for the dog to sniff. Red eyed her curiously, then came closer and pressed against Serena's knee. "Aw." Serena felt a surge of affection.

"You've got a new friend," Bonnie said.

"Whenever she hears the noise she holes up inside." Scout put the tray down and started filling a glass. "That run around the yard was just her weird way of doing a victory lap. Like she's conquered the mower."

"You know, Scout, it might be herding mentality," Bonnie said.

"That's true. But the mower is never going to let itself be corralled." He bent down and rubbed the dog's scruff. "You're a weird dog, but we love you."

Red gave a little whimper and watched Scout as he sat down in a chair.

"Go get your ball," Scout said. Red looked this way and that, and then walked over to the edge of the yard to retrieve a tennis ball.

"She found it," Serena observed.

"She's a pretty smart dog, except when it comes to lawn mowers," Scout said. Red delivered the ball to him, and he chucked it out into the yard. This time, the dog bolted out to fetch it.

"Where did you get her?"

The iced tea helped to cool Serena's nerves as Scout and his mother told her the story of how Red had found them when they went to donate old blankets to the local dog shelter.

"We weren't looking to adopt," Bonnie said, "but sometimes a dog finds you, and you just can't say no."

"Now she's part of the family," Scout said, throwing the ball again.

They talked and sipped tea for a few minutes before the conversation turned to furniture. "So you sell antiques?" Serena asked.

"Oh, heavens no. I'm more of a junk collector, but I just can't stand to see good furniture tossed into a junk heap. So I take things off people's hands and load them into my garage. My husband doesn't mind, but it drives Scout crazy."

"It would be nice to be able to use the garage for something besides junk," Scout said without looking up from Red.

"I like to think that creative clutter is a sign of an organized mind," Bonnie said with a smile. "And I'm not an untidy person. At work I keep my desk clean. But my garage junk is my hobby. So tell me, Serena, what sort of dresser are you looking for?"

Serena told her about the beautiful turquoise-painted dresser she'd seen at Joyful Gems.

Bonnie nodded. "That's a lovely shop, isn't it? I don't have anything like that, but you could get yourself some paint and get creative. How big?"

"My sisters and I need a place to store our clothes," Serena explained. "Right now we're living out of suitcases."

"One dresser for three young women? How about two?"

"There's not that much space. We're in a bunk room with my three cousins."

"It'll have to be a good size." Bonnie rose. "Let's take a look. Bring your tea."

Red followed them around the side of the house as they went to the front of the garage. The electronic double door lifted, and Serena's eyes opened wide at the mass of stacked furniture. "Wow." It was wedged in so tightly, she wasn't sure they could fit inside.

"I'll take a few things out, so we can move in more easily," Scout said. Serena helped him take out some wooden dining chairs, and he pulled out a large kitchen table and set it down in the driveway.

"I'll supervise from out here." Bonnie sat down at the table now parked in her driveway. "I like a chance to enjoy these old pieces."

Scout and Serena stepped into the little pocket of space and surveyed the furniture that towered around them. "Any large dressers will be on the bottom with other stuff stacked on top," Scout explained.

"What about that over there?" Serena asked.

He removed a nightstand and moved the dresser underneath so that she could see the front. It was dark, shiny wood, with gold knobs on the small drawers.

"The drawers are too small," she said, not wanting to say how unattractive the dark finish was. It seemed too glossy to be painted over.

"Look over to the left," Bonnie called from the table. "I think that's where most of the bedroom furniture is."

Scout moved a wooden wardrobe in the left bay, revealing a few dressers. "Jackpot!" he said.

With the wardrobe gone, there was enough space for Serena to inspect the furniture, though it didn't take her long. A tall, five-drawer dresser caught her eye. Although once painted white, it was scarred and dingy, missing half of the drawer pulls. There were round water stains on the top, and the drawers squeaked when she pulled them out.

Still, something about it stood out.

"It definitely needs paint," she told Scout. She ran her fingertips over a deep scar on the face of the top drawer. "I bet I could fill this in a little, then paint the crack metallic silver, like that one in the store."

"You could do that."

"It had these elegant crystal knobs," she said, "and I loved the way they caught the light."

"Pretty sure they carry that stuff at the hardware store," he said. "We can stop by and see, if you want."

"That'd be great." She smiled at Scout, grateful that he'd extended himself to help her with this project.

"Did you find something?" Bonnie joined them.

Serena gestured to the dresser. "I'd like to buy this one, if I can afford it. My aunt and uncle gave me thirty dollars to use, but I still need to buy some paint and knobs."

"Save your money for the hardware store. I'm happy to gift it to you. My whole point in collecting these things is to find a good home for them." Bonnie patted the side of the dresser. "I think you two are a match made in heaven."

Was she talking about the dresser, or her son? Serena's spirits soared as she dared a glance at Scout. He was nodding, his golden hair bobbing, a subtle smile on his face.

"Thank you so much," she said. For a moment, the Tanners' generosity and the joy of the moment overwhelmed her a little. That two people, two virtual strangers, would extend themselves and help her, out of the goodness of their hearts—that was daunting. She hoped that someday she could return the favor.

Together, Serena and Scout loaded the dresser into the back of his truck, and then systematically replaced the furniture in the garage. They grabbed lunch at Molly's Home Diner, where they decided to split a home-style fried chicken dinner. When Serena noticed that the restaurant seemed to be staffed mostly by Amish women, Scout explained that the Amish community was growing, and there wasn't enough land in Lancaster County to provide agricultural jobs for all the Amish men. "So people are spreading out, some moving to other places. Some Amish men and women take jobs in local businesses. But generally, the women end up working at home after they get married."

"And they work hard," Serena said. "There are a million chores to be done on a farm. My aunt Miriam is a whirlwind, but even when she sits down, she's working on some knitting or sewing."

While they waited for their food, they both looked up videos on ways to restore and paint furniture. "Chalk paint?" she said. "I've never heard of that."

"It looks pretty straightforward in the video," he said. "You don't even have to remove the other finish."

"Just fill the scars and paint. And then there's the sanding for the distressed look, if I want it."

"Step by step," Scout said. "Sometimes you just have to do the work."

"Usually, talk like that would scare me," she said, sipping her water. She wasn't really known as the worker in her family, but this seemed different. "Without my phone or the Internet or TV, I've got some spare time on my hands. It'll be nice to use it to get something important done."

"Don't you have homework? I mean, to fill your time."

"Please. Writing a book report or learning about old guys in history is not important." She pushed her hair back over her shoulder. "I wish I could get out of school like the Amish kids, but Aunt Miriam says it would upset my dad too much if I dropped out."

"Besides, you're a senior. If you stick with it this year, you'll have your high school degree," Scout said. "That counts for something."

"I guess," Serena said amicably. She didn't know where a high school diploma would get her, but then she didn't really know where she wanted to go in life. She was about to ask Scout about his dreams, but then the fried chicken and mashed potatoes arrived. Time to dig in.

When they were finished, Scout paid for her meal— which made it seem more and more like a date. *(Yay!)* She so wanted it to be a date, because he was so easy to talk to, so kind, and she always felt a glimmer of excitement when they were together.

The hardware store had a better selection of paints than she'd expected, and the salesclerk was able to direct her to the right grades of sand paper for her job. "Caribbean Blue Note" was the perfect color for the dresser—sort of a dusky turquoise. She paid for her supplies, realizing she would have to come back later with more money if she wanted those crystal knobs.

As she and Scout headed back to the dairy farm, a bag of supplies tucked in by her feet, Serena felt a little sad. "I'm sorry to see the day end," she said. "Time really flies when we're together, Scout."

"It does." He nodded, keeping his eyes on the road. "I'm glad we're friends."

"More than friends, right? What if I said I was falling for you?"

"I'd say wow. I mean, you're an amazing girl. But really, I'm not the guy you want to fall for."

Crestfallen, Serena turned toward the window as he continued to explain.

"I've got college, a job at the firehouse, another job on the milk truck, and a dog that's afraid of lawn mowers. That's way too busy to be in a relationship."

Too busy? What kind of a lame excuse was that? He wasn't going to slip away so easily.

"Everyone is busy," she said in a calm voice. "But people find time to be together when it matters. And it's important for us to find that time." She turned back toward him. "You come around every night, and I make it a point to come out and see you. It's the highlight of your night, right?"

"Absolutely."

"So we have a chance to see each other every day. I say we take advantage of that time and see where it leads."

"I just can't promise anything right now."

"No promises required," she said. "There's something special between us, Scout. I know there is. Don't you feel it?"

He shot her a quick glance, a restrained look in his blue eyes. "I do, but—"

"Don't say anything else that might hurt my feelings." She held up her palm to stop him. "Let's just stick with what we know right now. There's a chemistry between us. A spark." She smiled. "A sparkle. And we need to give it some time to grow. Especially because you're busy and I'm busy now that school is sucking up my quality time and I've got to learn how to paint furniture like, overnight."

He nudged his cap back slightly and nodded. "Okay."

"So I'll see you tonight?"

He nodded. "Looking forward to it."

She could tell he meant that. Proof that they were on the right track together.

That night, Serena stood in the circle of light cast by the battery lantern and struggled with a drawer of the old dresser. The woodshop at night was a little bit creepy, but Serena liked the fact that Uncle Alvin had given her a place to work apart from the activity of the rest of the family. She had spent time wiping down the dresser and scrubbing the inside of most of the drawers with a lemon cleaner so that they'd be ready for the sticky new drawer liners. None of the drawers glided smoothly, and one drawer seemed glued in place. "Try to cooperate," she said, tugging on the bottom drawer, which was stubbornly sticking inside. "Come on!" she fumed. "I can't paint you if you don't open up!"

But the drawer wouldn't budge.

She sighed. What was she supposed to do now?

A noise behind her made her flinch. She grabbed the lantern and moved behind the dresser as the door was nudged open.

"Serena?" Essie peered in and then entered, followed by Harlan, a quiet tower in dark pants and blue shirt.

Letting out the breath she'd been holding, Serena clutched her chest. "You scared the stuffing out of me."

"Sorry." Essie came into the circle of light, which illuminated her apron and patient face. "You're working so late. I heard you talking about the sticky drawers at dinner, and I thought Harlan might be able to help. He's a carpenter, you know."

"Really?" Serena said. "That would be a big help. I don't know what's wrong with them. The bottom drawer is the worst."

"Let me take a look." He gave a tug. "Hmm." He jiggled the edges of the drawer, which allowed him to pull it out a few inches. "This will need some help." He went over to the workbench and found a flat screwdriver. "The trick is to get them out, then repair the tracks and give the edges of the drawers a good waxing. Then they should be no trouble at all."

Essie moved closer to Serena and touched her shoulder. "See that? Harlan will get the dresser to cooperate."

So Essie had heard her chastising the dresser? Serena smiled and linked arms with her cousin. It must be late. Most likely everyone else was in bed and Harlan had come round for Saturday courtship night. And here were Essie and Harlan, spending their treasured time together helping her.

"You guys . . . you don't have to do this now," Serena said. "I can figure it out in the morning."

"We're here now," Essie said, "and Harlan can fix it one-two-three. You shouldn't have to do it alone."

Full of gratitude, Serena gave her cousin's arm a squeeze.

As they watched, Harlan managed to "tune up" all the drawers. He arranged them in order on the workbench, and then showed Serena how to inspect the tracks inside the case for splintered wood or obstructions. While she sanded the tracks on the sides of the drawers, Harlan sanded inside the dresser. After that, he showed her how to wax the tracks. "That'll make them glide smoothly."

"Thanks for helping me," she said. "And teaching me." It was nice to have the help, but even better that Harlan took the time to show her the ropes. She liked being treated as a peer.

"So what's next?" Essie asked, rubbing her hands together. "Are we going to start painting?"

"Not tonight," Serena said, realizing that it had grown later than she'd realized. She wanted to be sure to catch Scout on his milk run.

"Nay, but we should level the dresser." Harlan pushed the frame lightly to reveal a slight wobble.

"How do we fix that?" Serena asked.

"First, we figure out which side is longer. Then we turn the dresser on its side and shave it down till it's even." He sifted through the tools at the workbench. "I'm sure there's a level and a plane here somewhere."

Serena and Essie watched as Harlan made the adjustments. "He's pretty handy," Serena said. "Good to have around."

The lamplight shone in Essie's dark eyes. Or maybe it was her feelings for Harlan. "I always thought so."

"Stop, you two, or I'll get a swelled head," Harlan said without looking up from his work.

Serena showed Essie the color of the chalk paint she'd chosen, and Essie seemed so pleased. "When it's done, our room will be tidy and colorful. Good for you, Serena," Essie said. "Mem said you made a wonderful good choice, and she's right."

Serena's heart warmed to know that she'd made a good choice. Since Mom had gotten sick, she'd been so full of anger and pain. The panic in her heart couldn't be quelled by her father or sisters, and she'd tried other things to stop the pain. Hanging out late with friends who could get her alcohol, she'd tossed back plenty of drinks, pushing herself until a dark numbness took over. She'd flailed and struck at the universe—"acting out," Dad had called it. A series of bad choices.

It was so good to know she was on the right track.

Chapter Fourteen

On a cool September night, Miriam took out the quilt squares and enlisted the help of the girls. There was nothing like a sewing circle to get people talking and sharing. Serena had gone off to the woodshop to work on her dresser. They had learned to limit her tasks in the kitchen, but Serena had proved to be a hard worker. Miriam was thrilled she'd found something to occupy her hands and mind. Megan was upstairs in the girls' room, working on school assignments. Alvin had loaned her a headlight so that she could sit up in her bunk and have enough light to read. That one was serious about school.

Although Sarah's girls had made many adjustments, the youngest one, Grace, seemed to be the only one of the three who was still clinging to the idea of going back to the city. Miriam understood that Grace missed her father, but the girl seemed to have such a loneliness in her heart, a sadness that wouldn't be cured by spending most of her nights alone in the city. Grace needed an angel watching over her.

Miriam held the needle aloft as she surveyed the room of girls. It wasn't really a quilting circle, just Annie,

Lizzie, and Grace, sitting with her and stitching quilting squares. The fabric squares and batting had been precut weeks ago, and now Miriam was trying to drum up some enthusiasm for quilting. Quilts were beautiful and so practical, too! She was terrible at quilting—all thumbs—but she didn't want to discourage her girls from learning such a valuable skill.

"Feel that cool breeze," Miriam said to the girls, who had their heads bent over their stitching. "Autumn is surely on the way. One of my favorite seasons."

"I thought you loved the summer, Mem," said Lizzie.

"I do. Such sweet fruits and berries, and the endless blue of a summer sky. But then in the fall, when the weather gets crisp and cool, it's so easy to fall asleep at night. When the apples turn ripe and juicy and we press them for cider . . ." Miriam tilted her head to one side, considering. "It's truly hard to pick the best season."

"I like winter because of Christmas," Grace said.

"That is a wonderful holiday," Miriam agreed. "We get to spend lots of time with our family."

"We *always* spend time with our family," Annie pointed out.

"Do you think I'll get to go home for Christmas?" Grace asked.

"I don't know," Miriam said. "Maybe your father can come here? Wouldn't that be nice—having Christmas with all of us together? By December we're not going to want to give you up, even if it's just for the holiday." She thought she might get a bit of a smile from her niece, but Grace simply poked the needle and pulled the thread through.

"I guess," Grace said.

"How's your square going?" Miriam asked her.

"It's a lot of work to make the stitches even, when a machine could do it in seconds." Grace frowned at her square as she tried to line up the needle just right. "Can't you borrow someone's sewing machine?"

"We could," Miriam said, "but then it wouldn't be a hand-made quilt. And we need a special sewing machine on account of having no electricity."

"Right," Grace said. "I always forget about that part."

"Mem doesn't like to sew," Lizzie said. "But she gets credit for trying."

"Knitting is my hobby of choice," Miriam agreed.

"Can I be done?" Annie asked, holding up her square. The dirt under her fingernails caught Miriam's gaze. "I'm tired."

"Did you finish a square?" Miriam asked.

Annie handed her the square of cloth and batting she'd sewn together. The stitches looked a bit wide, more than an eighth of an inch, but it would do. "All done then. Are you going to bed?"

"I'm taking a bath first," Annie said, heading up the stairs.

"A good idea," Miriam called after her. Sixteen-year-old Annie had always been a big animal lover, preferring to spend time in the barn tending to the animals instead of learning how to cook and clean and tend house. So far, the chance to run with her friends during rumspringa hadn't really affected Annie, who still seemed to care more about the cows, horses, and chickens than young men who might court her. But as far as Miriam was concerned, regular bathing would be a step in the right direction.

"Who's going to put these squares together?" Lizzie asked as she moved the needle with some skill.

Miriam smiled at the implication that she wouldn't be assembling the quilt. Her daughters knew her lack of skill when it came to the detailed craft of a needle and thread. "There's going to be a quilting bee at Aunt Greta's."

Lizzie's brown eyes opened wide. "Can I go?" The children loved spending time with their aunt, and Lizzie enjoyed all manner of crafts and sewing.

"If it's not during school time."

Lizzie finished stitching and deftly knotted the thread, then peeked over at the square in Grace's hands. "That's very good stitching," she said. "Especially for your first time."

"Not as good as yours." Grace frowned at her stitching. "Mine is a little crooked. Ugh. It's so bad."

Miriam leaned forward to take a look. "Just a little bit different, but it will work just fine. It's like your signature. All of us sew a bit differently, but in the end, the patches are sewn together to make a comforting quilt. When a person sits under it, she won't see your patch or mine, she'll see a field of patches, all stitched with love."

Grace smoothed her fingers over the patch, as if seeing the potential for the first time. "That's actually really nice, a quilt stitched with love." This time when she looked up, she was smiling. "Do you think I could do another square?"

Miriam nodded. "As many as you like."

The day that Sully came out to visit was a good one all around. Miriam enjoyed bringing family together, and that night she had a houseful! Greta and Alvin's brother Lloyd were over to dinner with their children, as well as Alvin and Lloyd's mother, Esther, grandmother to so many. Essie was hosting her friend Sadie, as well as Harlan, who had become a regular fixture here. Most of the children were playing a game at the volleyball net, while the adults took to the gliders on the shady porch. Greta jostled her youngest, Andy, in her lap, while her twin toddlers built a structure of blocks with Sarah Rose on the other end of the porch.

Sam stared into the yard from the porch, his attention clearly split between the game and the porch conversation. Or was he watching Essie and Sadie put burgers on the grill? Miriam's heart ached a bit as she sensed that he was bothered by his younger sister's prospects of getting married before he found a bride. What could a mother do?

No one else seemed to notice Sam's concern, as they were wrapped up in Sully's tales of life as a police officer in the city. Grace sat on the glider beside her father, and from the devotion on her face, it was clear that she was spellbound by him.

And rightly so. Greta, Lloyd, Alvin, and Mammi Esther were equally charmed by Sully's stories. His daily life was far different from their activities on the farm. Alvin asked if Sully had ever been called to a car accident, and Sully told the group he'd handled a crash just last week.

"It was a single-car accident," Sully said. "The car had veered off the road and slammed into a light post. Even at a slow speed, that head-on impact is tremendous. The car was crumpled like an accordion, the front hood buckled up in the air."

Alvin and Lloyd moved closer, wanting to hear his account.

"I was the first cop on the scene. When I climbed on the hood to find the driver, I could see that the glass of the windshield had completely smashed and collapsed on the driver. But it was still intact, like a sheet of glitter. I reached in, and it lifted off like a blanket. It's amazing—the technology of shatterproof glass. The driver was a young woman, turned out to be a teenager. I was worried she'd gone out of the picture, bleeding from a head wound."

The listeners were silent, imagining the terrible scene.

"What happened next?" Lloyd asked, stroking his beard.

"She started talking to me. Told me her name when I asked. That's always a good sign." Arms folded, Sully leaned one hip against the porch railing. "The ambulance arrived soon after that. We got her out of the wreck, and they transported her to the hospital. Later I heard that she got to go home the next day. That's a good day on the job."

Esther looked to the sky, gaping in amazement before she patted Sully's arm. "Gott is good to see you through those difficult moments."

Sully nodded. "I'm grateful for that."

"You're a hero every day, Dad," Grace said, beaming a look of admiration to her father.

"A hero, indeed, he is," Esther said. "Thank Gott you were there to help that poor girl."

"It's my job to be there," Sully said.

"Crashes on the highway are a terrible thing," Alvin said. "It's always a concern when an Amish buggy gets hit by a car. The buggy weighs so much less, and it's really just a wooden box with paint and some lights and reflectors."

"I've never handled a crash like that," Sully said. "Does it happen often?"

"Too often," Lloyd said. "A fear years back a family in our church lost two children in a buggy accident."

"Such a heartbreak," Miriam said.

"But Sully's story has a happy ending," Esther said. "This would make a good story to send to one of my magazines."

"You should write about it, Mammi," Sam said. "Send it in to *The Connection*!"

"Yah!" Suddenly everyone was talking about hazards on the road.

It was a delight to see so much admiration for Sully. Miriam could tell Grace was pleased; her face was alight with joy.

Miriam had a smile on her face as she hurried over to the grill to help Essie tend the burgers and hotdogs. At times like this, she was grateful that she and Alvin bought large quantities of meat and stored it in their big gas freezer. Burger-making was one of the activities Alvin involved all the children in. He attached his patty-maker to the grinder and then passed each patty on to a child for packaging. Two hundred burgers at a time! Tonight they would need twenty or so.

"How's it going?" she asked Essie.

"Good. I put the hotdogs on a platter, and the burgers are about done. The ribs will take a little longer."

"I'll finish up. Why don't you go in and get the bread and salads? In the fridge you'll find potato salad and three-bean salad. And don't forget the pickled beets."

Beyond the grill, the low sun cast a lemony glow over the green fields and distant purple hills. Miriam took a moment to drink in the view—one of Gott's many gifts. The shouts of the children playing cornhole on the lawn brought a smile to her face. She was starting to remove burgers from the grill when Sully joined her.

"Let me give you a hand with that." He picked up the heavy platter and held it for her. "We don't want to lose any in the dirt."

She smiled. "You won everyone over with the stories."

"I try to keep people entertained. I have a question for you." When she nodded, he continued. "It's embarrassing, but the grandma—Mammi Esther? She isn't Sarah's mother, is she?"

Miriam gave a small laugh. "No, Esther is the mother of my husband Alvin and his brother Lloyd."

"Phew." Sully let out a breath. "That's a relief. I was worried that I'd have to win over Sarah's mother."

Miriam shook her head. "I forget that you never met our mem. Her name is Lois. Our father is David, and they've moved to Indiana." She stacked another burger on the plate, pointed to the second platter, and he made the switch. "I miss them, but I'm grateful to Gott for the family we have nearby. Alvin has four brothers and sisters, and his parents moved to the Dawdi House, that small house over yonder, when Alvin and I were first married."

The old two-bedroom Dawdi House, where elder parents usually lived on the farm, sat empty on their property, just a bit of a walk around the vegetable garden and on the other side of the woodshop. Esther had lived there with her dear husband Mervin. What a joy to have them close by when Miriam was having her babies and grateful for another pair of hands to put on the coffee or start the baking.

But four years ago Alvin's father Mervin had passed on, and Esther had felt ill at ease in the little house they'd shared. She had moved down the road to stay with her son Lloyd for a bit. There she'd been a blessing to Greta, who had three babies in three years after a long dry spell. Miriam hoped to have her mother-in-law move back one day, but the decision was up to Esther, who certainly knew her own mind.

"The girls seem to be adjusting," Sully said, drawing her back to the here and now. "I can't thank you enough for taking them in. It gives me a chance to pull in lots of overtime. I'm finally building up their college savings, and if you need more money for their food and expenses, I can do that."

"You've given us plenty of money to cover food," Miriam said. "If they need other things, I'll have them ask you."

"Are they doing okay, do you think?"

"We're so grateful to have them here. And I think they're all doing fine in their different ways." Miriam put the spatula down, and she and Sully carried the platters of meat to the long outdoor table. "Megan puts a lot of time into her schoolwork. Very dedicated. And every day, she goes on long walks. Sometimes Sam or Annie accompany her. I hear she walks for miles and miles. She says it's her therapy."

"That sounds like Megan. Exercise is a big part of her day, and, from all those years of soccer, she loves being outside."

"I have to say that Serena has surprised us all. One minute she wanted to buy a piece of furniture for eight hundred dollars; the next minute, she found something free that she's fixing up. What a turnaround! We had to push a little to get her to help around the house, but she's always cheerful."

Sully smiled. "She has that sunny quality that reminds me of her mother. She can fill a room with energy, but sometimes she veers off track."

"Serena likes working in the woodshop. School, not so much, but she goes on the bus every day."

"We need to get her through high school," Sully said. "It's important that she finish this year."

"She seems to know that. And Grace . . ." Miriam turned to Sully. "She misses her dat, but she's at the age when she really doesn't know what she wants."

He nodded. "I hear from Grace a lot. She texts me most mornings when she arrives at school. Sometimes phone calls. Of all my girls, she worries me the most."

Miriam looked toward the porch where Grace sat with the other adults. "Grace is at a crossroads, but if she knows you're worried, it will only scare her. I don't know if you're a man of faith, Sully, but worry is the opposite of faith. Some folks say: 'Worry ends where trust begins.' If we trust in Gott, who never makes mistakes, we can be comfortable that the outcome will be Gott's will."

Sully pressed a hand to his mouth, considering. "I kind of fell away from my faith when I lost your sister. I thought God let me down. Now I feel kind of petty for thinking that way. As if it was all about me. Sarah had her time on earth. She had a good life."

Sudden tears stung Miriam's eyes at the memory of her

sister, a woman so full of life. How she was missed! When Sarah's girls talked about her, their eyes filled with a special light, the love for their mother. "It was a wonderful, good life," Miriam agreed, "filled with a special love when she met you."

"She was the love of my life." His voice was raspy, tight with emotion. "I'm grateful for that. Sarah was like a sun at the center of the universe. She gave off more light in one day than some people share in a lifetime."

"She was a bright light. I'm glad your sorrow didn't rob you of all your faith."

"I'm back on track. I need to keep my head screwed on straight for my girls."

The image of a head being screwed on seemed cartoonish to Miriam, but Sully was right. "Your girls need you to be a steady influence for them."

He nodded. "But what you're giving them here—a family—that's what they need most right now."

"Mem!" Essie's arms were full of serving bowls as she passed the grill. "The ribs are going to burn!"

"I got distracted!" Miriam said, hurrying back to the grill with a smile.

Sully was right behind her, the first to pick up the grill tool. "Sorry about that." He turned a rib over with the tongs. "Looks perfect." He started stacking the meat on a platter.

"All right, then. I'll ring the dinner bell." The sweet chime of the bell brought the children running in from the field and the older ones ambling over from the porch. Miriam sent the younger ones inside to wash their hands, and then they all settled at the table and bowed their heads.

Gratitude filled her from head to toe at the delicious smells of the supper and the animated faces of the folk gathered around her, asking for Gott's blessing over their meal. Her own children, her trio of teen nieces, her pint-sized nieces and nephews, her dear friend Greta and brother-in-law Lloyd, husband, mother-in-law, and Sully, their special guest.

These were the people who filled her heart with love.

Her family.

Chapter Fifteen

For weeks, Serena spent every spare minute restoring the dresser. She had removed the drawer pulls and carefully applied two coats of chalk paint. Swishing the brush over every inch, she had let her mind relax into the beautiful new color that reminded her of tropical waters and cotton candy. And then she'd used a sanding sponge to distress the edges. And then the wax coating, and the new knobs. The work had been a kind of therapy for her, taking her mind off her old life, her schoolwork, and the social media friends who seemed unreal to her on the rare occasions when she checked her social media accounts.

It was late, but she still had a little time before Scout got here. She pulled on her sneakers, slipped one of Aunt Miriam's knitted throws over her shoulders, and set off into the night. The battery lantern was stark and bright, making the ground before her look like some strange planet. This had been her nightly trek, out to the woodshop to spend a little more time on the restoration.

She smiled at the thought of everyone who had helped her. Scout and his mom. Essie and Harlan. Even Uncle Alvin had given her a ride to the hardware store to pick up knobs and flowered paper to line the drawers, and he'd seemed pleased with what she was doing. It had been a true team effort.

Serena had tried to pull her sisters in on the project, but their minds were elsewhere now that school had begun. Megan was working hard to get accepted into a good college, and Grace seemed to be biding her time until Dad would let her go home. "It's fine here," Grace had told their father when he'd driven out to deliver clothes and visit last weekend. "The family is really nice to me, and I'm glad to be with Megan and Serena, but I still want to go home."

Home—that word again.

Right now Serena couldn't imagine herself back in high school in Philadelphia. The pressure, the parties, the popularity contests . . . She didn't really miss any of that. She did miss Dad, and his visit had been fun, but way too short. Of course, she didn't like doing without cell service or a computer, and it would be heaven to sit and watch a TV show. But she figured those things would happen someday when she left Amish country.

The door to the woodshop opened smoothly now, having been oiled by Harlan, and she held the lantern inside before stepping in.

There it was—the finished dresser.

She put the lantern on the ground, snuggled into the blanket around her neck, and stared at her masterpiece. Two months ago, if someone had told her she'd pour her energy into restoring a piece of furniture, she would have looked at them cross-eyed.

Not tonight.

Tonight she was happy with her accomplishment, grateful for the convenience the dresser would provide, and delighted by its beauty. She had the ability to turn an ugly piece of furniture into something really nice. A frog transformed to a prince. It felt good, and it meant that much more because of the obstacles she'd faced.

There were so many responsibilities that tugged on her time here. Household chores like making her bed each morning and helping with the dishes after dinner and helping with the laundry on wash day. School had also been a time-sucker. Her English teacher wanted a book report every month, and Serena wasn't a fast reader. But she had chosen a short book from the reading list and plowed through for September. Next month, she was determined to read *To Kill a Mockingbird*, even if it took extra time.

It didn't help that she was sometimes tired in class from staying up late to see Scout. She usually managed to stay awake, unless there was a film, and all the lights went out. More recently she'd taken to napping after school to boost her energy for the best fifteen minutes of the day, the time she spent with Scout. She could tell he enjoyed being with her, too, but she didn't want to pressure him too much by trying to pin down and define their relationship. For now, she was going with the flow.

She thought she heard a rumble outside, probably Scout's truck. Looping the yellow blanket around her neck like a jaunty scarf, she picked up the lantern and headed toward the milking barn. The red taillights of the milk truck glowed like a beacon, guiding her across the farm's wide lawn. The ground was bumpier in the dark, and a cool breeze stirred the leaves of trees lining the lane, scattering dried leaves, but nighttime on the farm didn't scare her the way it once did. She was getting used to the quiet darkness, and even appreciated the country nights that revealed thousands of stars in the sky.

"Hey Serena, how's it going?" Scout called as she drew close.

"How'd you know it was me?"

"That lantern gave you up."

"Oh my gosh, I forgot I had it." She held the lantern up, shaking her head. "Are you good on time tonight? I mean, can you get away for a minute?"

"Actually, I am a little bit ahead of schedule."

"Come with me." She waved him on. "There's something I want to show you."

As they walked, she told him that she'd completed the dresser. Her cousins, Pete and Paul, had been ready to haul it up to the bedroom so the girls could use it.

"But I asked them to wait one more day," she said. "I wanted you to see it, especially since you were so instrumental in getting me started with the project."

Scout shrugged. "I just knew my mom had a collection of old stuff that you might be able to fix up. You did all the hard work."

"But you got me started, and you delivered the dresser here, and I'm really grateful." Serena glanced over at Scout, but the darkness and the bill of his cap kept his face in shadow. "This is a new thing for me, this gratitude thing. I wasn't quite this nice back in Philly."

"Well, I'd say gratitude is a good fit for anyone."

As they approached the woodshop, Serena felt a tingle of excitement. "Are you ready for the big reveal?" she asked. "We need a drum roll."

Scout paused at the door. "How about this?" He started

tapping rapidly on the doorframe. "Ladies and gentlemen, presenting the fine artistry of Serena Sullivan!"

She laughed. "I love it!" She pushed the door open and stepped inside with the lantern. "Ta-da!"

"Wow. I mean, wow! It's really beautiful, Serena."

"And practical too." She stepped forward and opened and closed the top drawer, then the next one down. "Remember how the drawers used to stick? Now they glide, as smooth as silk."

"Who fixed them?"

"Essie's boyfriend Harlan. He's really good with carpentry. That's his job. And you know what? While they were helping me, I got to know them better. We sort of bonded. Did you know Harlan's father left his family years ago, and he hasn't been heard from since?"

Scout ran his palm over the waxed surface of the dresser. "I didn't know that."

"And Essie told me on the sly that he's been trying to find his dad, but no one has any leads for him. It makes me sad for Harlan, but he just powers through it."

"That must be tough. Well, you did a great job, and now you have two new friends and a dresser to show for it."

She threw her arms out wide. "I can't wait to start using this, but I have to say, I'm going to miss having a project. It was time-consuming, but the work was sort of therapeutic. You know?"

He nodded. "Work can be good for the soul. In your case, the end product is pretty spectacular. Looks like you found your hidden potential. I believe there are special abilities in all of us. You just need to find them."

"That is so sweet." She gave him a playful nudge. "I think you might be right."

"I'm going to take some photos to show Mom. She'll be thrilled that one of her furniture rejects has been transformed."

Serena basked in the joy of accomplishment as Scout took out his cell and photographed the dresser from different angles. Funny, but she'd taken on the dresser as a way to get closer to Scout. In the long run, she'd learned how to find some alone time with peace in her heart.

"I can't get a signal here, but I'll send them to Mom later," Scout said.

"I'll let you get back." She picked up the lantern. "We need to keep the milk truck on schedule."

Walking back beside Scout, in the limited light of the lantern, Serena's senses were alive. The coolness of the air, the smell of damp leaves, the warmth of his body beside her. There was a coziness between them, as if they were the only two people on earth.

"I was just thinking," Scout said. "Since you liked working on the furniture, and my mother has a garage full, maybe she'll want to give you a few more pieces to work on. You could sell them when you're done, and give her a share of the money."

Serena whirled toward him. "That would be great!"

"I'll talk with her tomorrow."

They were no longer walking, but faced each other on the broad lawn in front of the house. Scout reached toward her, his arm brushing her shoulder for a moment as he pulled the knit blanket back in place. "Your shawl was falling off," he said, smoothing it over her shoulder.

His touch left a sweet, tingling sensation in its wake. It gave her the nerve to step closer to him and place her free hand on his chest.

Her palm glided over the buttons of his denim shirt as she drank in his gaze. "You have such a good heart." She pressed her hand closer. "I can feel it beating."

He smiled. "Beating a little fast. That happens when I'm with you."

"Aw." She leaned into him, and he touched his fingertips to her cheek. She longed to toss the lantern aside and throw her arms around him, but the lantern might break, and she couldn't do that to her aunt and uncle. "Thanks for your help, Scout. I don't know where I'd be without you."

"You don't have to thank me. Friends help friends." He cupped her cheek, staring down at her with affection.

"But we're more than friends," she said. "Everything is special when we're together. The world is, I don't know, kind of sugar-coated. Covered in glitter."

He sighed. "You're really wearing down my resolve to keep this friendly."

"Good." Her free hand reached up to his shoulder as she rose up on tiptoes. Holding her breath, she let her eyes close as she lifted her lips to his.

The brush of his lips stirred feelings inside her, but it was a fleeting touch. A butterfly kiss.

Disappointed, she was lowering herself to her heels when his arms surrounded her and lifted her off her feet. The second kiss was deeper and more fulfilling. Her lips parted slightly, and he let her in, allowing her a connection to the vibrant energy that defined him. He was a tall, grand tree in the forest. A mountain of rock that held the wisdom of the ages. A river cutting through stone and field, ever moving, ever changing.

One kiss, and she felt that she knew him that well.

Chapter Sixteen

The late September sun was not quite warm enough to chase away the chill in the air as Essie drove the buggy out of town. Serena sat beside her, a fine companion on a busy day. Their horse Comet walked past the bank, where Essie and Harlan often enjoyed easing through the drive-through lane. Essie would have liked to stop and deposit the money tucked into her shoe. . . .

But not today. That could wait until Essie was in town with Harlan. Today Essie and Serena had just delivered items to a shop in Joyful River, and both girls were abuzz with excitement over their new cottage businesses.

"I'm just texting Scout and his mom to tell them the news and see if Bonnie has any more nightstands and small tables." All business, Serena's fingers tapped her phone. "Everyone seems to want small, light furniture."

"It takes up less space in the shop, and it's easier to move," Essie said. While waiting at a traffic light, she pulled the blanket onto her lap, though Serena waved it off. Dressed in blue jeans, boots, and a short, red and blue jacket that said "Phillies" on the back, Serena probably didn't notice the cool gusts of wind that made it clear autumn was here. When she was floating on a cloud of excitement, Serena didn't notice much.

"Did you hear what she wants to charge for the furniture?" Serena said. "And she loved the robin's egg blue paint. I bet those nightstands will sell in no time."

"I bet they will," Essie agreed. They had just dropped off a case of strawberry rhubarb jam and two pieces of furniture at Joyful Gems. Janice had been thrilled to have the items. "Bring me more!" she had said. Shifting her feet on the floor of the buggy, Essie could feel the wad of money Janice had given her, safely tucked away in her shoe. The second case of Essie's jam had sold out quickly, as had the jam placed in other boutiques in nearby towns.

Last Saturday when Harlan had come courting, he and Essie had gone over the numbers together and hugged each other in glee. With the way they were making money, they would reach the goal in their savings account within a month.

That meant one wonderful good thing.

"We're getting married in November," Harlan had said, taking her hands and planting a kiss on her knuckles.

"Gott in heaven has blessed us," Essie had said, tucking away their bank statement into a little book the bank had given them. "Our marriage is truly meant to be." She had leaned into Harlan, settling in as he put his arm around her. "I have to admit that I feel like I've been waiting for this moment for years."

"It feels that way because it has been years," Harlan had teased her.

"Well, you're worth waiting for, Harlan Yoder." She had tipped her face up to his, and their lips had touched in a sweet kiss.

"We'll tell our parents next week, before September's out," he had said. "I know it doesn't give them much time for planning, but they'll have to make do."

"Planning?" She had laughed, so joyful that their dreams were about to come true. "There's been lots of planning going on, even without our announcement. My mem has a garden full of celery and a gaggle of friends who will cook and bake and clean for our big day."

"How did she know?" he had asked. "Did you tell her?"

"A mother can tell when her daughter's fallen in love," Essie had said, nuzzling his smooth chin with her nose.

"Then she's wiser than I knew." Harlan had paused, scratching his head. "Do you think my mem knows, too?"

"I'm sure she does," Essie had said with a smile.

Harlan was smart and precise when it came to woodworking, fitting a dowel, or carving a flower. But when it came to the behavior of those around him, he was like a horse with blinders on, focusing only on the road in front of him.

Thinking back on that special moment, Essie smiled, her heart content as she listened to the clip-clop of Comet's hooves on the road.

Come November, she'd be Harlan's wife.

She realized Serena was still chatting about Scout and his mother and refinishing furniture, and she forced herself to concentrate on what her cousin was saying.

"As soon as those pieces sell, I'm going to pay Harlan for his work," Serena said. "Thank you so much for helping me deliver them to the store!"

"You know I'll do what I can to help you," Essie said.

"Aw!" Serena threw her arms around Essie, who had

to stretch her neck to the side to concentrate on driving. "I love you, cuz!"

"Me too." Essie was surprised by the sudden affection while sitting in the driver's seat of the buggy, but she hugged her cousin back. There was no denying the happiness brimming over in her heart as Serena hugged her. When her cousins had arrived a month ago, appearing so odd and scary and pushy, Essie had gritted her teeth and vowed to endure them. By the grace of Gott, the days and weeks had taught her new ways to find common ground with other people. She'd learned to help the girls in small ways and to enjoy the kindness and love that had developed as their hearts had slowly softened to Amish living.

"When we get home, we'll start planning our next furniture project," Serena said. "And maybe we should ask Harlan what he thinks a fair price is for his help?"

"We could do that," Essie said, slowing the horse at the sight of red taillights on the road ahead.

"And you should get a part of it for all your help. We'll figure out your cut when the nightstands sell," Serena said. "For now, just know that some money is coming to you and Harlan." Serena turned to Essie, her cheeks rosy and her eyes bright. "I just can't thank you guys enough. I love this furniture thing. I mean, I think it saved me from a dreaded job in the pretzel factory. Phew! But most of all, I love doing it. I feel like a famous designer, scoping out each piece and deciding how it should look. It's so artistic. I've found my thing!"

"I'm glad for you." Although Essie tried to keep the swell of enthusiasm tamped down as she focused on the slow-moving traffic, Serena's joy was contagious. Essie couldn't help but smile and laugh with her cousin as they talked about the prospects for the future. The furniture business was giving Serena a sense of belonging, and drawing her closer to Essie in a surprising way. Their new relationship had shown Essie that you never knew what sort of blessings Gott was sending your way.

On the outskirts of town, they came around a curve, and traffic stopped abruptly. "Whoa!" Comet halted, as flashing red and blue lights came into view. *Emergency vehicles*, thought Essie. Flashing lights rattled her nerves, and sometimes they disturbed the horses. She wished Harlan were driving now. "Something's happened up ahead," she said, but she couldn't see over the tall vehicles waiting to pass the scene.

"Looks like an accident," Serena said, stretching out the side of the buggy. "But I can't see much besides the flashing lights."

"I hope it's not a buggy," Essie said, thinking out loud. "Buggies are so easily damaged by cars." She held the reins, keeping the horse in check as they waited for vehicles to move. She tried to remain calm, lest Comet sense her rattled nerves and become agitated.

"Why don't you guys have cars, anyway?" asked Serena.

Essie squinted at her cousin. "You're asking me this now, after you've been riding in buggies with us since we were little?"

Serena shrugged. "I never thought about the reason for it."

"It's not permitted by the Ordnung, our church rules. Dat says it's because if you own a car, it can take you far, far away from your church and family, and that's how people lose their way. Leaving their family and their community."

"So how did you guys get to Mom's funeral in Philadelphia?"

"In a hired van. We use other transportation for long distances. We're allowed to ride in cars, but we can't own them. It limits your travel when you have to pay a driver every time you go a long distance. Our church allows members to ride trains and busses, too."

"A van . . . That makes sense. I was so happy to see you that day." There was a raw pain in Serena's voice. "Thank you for coming."

"It was a sad time," Essie said, remembering. The loss of Aunt Sarah had hit them all hard. Essie had tried to avoid going to the funeral in the city. She'd wanted to avoid things that reminded her of her English aunt, and she'd always felt out of place in the city, where English folk stared and children pointed at their clothes, their hair, their head coverings. Now she felt a twinge of guilt over that day. Good thing Mem had made her put on her church clothes and go on the trip to Philly.

Serena chatted on, but Essie wasn't really listening as they moved ahead another ten feet, and then another. Comet didn't mind the slow pace, and Essie knew the best way to preserve a horse's energy was through a combination of trotting and walking.

At last, they drew close enough to see the roadside, where debris seemed to be scattered. The cracked wooden shell of a buggy lay sideways on the dirt. There was exposed wood and fiberglass. Twisted metal. A bent wheel.

"A buggy accident." Essie pressed her fingers to her

lips as panic squeezed her throat. What had happened to the folks riding in that mangled buggy?

Serena was squeezing Essie's arm, pointing to the crash. "Oh gosh. That looks so awful. Do you think . . . Is everyone okay?"

Essie looked to the two police vehicles, parked at odd angles to block the traffic. The door of a third vehicle slammed, and the bubble light on its roof began flashing as it pulled off and sped away. "That ambulance just left," she said. "Please, Gott, let the passengers of that buggy be healthy and whole."

The traffic moved again, and now Essie could see one of the police officers trying to comfort the animal that still wore its harness from pulling the buggy. A small horse . . . No, a mule.

"Dear Gott in heaven," she said on a shallow breath, staring at the mule and the officer. "That's Harlan's mule, Beebee."

"What?" Serena turned to look at the braying animal. "Are you sure?"

Unable to answer, Essie gritted her teeth and guided Comet through the traffic, moving their buggy beyond the police vehicles before pulling over to the side of the road. She tied off the reins and opened the door. "Wait here."

"I'm going with you," Serena said. "I got your back."

The strings of Essie's kapp trailed behind her as she ran to the first officer she could find, a tall woman, wearing a helmet. The officer was trying to walk toward the wreckage, but Essie blocked her path.

"Officer, please help me. The buggy that crashed belonged to my friend, Harlan Yoder. Is he all right?"

The cop shook her head. "The passengers in the buggy were two females."

Harlan hadn't been in the buggy. Yah, that made sense. He was at work now. Essie felt a quick rush of relief, and then a new anxiety. The buggy must have been occupied by Harlan's mother and sister. "The women in the buggy—what happened to them?" she asked.

"They were both injured. One more serious than the other. They've been transported to Lancaster Hope Hospital."

Serena touched Essie's arm. "So it's not Harlan's buggy?"

"It is. It was probably his mother and sister driving it," Essie said as she moved toward the mule, which was being watched by another officer. The woman's words echoed in her head: Both injured.

"Beebee." She approached the mule slowly, not wanting to spook her any more than she was. "It's me, Beebee. Are you okay?"

She wasn't; Essie could see she was anxious. The mule's muzzle was tight, her eyes so wide-open that Essie could see the white part. Her ears were flicking back and forth, a sure sign that she was overwhelmed. But despite the mule's panic, Essie didn't see any obvious signs of injury. Essie touched her, stroking her neck as she looked to the police officer, a dark-skinned man with warm amber eyes.

"The horse seems to like you," he said. "That's good. I was trying to calm it down, but I don't know beans about horses."

He didn't know enough to realize Beebee was a mule, but Essie was too overwrought to correct him. "Her name is Beebee. She belongs to my friend. What's going to happen to her?"

"We've got a vet coming with a cart. A Dr. Evan Foster. He'll take her in and check her out, keep her boarded for the time being."

Essie nodded. She tried to brand the vet's name in her memory so that she could help Harlan find Beebee, but right now there was a greater worry.

Two injured.

Her throat felt thick and dusty, and she felt about to cry. But there was no time for tears.

"Come," she told her cousin. "I've got to get to the hospital."

Chapter Seventeen

As soon as they pulled away from the scene of the crash, Essie realized she couldn't just drive to the hospital. "What if no one has told Harlan?" she asked Serena. "The most important thing right now is for Harlan to be at the hospital with his mem and sister."

"Okay." Serena frowned. "So do we drive over to the furniture workshop and break the news?" She pulled her phone out of her pocket. "Or is it okay for us to call him? I still have cell service; we're close enough to town. And I'm sure I can get the number for the furniture place."

"Yah, call him," Essie said, nodding brusquely. She gave Serena the official name painted on the sign outside the workshop, and within a minute Serena had someone from the factory on the line.

"Hold on," Serena said, handing the phone to Essie. "It's the factory foreman."

"Hello?" Essie had never liked talking on the telephone in their phone shack. She always found it hard to absorb everything another person was saying without watching his or her movement and looking in his or her eyes. "This is Essie Lapp, trying to reach one of your workers, Harlan Yoder."

"I can't really pull him off work for a phone call, miss."

"It's an emergency," she said. "There's been a terrible accident on the road, and his mother and sister have been taken to the hospital. He needs to go to them, to Lancaster Hope. Can I talk to him, please?"

The foreman apologized, and went to fetch Harlan.

A few minutes later when she heard Harlan's tight voice, Essie's heart sank. "Jerry told me what happened," he said. "How badly hurt are they?"

"I don't know, but I'll come pick you up and take you to them."

"No, I have a ride. Jerry here is going to take me in his car."

She longed to be with Harlan now, but she knew that a ride in a car would get him to the hospital sooner. "Then I'll meet you there," Essie said, wishing to stand beside him to offer him strength and support. Harlan needed her now.

She handed the cellular phone back to Serena.

"Who should we call next?" Serena asked.

Essie considered the question a moment, then shook her head. Harlan didn't have much family in this area. His dat had come from a settlement near Erie, and his mem's family was mostly in Ohio. "We need to go home," she said. "Mem and Dat will want to come to the hospital with me, and we might need to use another horse."

The rest of the trip home would have been agonizing but for Serena's encouraging chatter and questions about Harlan's family. Did Essie know them well? Did she get along with Harlan's mother? How old was his sister? Did he have other siblings?

Serena's questions gave Essie a chance to think about the two women who would soon be part of her family—at least officially. Collette Yoder, Harlan's mem, was a kind, soft-spoken woman with dark hair and a load of worries on her shoulders. Although Collette was in her late thirties like Essie's mem, the sorrow that clung to her made her seem older.

Harlan's sister Suzie was a different story. Just fifteen, she had a sunny disposition that mixed well with her mother's serious streak. Sometimes, seeing how dutiful Suzie and Harlan were, Essie felt sure that Collette Yoder didn't know how good she had it. If Collette could see the chaos and arguments that went on in the Lapp home, she would thank Gott ten times and again!

Essie shared her observations of Harlan's family with Serena, and they were still talking when they pulled into the lane that led to their home.

"It sounds like Harlan has a very nice family," Serena said. "I hope everyone's okay. Do you want me to go to the hospital with you?"

"It's okay. You don't know them, and Mem will want to go." Essie tied off the reins and started to climb out of the buggy. "You've got your schoolwork, I'm sure, and you'll be needed here to help get supper on the table."

"Okay," Serena said cheerfully, though Essie knew that cooking was not one of her talents. "Whatever needs to be done." She held her arms out. "Hug?"

Essie moved into her cousin's arms and felt a new strength coursing through her. How was it that Serena had been with Essie today of all days, when she needed her most? *Gott makes no mistakes*—that was what Mem always said.

The trip to the hospital seemed maddeningly slow, like trying to empty the last of the molasses from the bottle. Essie was glad that Dat was driving this time as they approached the wreckage of Harlan's buggy.

"There it is," she said.

In the front seat, Mem and Dat turned to look. Even little Sarah Rose leaned in front of Mem to see what had captured their attention.

"What's that?" she asked. "What happened, Mem?"

"It's the buggy Collette and Susan Yoder were riding in today," Mem said. "They had an accident and got hurt. That's why we're going to see them at the hospital."

"I get hurt sometimes," Sarah Rose said thoughtfully. "Did you bring the bandages?" She had gone through a phase of wanting attention for her cuts and scrapes. Once, when no one was looking, she had opened the box of bandages and taped a dozen of them to her bare legs.

"They have bandages at the hospital," Mem said.

Essie turned to stare back at the remains of the buggy. The pieces had been pulled off the road onto the edge of the fallow field with knee-high dried weeds, but Essie could still make out the pieces. The overturned bench where she'd sat with Harlan countless times. The gray cab that had been shorn off the platform and cracked in half.

The sight of the debris gave Essie a stab of uncertainty; she wouldn't be able to take a deep breath until she knew that Suzie and Collette were fine. As the Lapp's buggy rolled past the heap of mangled wood and fiberglass,

Essie thought back to the buggy accident that had rocked their church a few years ago, the crash that had killed two little kids.

And there was her sister Sarah Rose, sitting in the seat in front of her. It scared Essie to know that terrible things could happen in an instant.

The stress and controlled panic of the day suddenly flared inside her. Tears filled her eyes, and before she could put her feelings in check, she was crying.

Sarah Rose turned around and rested her chin on the back of the seat. "Why are you crying?"

Essie sniffed, shaking her head. But now Mem was turned around, studying her. "I know, Essie. All of us are concerned about the Yoders."

"It's so scary, Mem. One minute they were traveling down the road; the next they were . . . Their buggy was smashed to pieces."

"I know, daughter. We can't understand why these things happen, and it's so upsetting; it is." Mem reached back and patted her knee. "We just have to trust that God Almighty will get us through, and you know he will."

"I know," Essie said, wiping her damp cheeks with one hand. Mem's words were reassuring, as always. Her quiet strength had a calming effect, taking some of the barbs of anxiety out of Essie's chest. But even though Essie had faith in Gott, she couldn't help but worry. How did you let go of the terrible possibilities, the bad twists and turns in life that you couldn't control? She wasn't sure, but she knew that her fears were allayed in the safety of Harlan's arms. They couldn't get to that hospital fast enough.

At last, they turned into the hospital entrance. Dat let them out at the main doors, and went around the building to find the horse and buggy parking. The kind woman at the information desk directed them to the emergency room. Mem and Sarah Rose waited at the entrance for Dat, while Essie hurried down the long corridor, her heart racing as she followed signs to the ER.

Harlan stood out in the busy waiting room. He was the only Amish fellow there, pacing in front of two shiny snack machines. Although his brow was knit with worry, the steely resolve in his demeanor reminded her of how strong and determined he was.

"Essie . . ." He cut through the room and took her hands, relief evident in the way his shoulders relaxed. "It's good you're here."

"How are they?"

He swallowed hard, then took a deep breath. "They were both injured in the crash, but they're in good spirits."

"Thanks to Gott in heaven!" she whispered. At last, she could breathe a sigh of relief. She hugged him for a brief second before she realized other people were watching. Public displays of affection were discouraged by the Ordnung. When she stepped back, Harlan seemed a little less tense. "What are the doctors saying?"

"Suzie has a bump on her head that they're checking out. I just talked with her before they took her off for a CT scan. She's a little scraped up, too, getting some stitches. Mem's a bit worse off. Her thigh was broken, and she may have injured her pelvis, too. She'll have a longer road to recovery, but the doctors say everything can be treated. They've moved her upstairs, and they gave her pain medication. She'll probably sleep for a bit."

"It's a miracle they survived." Having seen the ruins of the crash, Essie truly believed this. Gott had been merciful.

Behind Harlan an English man with a gray crew cut and a craggy face rose from a chair and joined them. "I'm Jerry. The foreman at the furniture shop."

Essie nodded, introducing herself. "Thank you for your help."

"I appreciate the ride," Harlan said, "and the afternoon off."

"It's the least I could do." Jerry wore a navy T-shirt and jeans and smelled heavily of cigarette smoke. "I didn't want to leave Harlan here alone, but if you're staying, I'm gonna get back to the shop."

"I'll be here, and my parents are right behind me."

"Okay, then." Jerry patted Harlan's shoulder. "You take care, and let us know if there's anything you need."

Harlan nodded. "I'll be at work in the morning."

"That would help us stay on track with the delivery schedule, but let me know if you can't make it."

"I'll be there," Harlan said, a steely resolve in his amber eyes.

Watching Jerry walk away, Essie wondered if Harlan was in shock. "Maybe you should take tomorrow off. Your mem and sister might need you."

"I can't," Harlan said. "We're on a tight deadline, and I'm the only one who can do the hand-carving on it. Besides, I won't get paid if I take the day off, and my family is going to need the money, now more than ever."

Essie understood about needing the money, but right now the priorities were caring for Collette and Suzie. Before she could pursue the topic, her parents came into the waiting room, Sarah Rose following with a rag doll she carried by one leg.

"Harlan?" Sarah Rose touched his hand. "What happened to your buggy?"

He got down on one knee so that they could be face-to-face. "I don't know what happened, but it was in a crash."

"Can you bandage it together?" she asked.

He shook his head. "That won't work."

"Maybe you can glue it," she said, finding an empty chair.

"I might try that," he said.

Watching them, Essie appreciated the way Harlan could chat with a child even in the worst of circumstances. When he turned to Essie and winked, her heart melted with love for him.

Mem and Dat spoke with Harlan while Sarah Rose played with her doll, letting it slide on a slippery plastic chair. Mem wanted to visit with Collette, but Harlan explained that she was sleeping right now, sedated because of her pain. Dat wondered how the accident happened, and Harlan said he didn't know yet. A police officer was supposed to come back to complete the report, but Harlan was thinking it had been a hit-and-run, since there hadn't been a second vehicle at the scene.

"Right now I'm grateful that Mem and Suzie are each in one piece, soon to be on the mend," he said. "Once I know they're squared away, I need to see about our mule. Suzie told me that Beebee didn't seem to be hurt, but the police were carting her off. I'll have to track her down tomorrow."

"No need," Essie said. She explained that the police officer at the scene of the crash had given her the name of the veterinarian who had taken her in. "A Dr. Foster. When we left, Sam and the twins were harnessing up our horse cart to go pick her up. Beebee will be fine in our barn till you're ready for her, and there shouldn't be any boarding fee."

Relieved, Harlan pressed a palm to his heart. "That's a burden lifted. Denki, Essie."

She nodded, wishing she could do more. *Don't you know I would do anything for you?* she thought. When you loved someone, there was no limit on giving.

Dat offered to get some coffees from the cafeteria, and Mem popped open a bin of homemade "z-cookies," one of Miriam's creations. "There's zucchini in them," Mem said, trying to add a lighter note. "So I like to think they're good for you."

"If you don't count the chocolate chips," Essie added.

Harlan was too distracted to get the joke, but he bit into a cookie and thanked Mem. Dat returned with coffee for the adults and milk for Sarah Rose, and she sat in a chair to drink it down, pretending to share it with her doll.

"Harlan Yoder?" One of the nurses told Harlan that he could see his sister.

Harlan motioned Essie to come along—"Suzie's always happy to see you"—and they were led down the hallway to small examining areas separated only by curtains on hooks.

The nurse grabbed hold of the edge of the curtain and called into the small space. "I have your brother here," he said. "And a friend."

Essie moved forward and peered in to see Suzie sitting back in an upright bed, looking small and forlorn. A red bump sat over her right eye, and the cheek below it had been stitched closed and then fastened with a row of tiny bandages. Except for the bump, her face seemed washed out and pale.

"Suzie . . ." Essie rushed to her bedside and took her hand, only to find a clip on Suzie's finger. "How do you feel? That's a nasty bump."

"I have a headache," Suzie said, "but they don't think it's—what did you call it? A combustion?"

"Concussion. The doctor ruled out concussion with the CT scan," the nurse said. "But you need to take it easy. Any vomiting or seizures would be warning signs. And you'll want to keep those stitches dry for 24 to 48 hours, then apply petroleum jelly. I'll give you an instruction sheet on that."

"And you said I can go home soon?" Suzie said to the nurse.

"The doctor plans to release you, but you can't be home alone. Is there someone at home who can watch over you? At least for the next twenty-four hours."

"I can take care of her," Harlan said.

"But Mem might need you here," Suzie said, gingerly touching her chin, as if to check that it was still there.

Harlan and Essie exchanged a look. "She can come to our house," Essie offered. "There's plenty of people to keep an eye on her there."

"Do you want to stay at the Lapps?" Harlan asked.

"Yah, that would be good," Suzie said, leaning back against the bed again. She closed her eyes and sighed. "Most days I'd be tickled to spend the night away, but right now my head hurts too much to be happy."

"We'll make sure you get rest," Essie said, rubbing Suzie's arm.

"All right," the nurse said. "You chill here, and I'll be back when the doctor signs off on your release."

Essie remained close to Suzie while Harlan stood at the foot of the bed, his arms folded as he looked over his sister.

"Don't worry, Suzie," he said. "The Lapps will take good care of you."

"What about Mem?" she asked. "When's she coming home?"

"It sounds like it might be a while," Harlan said. "She might need a surgery or something called traction, when they lift your leg on a pulley to help it heal."

This was the first Essie had heard of those possibilities, and she wondered if Harlan was down-playing Collette's condition to soften the news for Suzie.

Still, Suzie winced. "That sounds terrible." She sighed. "I just want the three of us to go home together."

"It'll be a while until that can happen," Harlan said. "Till then, we'll make sure you've got someone taking care of you."

"Okay, Harlan." With her pale face and slender hands curled under her chin, Suzie seemed so small and delicate in the hospital bed. Essie longed to cover her with one of Mem's soft, knitted throws.

"While you're resting, can you tell me what happened there on the road?" Harlan's face was shadowed with rue. "Was it a hit-and-run? Or maybe Mem took a bad turn over a pothole?"

"It wasn't anything like that." Suzie opened her eyes, but kept her head on the pillow. "There were no cars nearby, and Mem didn't do anything wrong. One minute we were talking; the next the buggy was tipping over, tumbling to the ground on one side. I think the bad wheel—the noisy one—it just let loose."

The bad wheel . . . Oh, no. It couldn't be.

A stricken look darkened Harlan's face. "That wheel . . ." He pressed a hand to his cheek. "I tried to fix it a dozen times. I should have known better. I should have bought a new buggy."

"Who can afford that?" Suzie said.

"It's not your fault," Essie told Harlan. She moved toward the foot of the bed and put her hand on his shoulder. "These things happen."

"Not when you've got a brand-new buggy that doesn't click or squeak or lose its wheel on a busy road." His fingers curled as he squeezed his eyes shut for a moment. "I should have replaced that wheel. Should have junked the whole buggy and gotten a new one. It was up to me to keep you and Mem safe. I'm the man of the family. It was on my shoulders."

He whisked the curtain open. "And now it will be on my conscience."

And with that, he was gone.

Chapter Eighteen

Serena put her hands on the kitchen counter and stared around her suspiciously. This was definitely hostile territory, but she needed to conquer it, and fast.

Before Aunt Miriam had left, she'd asked Serena to handle tonight's dinner. "I'll leave it up to you to make sure everyone gets fed." Preparing to leave, Miriam had propped a plastic container of homemade cookies under one arm and handed a doll to Sarah Rose with the other.

"Me?" Serena had been surprised, and a little annoyed. Everyone knew she was like a tornado in the kitchen. "That's a dangerous idea. Why don't you ask Megan?"

"She's at the library in town, trying to finish a school assignment," Aunt Miriam said as she hustled Sarah Rose out the door. "Annie will be helping with the evening milking, and I don't think Grace is quite up for it. But ask for help. Ask the others to pitch in."

Serena had pressed her lips together to keep from objecting. She didn't want this assignment, and she knew she would fail. But someone needed to step up at this time when Essie was on the verge of tears and they all were holding their breath, anxiously waiting to hear how

Harlan's mother and sister had fared. Tension abounded. And at the moment Serena couldn't shake off her dad's favorite expression: *Lead, follow, or get out of the way.*

"I'll take care of it," Serena called from the front doorway as Essie, Miriam, and Sarah Rose climbed into the waiting buggy. "Don't you worry about a thing here." She hoped she sounded more confident than she felt as Uncle Alvin called to the horse and the buggy started rolling down the lane. From the backseat, Essie peered back sadly, and Serena gave her a thumbs-up. Essie's face disappeared, but her hand emerged with her thumb in the air. Serena hoped things went well at the hospital.

Back in the kitchen, Serena looked from the stove to the fridge, as if a meal might be waiting there to heat and serve. No such luck. How long would it take to make dinner for all the Lapp kids? At the big table, Grace and Lizzie sat together doing their separate schoolwork assignments. Lizzie's schoolwork never seemed too taxing, but she seemed to enjoy reading, especially books about the big brown dog Scooby-Doo.

Serena opened cupboards and stared at the contents, searching for inspiration. What had Aunt Miriam been planning to serve tonight? In one cupboard she found a jar of Essie's berry jam, as well as the delicious Amish peanut butter spread that had marshmallow mixed through it. Over the past few weeks, Serena had noticed that Sunday dinners were usually do-it-yourself sandwiches, the opposite of the big Sunday feasts Dad had always enjoyed at home. When she had asked about it, Miriam had explained that they believed God wanted Sunday to be a day of rest, so they didn't do big tasks, and they took a break from cooking.

Maybe tonight could be a sandwich night, too?

"Serena . . ." Lizzie called in a sing-songy voice from the next room. "What are you doing? Are you making food? I'm hungry."

"I'm just trying to figure out what to make for dinner." She opened the propane-powered refrigerator and tried to look for something obvious, like a plate of roasted chicken or even burger patties that could be cooked. There were jars of pickles, beets, and juice. Half a jar of red sauce was marked "pizza sauce." There was a fat slab of bacon, and a large bowl of leftover mashed potatoes. Unfortunately, there was nothing ready to serve.

"Looks like it's going to be sandwiches for dinner," Serena said.

"Oh, goody." Lizzie smiled. "Are you going to bake bread?"

"Sure," Grace said without looking up from her notebook. "Start now, and we might be able to eat by midnight."

Serena looked behind her. "What's wrong with the bread we have?"

"Nothing." Lizzie shrugged. "Except we ate it all up."

"Are you kidding me?" Serena put her hands on her hips.

"Look in the bread box." Lizzie put her book down. "Here. I'll show you." She strode into the kitchen and showed Serena the wooden container where they kept bread. Of course, Serena had pulled fresh bread from there to make toast. As luck would have it, the container was empty.

"Oh, come on." Serena stamped one foot on the floor. "How are we going to have sandwiches without bread?"

Lizzie smiled, as if it was the funniest thing that had happened all week. "I guess we can't have sandwiches."

"Grr." Serena raked back her hair. "Okay, Lizzie-doo. What do you suggest?"

Lizzie giggled. "Do you know Scooby-Doo?"

"I've never met him personally, but I used to watch the cartoons when I was little."

"I like his books."

"I've noticed. So, you know your way around this kitchen. You've been here, what? Ten, eleven years?"

Lizzie giggled again. "Ten."

"What do you think we should make for dinner?" Serena asked. "And notice that I said *we*. Because a Lapp family dinner is too much for one person to handle."

"Why don't you make a casserole?" Lizzie suggested.

"Nice idea." Serena folded her arms. "How would we do that?"

Lizzie held up her hands. "With a recipe!"

"Well, since I can't just go on YouTube to find one, what do you suggest?" Serena asked. "Where does Aunt Miriam keep hers stashed?"

"In that drawer over there." Lizzie pulled out a drawer and showed Serena several bundles of index cards secured by rubber bands. "There you go."

"Now we're cooking." Serena sifted through the bundles and chose one that seemed to have dinner recipes. "You've been a big help, Lizzie," she said, leafing through recipes. "Tell me, how are you at chopping?"

Lizzie reached into a lower drawer and pulled out two cooking aprons. "Mem says I'm a big help in the kitchen."

Serena tied a green apron on and smiled. "Music to my ears."

Serena and Lizzie found one of Miriam's recipes that used leftover mashed potatoes. The dish was called potato squares, and it called for leftover mashed potatoes covered with a seasoned ground beef crumble. Since the only ground beef in the house was frozen, Serena decided to leave it out, but Grace and Lizzie thought that would be too bland.

"How about a bacon crumble instead?" Serena asked, staring into the refrigerator.

"Everybody likes bacon," Grace said.

"Scooby-Dooby bacon!" Serena joked as she took the slab out and put a griddle on the stove to heat. Lizzie found it enormously funny.

Sam and the twins returned from the veterinarian with Harlan's mule. "We're going to get her settled and then milk the cows," Sam said. "What's for dinner?"

"It's a surprise," Serena said.

"A bacon surprise," Lizzie added.

"I don't like surprises," Sam said, pausing at the door, "but I do like bacon."

As they tried to follow the recipe, the bacon sizzled and popped in the pan. One pop sent something hot onto Serena's arm, but she rubbed the pain away and lowered the fire a bit. Lizzie was helpful when Serena struggled to find the different ingredients like brown sugar, paprika, and Worcestershire sauce. Who knew that onions would be stored down in the cooler cellar? Grace pitched in to finish chopping the onion when Serena's eyes were so full of tears that she could no longer see.

"It's so sad! I have to chop an onion!" Grace said, pantomiming tears when Serena complained. "Wa-ha-ha-ha!"

Serena sniffed, a little annoyed as she went to rinse her hands. But Lizzie's laughter was contagious, and Serena quickly got over it and laughed along. When they spread the mashed potatoes in a cake pan and covered them with the seasoned bacon crumble, Serena felt as if she'd had a hand in creating a masterpiece.

"This is going to be fantastic," she said, sprinkling on the last of the bacon.

"We'll see about that, Martha Stewart," Grace said.

The dish was heating in the hot oven when Annie, Sam, Pete, and Paul came in from milking the cows.

"Dinner will be ready in ten minutes," Serena said. "You guys can go wash up."

"Smells good," Sam said as he headed upstairs.

"Let's hope it's edible," Serena said under her breath.

Grace stowed her books in her backpack and set the table, while Serena cleaned up from the dinner preparation. Lizzie set out a pitcher of lemonade and one of water, as well as a platter of fresh veggies from the garden. As everyone assembled at the table, Serena shoved oven mitts on her hands and paced in front of the stove. At the ding of the timer, she removed the steaming pan from the oven and faced the audience gathered round the table. Megan came in just as Annie was showing Serena how to cut rectangular portions with the edge of the spatula.

"You made it in time for Serena's creation," Grace said.

"Actually I was just trying to get home on the scooter

before dark. I'm still not done, but I think I have enough information to finish here." Megan's AP classes were more difficult than Serena's. Many of them were college level, which required a greater time investment.

"Wash your hands and have a seat," Serena said, dishing up another portion. Once everyone was served, they silently gave thanks for the food and then dug in. Serena watched as the boys attacked the meal quickly, while the girls took their time. Serena watched for their reaction.

"Good," Pete said between bites.

"Wonderful good," Sam agreed. "You need to give Mem your recipe."

"See?" Lizzie smiled at Serena. "I told you everyone would like it."

"It's actually not bad," Megan said.

"I'm so glad you guys like it," Serena said. "I was so worried. You know cooking is not my thing. But Lizzie was a big help. Grace, too."

"Can I have more?" asked Paul.

Serena smiled as she gave out second helpings.

With the pressure off, she lifted her fork and took a bite. The brown sugar added just the right touch of sweetness to the bacon, and the bacon fat gave the potatoes moisture and a smoky flavor. Not bad for a first try.

The feeling of accomplishment was amplified by the fact that Essie and Aunt Miriam had needed her to cook so that they could attend to Harlan's family at the hospital. At least, Serena now had one recipe in her repertoire.

Not long after the kitchen cleanup Aunt Miriam arrived home with Sarah Rose and Harlan's sister, Suzie. Serena hung back as Lizzie and Annie greeted Suzie warmly, but she was obviously weak and tired, moving slowly.

"Let's get some food in you, and then up to bed," Aunt Miriam said, guiding Suzie to the table. "You can take a bed in the nursery with Sarah Rose. More quiet for you."

Annie brought Suzie a glass of milk and sat down beside her. Miriam went into the kitchen and called out, "This casserole will be the perfect thing."

Once the food was reheated, Suzie took a few bites as the younger girls asked her about her injuries. Did her head hurt? What were those tiny strips on her face?

"Mem has more bandages if you need them," Sarah Rose offered.

Serena smiled, but Suzie seemed to be falling asleep at the table.

"Annie, take Suzie upstairs and show her where she can wash up," Miriam instructed. "I'm sure you can find an extra nightgown of Essie's to fit her. Essie won't mind."

Serena watched the girls go upstairs, and then followed Aunt Miriam into the kitchen. "Is she going to be okay?"

Miriam nodded. "She was spared a concussion, thanks to Gott, but we need to watch over her."

"How is Harlan's mother?"

"Sorry to say, she's worse off. They think it's a broken leg, and it sounds like she'll need to stay in the hospital a few days. Surgery might be necessary. Harlan was waiting to talk with her doctor when we left. I would have stayed longer, but Suzie needed to leave that uncomfortable hospital and get rest."

"It's really nice that you're taking care of her."

Miriam smiled and put a hand on Serena's shoulder. "That's what we must do. Love your neighbor as yourself."

As her aunt helped herself to a small serving of the casserole, Serena wondered if Miriam had always been this way—generous, unassuming, and cheerful. It wasn't just the fact that she did nice things for people. A lot of people did favors for others. Aunt Miriam committed acts of kindness joyfully, as if it made her the happiest person on earth. And maybe, just maybe she was.

That night Serena wrapped a blanket around her shoulders as she set out to greet Scout. In the time since she'd arrived here the nights had become noticeably cooler, and Serena wondered if there might come a day when she was traipsing out here to see Scout in the snow. Well, even a blizzard wouldn't stop her from visiting with Scout.

Their nightly meetings were usually the highlight of her day, as they used their short span of time together to catch up on each other's joys and disappointments. And tonight, she had a bazillion things to tell him about the events of the day. The agitator had been shut off, and he must have finished testing samples of the milk, as he was hooking up the hose when she approached. The warm smile on his face let her know how happy he was to see her. Every night, Scout had that smile. She'd never had a boyfriend who'd appreciated her this much. As soon as the milk was pumping, they walked to their usual spot— the picnic table on the lawn—to get away from the noise of the truck.

"I got your text about needing more furniture," he said.

She had forgotten about the message she'd sent earlier that day. It seemed like weeks ago.

"Mom says you're welcome to anything in the garage. She's actually really pleased with the way you restored the pieces you worked on. Very 'of the moment,' that's what she calls the style. So you should come over this weekend and pick out more furniture."

"That would be great. But I've had such a crazy day." Serena sat beside him on the seat of the wooden picnic table. "Right after I sent you that text, Essie and I were stuck in traffic. Turned out it was a crashed buggy, and Harlan's mom and sister were inside. They both went to the hospital, and poor Essie . . . I felt awful for her. I know that fear, when someone you love is in the hospital and you don't know what's going on. I went through that with my mom, more than once." She told him the latest news on Suzie and Collette Yoder.

"I'm sorry to hear all that," Scout said. "I wish them both a speedy recovery."

"It's so hard on Harlan and Essie. They're still at the hospital now! Aunt Miriam said she wouldn't be surprised if they stay the night there."

"I don't like hospitals."

"I don't either." She adjusted the blanket on her shoulders and let out her breath in a huff of air. "My mind is kind of buzzing and spinning. It's hard to push back the worry and stress."

"That's when you know you've got to kiss things up to God." Scout kissed his fingertips and lifted his hand to the sky.

"I wish it was that easy."

"It *is*," he insisted.

He climbed up to the tabletop, took her hand, and helped her climb up beside him. Side by side, they stretched out on the tabletop facing the sky. This had become one of their nightly rituals, lying shoulder to shoulder and staring up at the night sky to soak up the moon and the stars. Tonight she was conscious of the warmth of his body along her right side, and she snuggled closer to him.

"Cold?" he asked.

"A little."

He sat up a second to slip off his leather jacket, and then spread it open over the two of them. Serena loved the way it had captured his warmth, and the leathery, clean smell reminded her of Scout.

"That's cozy," she said. "Look at that. . . . Plenty of stars out tonight."

"Yeah, they're always in the sky. We just can't see them because of cloud cover, light, and pollution."

"Such a scientist you are."

"Science is life. When my mind is spinning and I have trouble thinking straight, I look at the stars. The sky is where science and God converge in a wonderful way. We can study the universe from our planet, but despite telescopes and great innovations, there are still countless mysteries in God's universe."

"That's such a beautiful thought," she said.

Under the jacket he linked his fingers through hers and held her hand to his chest. "Thanks. It gives me comfort."

She took a deep breath, her cheek resting against Scout's shoulder. It did calm the flurry in her mind, sky-gazing with Scout by her side. The air was just cool enough to make her burrow closer to him. "Teach me about the stars," she said. "I know it's complex, but what would you cover in lesson one."

"Lesson one. Well, most people would start with the Big Dipper. It's easier to see in the spring, but I'll bet we can find it tonight. Let's see. If we can find the North Star, we can find the Big Dipper."

"I've heard of the Big Dipper," she said. "When I was in school I learned that black slaves called the Big Dipper the Drinking Gourd. I think they used it to navigate to the North, to escape slavery in the South."

"See? You can do astronomy," he said. "And you've soaked up some important history, too. So to find the Big Dipper, you start out by looking north, which is that direction." He pointed toward the barn. "The North Star, also called Polaris, stays stationary in the northern sky. That's why sailors used to navigate by it. See it there?"

She did. "I got it."

"So the Big Dipper is going to be near the North Star. It rotates around it. The bowl of the Big Dipper is four stars, sort of an irregular square. And the handle is three stars." He paused. "Right now it's sort of tipped down, like someone's pouring water out of it."

As he spoke, the shape of the constellation seemed to pop in the dark sky. "I see it!" For a moment Serena lay beside him gazing up at the inky dark sky and the tiny lights that were suns bajillions of miles away. It wasn't just awe at the sparkly stars. It was the realization that people had stared up at this same sky for thousands of years, charting the stars and seeing the figures of animals and archers and drinking gourds there. Stargazing was a timeless occupation, and she was just one of countless people who had looked to the sky.

It made her feel incredibly small but significant, all at the same time.

This same sky, with its mysteries that Scout believed God had the answers to. It comforted her to think that someone was in the heavens, watching over the world and lending people moments of grace.

She sure hoped it was true.

Chapter Nineteen

It was after ten, and although Essie was beginning to feel like today was the longest day she'd ever lived, she pushed herself to stay awake and socialize with the other folk in the hospital waiting room.

After suppertime, Amish visitors had begun to stream into the hospital, as was the tradition in their community. Parents came with their children, filling the waiting room and staying late, often until the staff sent them home at night. Amish folk followed instructions, but they'd be back early in the morning, as soon as visiting hours started again. Essie had been concerned that Collette Yoder didn't have much family in the area, but she needn't have worried. Dat's brother Lloyd had come with his wife Greta and their two youngest, giggly toddlers who enjoyed playing in the new waiting room, this one upstairs in the orthopedics department, where Collette had been assigned a room.

Smitty, the man who owned the pretzel company where Collette and Suzie worked, had come with his wife, sister, and three children ranging from nine to fourteen. They'd brought two tubs of pretzels, which were salty and delicious. "Where's Suzie?" asked Smitty's fourteen-year-old daughter Christina. The two girls worked together forming pretzels at the factory.

"Suzie went home with my mem," Essie told her. "She injured her head, and the doctors want her to rest."

"I wanted to see her," Christina said, looking down at the floor. "We never get to spend time together outside the factory."

"Maybe you can come visit her while she's on the mend," Essie said. "I'm sure she'd like to see you." They made plans for Christina to visit the following evening. By then, Essie hoped that Suzie would be feeling better and Harlan would have stopped blaming himself for the accident. His earlier outburst had been understandable, but she had warned him to control his anger for his sister's sake. "You're upsetting Suzie, and the doctors say she needs peace and rest right now."

Harlan had apologized and tamped down his guilt. A good thing, because he wouldn't have wanted all these visitors to see him like that.

Especially not their bishop, Aaron Troyer, who had come to the hospital with two of his daughters. At thirteen and seventeen, the Troyer girls were interested in the social chatter of the others their age. Bishop Troyer had lost his wife Dorcus two years ago from cancer, and Essie sensed that it required extra effort for the Troyer family to visit the hospital where their wife and mother had spent so much time in treatment and surgery. Aaron Troyer sat with the men, imparting words of concern and faith, but the tension was obvious in his tight lips and rapidly blinking eyes.

A glance at Harlan told Essie he was equally tense, but she understood why. In the past few years, Harlan had become nervous around the bishop. "He seems to visit our family more than most," he had confided to Essie. "I think he's watching for me to do something wrong. Or maybe he disapproves of Mem because Dat left her."

Marital strife was frowned upon in Amish communities, but Essie didn't think the bishop would punish Collette for the sins of her husband. "I don't think he's out to punish your mem or you," she had told Harlan. "You've always followed the rules. And the bishop has his own problems with Mose." The bishop's nineteen-year-old son had truly run wild on his rumspringa, hosting parties that were the talk of Amish teens until Mose hitchhiked away. He'd been gone for months now, and though the unbaptized were free to go, it always left a bit of a taint on the parents who raised them.

Seeking to save Harlan from a long engagement with the bishop, Essie picked up the basket of sandwiches that Greta had brought from home, and took it over to the men.

"Who wants a sandwich?" she offered. "There's peanut butter spread on the left, and this side is cheese and pickles." She went down the line of men, waiting for each to pick until she got to Harlan. "I think Greta has some more cheese over there," she told him. "Come."

He followed her to the other side of the waiting room, where they took two sandwiches, chatted with Greta, and then took seats together.

"Denki," Harlan said quietly before taking a colossal bite.

"I sensed that you needed a way out."

"You have wonderful good instincts, Essie."

Harlan finished his sandwich in a few bites, and Essie got up to fetch more. "You need to keep your strength up," she said, handing him two more sandwiches.

"What would I do without you?" His amber eyes warmed her as they both continued eating. After such a long day, Essie was grateful to have something in her stomach. They were just finishing when a woman in a white coat, with short blond hair that seemed fine as duck fluff and black-framed glasses, called out Harlan's name. He rose, and Essie went to the edge of the room with him to meet Dr. Teddy Kiddle.

"All these folks are your family?" Dr. Kiddle gestured to the Amish folk, who now completely dominated the waiting room, but for one English couple who had been leaning on each other to rest.

"Family and community," Harlan said. "How's my mother doing?"

"You can see her now." Dr. Kiddle gestured for them to follow her down the hallway, where they passed a few open doors, an empty bed on wheels, and a cart with clipboards hanging from the side.

"Your mom has a fractured femur, that's the thigh bone, in the upper leg." Dr. Kiddle spoke in a casual manner as they walked. "We thought she also had a fractured pelvis, but fortunately that injury is less severe. A contusion. We've medicated her to reduce her pain, so Mom is too drowsy to discuss treatment tonight, but I can tell you that we think surgery is our best chance to correct the fracture. After that, she'll need in-patient rehab for at least five days. We can start it here, but you'll probably want to move her to another facility after we've cleared her for infection." She turned toward them, her eyes earnest behind the wide-frame glasses. "An extended hospital stay will be quite costly, and I know you don't have insurance."

This was the first time Essie had heard anyone mention

the costs of Collette's care here at the hospital. Money would be needed to pay for the doctors and medical care.

Money that Harlan's family didn't have.

"I'm confident that your mother can get excellent medical care at a rehab facility," Dr. Kiddle went on. "We'll give you some referrals, and you can get prices from the facilities. But please, don't skimp on rehab. Depending on the outcome of the surgery, she may need to learn how to walk again. Physical therapy will help her build up the muscles around the fracture and increase her range of motion. It could mean the difference between walking and needing assistance the rest of her life."

"I'll make sure she gets what she needs," Harlan vowed. "Surgery and physical therapy. We'll find a way to pay for it all."

"Keep in mind, it's going to be a long road to recovery for her. We're talking at least eight weeks of physical therapy. More if she needs it. And she'll need full-time care for a while. Is there anyone at home—a grandparent or a teen who could be with her twenty-four seven?"

"My sister and I both work," Harlan said. "But Suzie can take off from her job or . . . we'll hire someone."

"Folks from the community will pitch in," Essie explained. "We'll take care of her."

"Good. That's what she's going to need." Dr. Kiddle covered a few other details, talking so quickly that Essie had trouble keeping up. At last, Dr. Kiddle paused in front of a closed door. "You can go in, but she's probably still groggy. I'm going to check and see if some of her lab results came back."

Harlan thanked the doctor, set his jaw, and then opened the door.

Following Harlan into the room, Essie forced a smile, determined not to be put off by the blinking and beeping machines in the hospital room. Such strange things had frightened her as a girl when her dawdi had been in the hospital, but now she knew that the machines were there to help doctors and nurses treat the patient.

Underneath the headboard of screens with squiggles and flashing lights, Collette Yoder lay in bed, her eyes closed as if she were having an afternoon nap. Her white, heart-shaped kapp had been removed, but her dark hair was still pulled back into a twist. Essie had expected to see Collette's leg in a big white cast; instead it lay atop the sheet, strapped into a plastic tray that resembled a snow sled.

"Mem?" Harlan rubbed the back of her hand. "It's Harlan. I'm here with Essie. Can you wake up?"

Collette's eyelids drifted up, and her face turned toward her son. "Oh, Harlan, I've been waiting for you. It's time to go."

Harlan looked at Essie, who shrugged. "Must be the medication," she said quietly.

"How are you feeling, Mem?" Harlan asked. "I'm sorry you have to go through this pain."

"I can't stay here any longer," she said. "Now help me pack up so we can go."

"We can't go home, Mem. The doctors say you need to stay here at least for a few days. You need to have surgery on your leg to help you heal."

"I do? I don't have the time for that now, do I?" She drew in a breath and tried to pull herself up in bed, but the movement produced a gasp of pain. "My leg. How am

I going to pack up the apartment when it hurts to move? We'll never make it to Ohio."

"Ohio?" Essie said softly. "Why do you want to go there, Collette?"

"My brothers . . . they'll take care of me."

Just then the door opened. "How's it going?" Dr. Kiddle asked. "How's your pain, Collette? On a scale of one to ten?"

Collette squinted at the doctor, not recognizing her.

"Can you show me on this chart?" The doctor pulled out a plastic-coated card from a pocket on the wall. It showed various cartoon faces, their expressions ranging from a frantic face at ten, to a happy face at the number one.

Collette stared at the chart. "Is that supposed to be me?"

"Can you point to which one describes your pain?"

"Just leave me be." Collette turned away and closed her eyes.

"Mem, the doctor is trying to help you."

Essie patted the back of Collette's hand, trying to encourage her, but she didn't respond.

"She hasn't been making sense," Harlan told Dr. Kiddle. "This is not like her."

"Sometimes trauma makes people irrational for a period of time after the incident. But more likely it's the pain meds," the doctor said. "I'll make sure the dosage is correct, but since she's in bed and on monitors, I'd rather have her well medicated to control her pain. That's the best we can do for her until the surgery." The doctor opened the door and motioned them out. "And you two probably need a good night's sleep."

Sleep would be welcome, but Essie wasn't sure that it would come easily. Now that she'd seen Harlan's mother, she had more questions and concerns than reassurances. She said a quiet good-bye to Collette, and then went out to the nurse's desk, where Harlan had to read through pages of forms involving his mother's care, permission for the surgery, and assurance that the hospital bills would be paid.

There was no question about paying for whatever Collette needed. Amish folk used the advice and treatment of doctors when they could.

"I might be paying for the rest of my life," Harlan said as he signed his name to the form. "But I thank Gott that Mem will get the treatment she needs."

"You're a good son," Essie said.

From the stony look on his face, she could tell that he didn't believe her.

Chapter Twenty

It was late. The wood in the potbelly stove had long ago burned down to embers, but it still gave off enough heat to keep the main room cozy on this October night. Miriam was one of the last ones up, along with Serena, who had come in from the woodshop with streaks of lavender paint on her hands. By the light of a large kerosene lamp they chatted and lost themselves in their repetitive tasks.

"I'm so tired," Serena said as she wound the yarn from the skein into a growing ball. The task was a big help to Miriam, who had learned the hard way that skeins got tangled in the knitting process. It seemed that the busy work eased Serena's mind. "I should go to bed," Serena said.

"You should," Miriam said. "But then you'd miss the best part of your day—the arrival of the milk truck."

Serena smiled, peering at Miriam through a lock of dark hair that had fallen loose from her ponytail. "You don't miss a trick, Aunt Miriam."

"Seven children before you have taught me a thing or two." Miriam's fingers moved automatically, the knitting needles clicking away as her thoughts went to her three English nieces. Grace, whom she was knitting this scarf for, seemed to have settled into a content pocket with school and the family to keep her busy. Megan was the hard worker, a serious student with her mind set on college. Lately she had taken to going on short runs instead of those long walks. A sign that her knee and her mind were healing.

And bubbly, daring Serena, who now expended so much of her energy on old furniture, turning the beast into a beauty, as the fairy tale went. The girl who'd once said she hated old things was giving them new life. Miriam was happy for her.

"You're not usually up this late," Serena said. "Wassup, Auntie M?"

It was true. And despite the warmth of the stove, Miriam wished she was upstairs snuggling next to the warmth of her husband. But Essie was out late, another night at the hospital, and Miriam had decided to stay up until she got home. The girl's energy must be about whittled down to nothing, and Miriam wanted to encourage her. "I'm waiting up to see Essie," Miriam said. "She's been tirelessly attending to Collette all this week."

"I've barely seen her at all," Serena agreed. "But aren't Amish parents supposed to look the other way when their teenage kids are out late?"

"You've learned a few things about plain living." Miriam nodded. "It's true that during rumspringa, parents go to bed and hope their children stay safe. But Essie is finished with all that. She and Harlan are both baptized members of the church now, committed to following church rules." Her needles clicked away steadily. "And when her daughter is out late caring for folks in the hospital, a mother wants to make sure she's taking time to take care of herself, too."

"That's sweet." Serena wound the yarn slowly. "She's lucky to have you as a mom."

"I'm the one who's been blessed. A big family fills a home with love," Miriam said. "And a good deal of noise, too."

The clip-clop of hooves let them know a buggy was coming. "That'll be Harlan bringing her home."

"It was nice of you guys to lend him a buggy."

"Well, he needed a way to get around, and we had an old one in the buggy barn. There's so much for Harlan and Suzie to do, going back and forth to the rehab center and tending to their jobs. The least we could do was help with transportation."

Miriam and Serena remained in place as the noise from the buggy stopped. After dropping Essie off, Harlan would return to the apartment in Joyful River, where he would have to park the buggy, remove Beebee from the harnesses, and brush her down. Miriam couldn't imagine how exhausted the young man must be, working at the furniture factory by day and then spending his nights visiting his mem at the care facility. She was grateful that the women of their church had organized a food train so that someone was bringing a nice meal to Collette, Harlan, and visitors at the facility each night.

When Essie came in the door she seemed surprised to see anyone up on this Saturday night before church. She hung her cape on the hook by the door and came over to sit by the potbelly stove. "You're up late."

"We didn't want you to come home to a cold, dark house," Miriam said. "How did the day go for Collette?"

"She seems to be feeling a bit better every day." Essie seemed worn to the marrow as she removed her shoes and sank back in the chair. "The doctor said she can be released Tuesday and continue her physical therapy as an outpatient. But there's no place for her to go. She won't be able to tackle those narrow steps to the apartment for a long time."

"I wish we could have her here," Miriam said.

"I know, but she would struggle at the front porch, let alone getting upstairs to the bedroom. No, the doctor wants her living on the ground floor of a house. Harlan and I spent a few hours today looking for a new rental for Collette, Suzie, and him, but no ground floor units were available." She sighed. "I feel sorry for Collette. Her heart's set on getting out of there Tuesday, but she has nowhere to go."

"Can't she stay in the rehab place for a while?" asked Serena.

"It's too expensive," Essie said, "and she longs for the freedom and comfort they can't allow her there."

"I'm sure something will turn up," Miriam said.

"I hope so," Essie said. "The bishop was visiting tonight, and he said he's going to pray on it."

"We'll all pray, and an answer will come." Miriam stopped knitting. "You look tired, daughter. Shall I make you a snack?"

"I've no appetite." Essie shook her head. "All of this commotion over the crash has gotten in the way of things. My plans with Harlan . . ." She bit her lower lip, trying to keep from crying.

"What is it, Essie?" Miriam prodded.

"It seems selfish to be sad for myself when Collette is suffering so, but . . ." Essie's words were cut off by a sob. Quickly she caught herself, sniffing and wiping away her tears. "Harlan and I are getting married in November.

At least that was the plan until the accident. We were going to tell you and Dat and Collette . . . and then the crash happened."

"Oh, daughter!" Miriam kept her voice low, but she could not deny that she was thrilled by Essie's news. "That's a joyous announcement."

"But with everything that's happened, I don't know what Harlan is planning to do. Collette is still talking about leaving Joyful River. That first night at the hospital we thought she was in shock, but now, with a clear head, she's still talking about it. She said she's been thinking of leaving Joyful River for some time now. That it's just too hard to make ends meet, and she wants a good life for her children."

"But Harlan has a good life here, with you," Serena insisted.

Leaving town? It was the last thing Miriam would expect from Collette Yoder, who seemed like the sort who loved her routines and familiar paths. "Where would they go?" Miriam asked.

"To Ohio, to live with one of her brothers."

"Ah, yes, Ohio was where her brothers went to find work when the farmland began to get so scarce here," Miriam said, hoping the light chatter would calm her oldest daughter. "Collette has visited there for weddings. She said her brothers found a church that accepted them years ago, and they feel very much at home now. They wanted her to join them, but at the time she insisted that Joyful River was home. But you say she's changed her mind now?"

Essie frowned. "She says they need to go. Harlan is torn in two. I know he wants to stay. . . ."

"Harlan can't leave Joyful River," Serena insisted. "What about your plans? That would ruin everything."

"But his mem expects him to go, and you know he's a good son. Besides, he still thinks the buggy accident was his fault. He can't forgive himself. It doesn't help that the police determined that the crash was caused by a malfunction of the Yoder buggy. Harlan feels responsible, and he'll do anything to make it up to his mem and sister. He might even have to go to Ohio with them."

Miriam touched her daughter's hand. "Would you go with him?"

Another tear coursed down Essie's cheek. "I don't know, but so far I haven't been asked."

Miriam squeezed her daughter's hand. Essie's heart was hurting, and Miriam hated the fact that a remedy for the situation was out of her hands. "So many mountains to climb," Miriam said, searching her daughter's shiny brown eyes. "But still, the journey must begin with a single step. This, I know you can do."

Essie sniffed and nodded.

"Talk to Harlan," Miriam said. "That's where I would start. You two are planning to take a major step together. You need to make sure you're walking the same path."

The next morning came all too soon. Church day, and though Miriam longed to stay in bed, there were the little ones to corral into their church clothes, and a quick breakfast to fit in after the milking and before it was time to leave.

On the way to church the twins started complaining. "I

wish I could sleep all day, like the English cousins," Paul said.

"Sleep all day and skip church," Pete agreed.

Paul argued that if they skipped church, they wouldn't get to see their friends. Pete insisted he didn't care, and that led to a petty back and forth of:

"Yes, you do!"

"No, I don't!"

"Boys, please, save your bickering for something that matters," Miriam said. "And don't blame your cousins for who they are. I'll have you know that Serena was up late working on her furniture business, and Megan and Grace put a lot of time into their schoolwork. Gott gives each of us different paths and burdens. Yours is not to judge."

"Sorry, Mem," the boys said quietly.

After that the buggy was silent, a few moments of quiet. A blessed peace! Alvie touched her knee and winked, grateful for the interlude. All too soon they turned into Alice and Noah Yutzy's driveway, in line with other buggies arriving for church.

As the singing began in Hoch Deutsch, the traditional language of Anabaptist church ceremonies, Miriam felt a swell of gratitude to be here amongst good people gathered together in glory to Gott. Noah Yutzy's large workshop had been cleared for the gathering, and a white tent outside extended the area for folks to sit on benches without getting wet, if it should rain. She looked to her left, where Essie sat beside her in the women's section. It was hard to see her daughter going through troubled times, but Gott in his wisdom would see Essie through.

This, Miriam knew.

* * *

"Such a wonderful good sermon today, don't you think?" Linda Hostetler's small round eyes scanned the group of women before her gaze landed hard on Miriam. "Temptation can be a problem for us when we stray from the rules of the church."

"So true," Greta said, and everyone agreed.

Miriam nodded, feeling like a rabbit frozen in caution under the watchful eyes of a fox. She'd been lured into Linda's social traps one too many times before.

"It's good to have a reminder that possessions are not what matter in the world," Linda continued. "We live plain by choice, and once we make that choice we must—"

"Ach! Ezra!" Rose Graber got up from the bench and crossed to the food table, where her nine-year-old son was struggling with a pitcher. "You're spilling that iced tea everywhere."

Miriam smiled, noticing how the interruption had diverted everyone's attention. All for the best. The women had listened to one sermon today; they didn't need to hear another one from Linda.

"Good thing we're still having church outside," Greta said as she rose and started collecting empty paper plates.

"Tell me, Miriam," Linda said, taking Rose's empty spot on the bench. "Is your oldest daughter here?"

"Essie? Yes, she's here somewhere. Probably talking with the younger ones."

"The topic of temptations made me think of her. Does the bishop know she has a cell phone?"

"Essie?" Miriam held her smile, despite the nettles of

Linda's accusation. "My Essie doesn't have a cell phone. She's beyond rumspringa. She was baptized more than a year ago now, and she follows the Ordnung."

"But I saw her talking on her cell phone, plain as day. She was sitting in one of your buggies in town, chatting away in broad daylight. I know it was her."

"I trust your memory," Miriam said. "But talking on a cell phone doesn't mean she owns one."

"Sometimes it's hard for a mother to see the truth about her child." Linda's beady eyes softened for a moment. "Too bad. I know what I saw."

Rose seemed wary of Linda's somewhat heated remark as she returned to their group. She seemed about to ask a question, but Miriam shook her head.

"We're getting to the age where many of us need eyeglasses," Greta said, catching up with the conversation. "Just the other day, Lloyd told me he couldn't tell if a gray bird in our oak tree was a gnatcatcher or a catbird. And there it was, only a few yards away from us. I'm sending him to get his eyes checked."

"Sometimes I have trouble seeing the street signs when I'm driving our buggy," Rose admitted. "Especially in the rain."

"Were you out in that storm last week?" Miriam asked.

"I was home, thanks to Gott in heaven," Greta said, "but I was running around the yard like a wild horse, pulling my laundry down from the line."

"The downpour left a river in our driveway," Linda said.

"The thunder really rocked the house. I think it moved a few inches," Miriam joked, glad that they had switched to a lighter topic.

They were laughing when Loretta Glick came along with a big smile. "I just heard the news about Collette Yoder," she said, squeezing Linda's arm.

"It was a terrible accident," Greta said, sharing a concerned look with Miriam. How could Loretta be so gleeful about a friend's suffering?

"Not that news! I heard that she's getting out of the rehab facility this week, all because you've offered to put her up." Loretta patted Linda's arm. "It's like the Good Samaritan in the Bible."

"I couldn't say no," Linda admitted. "Collette needed a one-story place to live, on account of her being in a wheelchair part of the time. That apartment they have, up a flight of stairs, it's no good. So Bishop Aaron came to me and asked if we'd put her up for a bit. I think she's moving in on Tuesday."

"That is good news," Rose agreed. "I know the family has been eager to get her out of that facility. They all cost so much. You're a blessing to the family, Linda."

Linda Hostetler, a blessing?

It sure seemed that way. Maybe Miriam had been too harsh on Linda. Truly, all men and women were Gott's creations, and he didn't make mistakes. Maybe Linda's act of kindness would persuade Collette to stay in the community where she was loved and appreciated.

Or maybe Linda's tendency to gossip would send Collette off to Ohio the moment she was healed. Time would tell.

Chapter Twenty-One

Monday morning, Essie was up before dawn helping Mem make breakfast. She had a small helping of scrambled eggs along with a slice of bread and jam, and then went out to the horse barn to hitch Comet to a buggy. When Lizzie, Peter, and Paul were ready, they climbed into the buggy, and off they went to school. Usually the Amish children walked to their nearby school, but since Essie needed to go into town, she thought she would give them a special treat. For once, they would be on time.

After the accident, Essie had put off all her errands to be with Harlan and his family. Today, it was time to catch up.

She stopped at the dry goods store and bought ten pounds of sugar, five pounds of flour, and four cases of mason jars. Mem had requested the flour, and Essie needed the rest for canning. Mem had also requested a few yards of discounted fabric in a solid color to be used for dresses and quilting. Essie found a pretty shade of blue, and the clerk measured and cut cloth from the bolt. The clerk, an English woman with short, curly hair and a bright red sweater, helped Essie load up the back of the buggy.

At the bank, Essie decided to forgo the drive-through, worried as always that Comet wouldn't mind her as they waited in line. Instead, she tied the horse to the hitching post and went inside the bank. While in line she once again counted the money she'd tucked in her shoe—a hundred seventy-two dollars. Had Harlan been able to collect money from any of the shops in nearby towns yet? Probably not. She would try to find a moment to ask him about it when she saw him later today.

Once all the money was in, they would have surely made their goal.

At last, it was her turn to step up to the counter and hand the teller the cash and deposit ticket. The young woman behind the counter had doughy pale skin and long dark ringlets of hair that she twirled around one finger as she talked.

"How's your day been?" she asked.

"Very good, thank you." Essie smiled as she handed over the deposit.

"Do you want a balance on the account?" the woman asked.

"Yes, please."

The woman typed in a few things, counted out Essie's bills, and then frowned at the screen. "Were you in here this morning?" she asked.

"No." It seemed like an odd question. "I haven't been here for a few days."

"I only ask because a transaction was made on this account this morning. A withdrawal."

Money had been taken out? Essie's breath seemed trapped in her throat. "Do you know if it was Harlan Yoder?"

The young woman pushed her curls over one shoulder

as she pursed her lips. "He's the only other person on the account, so it must have been him. Here. I'll print out a record of recent transactions."

Why had Harlan come here without telling her? Essie wouldn't have stopped him from taking any of the money if he needed it, and he had to know that. It worried her that some imposter might have come in to rob their account. It also hurt to think that Harlan might have withdrawn the money without telling her.

"So here's your balance—$2,738.59. A withdrawal of $2,500 dollars was made this morning. Is there anything else I can help you with?"

Essie studied the slip of paper, calculating in her head. That had to be it. Decision made, she looked up at the young teller and slid the paper across the counter. "If you please, there is one more thing I need to do."

The White Dove Rehabilitation Hospital was a cluster of low-slung buildings set atop a grassy knoll that had at one time been farmland. Although Collette's treatment there was still costly, it was a fraction of the price of the main hospital, and the rehab center was far more homey and friendly. Essie enjoyed passing through the wide glass double doors that quietly whooshed open and shut when she approached with her arms usually full of food, treats, Collette's laundry, or books.

Today she carried a bag of clean clothes, a jar of her homemade berry jam, and a small batch of gmay cookies that had been left over from yesterday's church gathering. Collette had longed to attend church yesterday, especially since she was a friend of Alice Yutzy, their host, but the doctor had advised her to wait another two weeks. By then, she would be out of the wheelchair and moving with the assistance of a metal walker. "You're coming along great," Abby, the physical therapist, had assured Collette. "But part of the process of healing is accepting the things that you can't do for now."

Essie paused at the desk to sign in and deliver the small bag of cookies to Gilda, the receptionist, who always had a kind word for folks passing through. "Thanks for the cookies," Gilda said. "I'm going to try to take them home to my husband, mister skin-and-bones. I'm afraid the perks of the job are going right to my waistline!"

"We all have our challenges," Essie said. "Have you seen her this morning?"

"Oh, yes. She was out here a few times, soaking up the morning sun." Gilda nodded toward a corner of the lobby near the double doors where the rooftop had skylights that allowed light to shine through. "I keep telling her that she's going to get a speeding ticket if she doesn't slow down in that wheelchair."

Essie smiled. "That sounds like Collette." Harlan's mother had born up better than anyone had expected through the pain and physical challenges of her injuries. Normally a quiet homebody, Collette seemed to enjoy the social aspects of life in a facility. Reaching out to other patients, she had developed a new awareness of and sympathy for the difficulties other people faced. In her own course of treatment, she had done every exercise her therapist prescribed, pushing through each challenge.

"Is she still scheduled to leave tomorrow?" Essie asked.

"That's what I hear. We're going to miss her around here."

Essie would miss coming here. Besides saying good-bye to the cheerful staff of this facility, Essie dreaded having to deal with Linda Hostetler every time she visited Collette. That woman seemed to have a knack for saying things that hurt people's feelings. But Essie would have to grin and bear it and learn to appreciate the help Linda was providing to Harlan's family.

"I'm sure Collette will come back and visit you," Essie promised. "And she'll be sure to bring cookies."

"Music to my ears!" Gilda exclaimed.

Peeking into Collette's room, Essie found her bed empty. She dropped off the laundry and jam, and then proceeded down the hall. The small solarium had a view of the garden, as well as trays of potted plants along the windows that patients and staff tended to. Collette was showing another patient in a wheelchair how to mist an African violet.

"Not too much," Collette instructed. "You want the soil to be moist, but never soggy."

"Such a pretty plant," the other woman said. "I love that shade of purple."

"One of Gott's beautiful creations," Collette agreed. "But it's such a delicate thing. African violets need to be kept away from cold drafts and doorways. Like a colicky baby."

Both women were laughing as Essie joined them. "The greenhouse plants will be happier from all the care they're getting."

"I do miss having a garden," Collette admitted, smiling up at Essie. "Thank you for coming. It's always good to have company."

"I'm sure Harlan will get here after work," Essie said.

After the accident Essie and Harlan had agreed to stagger their visits so that Collette would have someone attending to her day and night. Essie came to visit during the day, Harlan in the evening after work. Although the plan provided Collette with companionship, it had created a schedule in which Essie and Harlan rarely crossed paths. "But in the meantime, I've brought some clean laundry and church cookies."

"Denki. I handed out the last of those chocolate marshmallow bars last night after dinner. Folks round here sure liked them." Collette seemed to derive joy from handing out delicious treats to everyone in the facility. "But we'd better get back to my room. I'll need your help packing up my things for the move to Linda's spare room." She turned to the other woman to add: "Looks like I'm leaving tomorrow."

"Good on you!"

"We'll drop off some church cookies in your room," Collette promised her acquaintance. Wheeling Collette back to her room, Essie considered how this experience had brought Harlan's mem out of her shell. Funny how you never knew what Gott had in store for you.

Back in the room, a nurse helped Collette move from the wheelchair to the hospital bed, which cranked up and down for convenience. Then, under Collette's direction, Essie loaded most of Collette's clothes and belongings into paper shopping bags. "Just be sure to leave my nightgown out for tonight," Collette instructed.

It didn't take long at all, and as Essie folded and tucked things away, Collette explained her long-term plans. "I know you and Harlan thought I'd gone crazy after the crash when I talked about going back to Ohio, but that's my plan. The more I'm around folks, the more I've realized how lonely I was, cooped up in that apartment with church and the pretzel factory being the only activities I could look forward to. I was lonely and always worried about money. That's not where Gott wants our thoughts to be."

Essie nodded, thinking about her worries over the money missing from their bank account. Dollars and cents were not meant to be the focus of any person's life. "It's good that you've learned these things about yourself," Essie said, choosing her words carefully. She wanted to speak her mind to Collette, but she didn't want to seem disrespectful of Collette's plans. "But moving all the way to Ohio, leaving your friends and church behind, isn't that a bigger step than you need to take?"

"I don't see any other way," Collette said. "I've sent a letter to my brother, asking him to prepare for us to move in sometime in the next few months."

Essie turned toward the window so that Collette wouldn't see the tears in her eyes.

"At least, living with my brother, we'll have a roof over our heads," Collette added, "and we'll be surrounded by family. Something we don't have here."

Essie finished folding a blanket and dashed her tears away as she ducked down to put it in the bag.

"What if you had a place to live here—a place you didn't need to rent?" Essie imagined a house big enough for Harlan and her, with rooms for his mother and sister. It wouldn't have to be so big. That way Collette could be with her close family, near to friends she knew well.

"That would be nice, but wishing doesn't make it so," Collette said. She gathered three paperback novels from her tray table and handed them to Essie to pack. "I've lived in worry too long, wondering how we'd make the rent and have enough to buy meat and feed for the mule. Maybe the crash was Gott's way of telling me it's time for a change. Gott doesn't make mistakes, so there's something I'm supposed to learn from this bad situation."

Maybe you're supposed to learn to let your son go. Learn that your friends were always nearby, even when you were lonely, and that you were the one who pushed them away.

But Essie bit her bottom lip; she didn't dare share her thoughts.

The topic dropped quickly when other visitors arrived. Rose Graber had brought whoopie pies as well as her two little ones, a wobbly toddler and four-year-old Bitsy, who was immensely curious about the items packed in the bags. Mr. Smitty and his wife came with a tub of pretzels, and Bishop Aaron brought a soft shawl his daughter had knitted, in case Collette caught a chill at night.

Too upset to participate in the conversation, Essie was relieved to take Rose's children for a walk down the hall to give their mother a break. But as she took them to meet Gilda in reception, as she helped them split a cookie in half to share, she thought of the folks visiting Collette right now. Collette's boss, her friend, her bishop. It was but a smattering of the many people who valued Collette Yoder as part of the tightly woven fabric of their community.

Why didn't Collette see the loving friends surrounding her in this moment?

Trundling her family off to Ohio . . . Essie was sure it would be the biggest mistake of Collette's life.

A half hour later, Essie was at reception fetching a dinner menu for Collette when Harlan arrived. With smudges under his amber eyes, he was rundown. Her heart ached for him, but then she reminded herself that she'd been losing sleep, too. Working hard and saving money, only to find it draining from their joint account.

"Essie." His amber eyes were suffused with sorrow as he took her hand and led her toward his mem's room. "Thanks for coming."

"Harlan, hold on." She tugged his hand, stopping him in his tracks.

"What is it?"

"We need to talk." She nodded in the other direction, toward the warm solarium. "Come."

He gave in easily, weaving his fingers through hers so that they walked hand-in-hand, the way they once had along the banks of Joyful River. Ah, how the summer seemed so long ago! The carefree afternoons when they'd walked barefoot and waded in the frothy cold river.

She was relieved to find the solarium empty. They went to the window overlooking the gardens, and he immediately pointed to two tall oak trees that stood on either side of the path but had grown together into one canopy overhead. "Look at those two trees. That's us. Two separate trunks twining into one."

"Every time you see two trees you think of us," she said.

"I do. And since there are many trees in Lancaster County, I think of us often."

She smiled, despite her annoyance with him. How could she not laugh at his little jokes?

"Tell me what's wrong, Essie. I see storm clouds in your eyes."

She kept her eyes on those two trees in the garden. "I went to the bank this morning to make a deposit. When

I was there, I learned that a withdrawal had been made from our account. More than two thousand dollars was taken out."

"I took the money. I was going to tell you, but we never get a chance to be together these days. But I only took out half of the money—my half—to use toward Suzie and Mem's hospital bills."

"That's a relief. I was worried that someone else took the money."

"Who else could have taken it? It's safe and secure in the bank."

She lifted her face to look him in the eye. "Why, Harlan? Why didn't you tell me?"

"I didn't have a chance, with everything going on. And this weekend, we got the first bill from the hospital emergency room. I knew I would need my money from the bank to make a payment. But I only took what was mine."

It bothered Essie that he saw a part of the money as his, when truly the whole account was *theirs*. Their savings as a couple. Two people who made all their important decisions together.

"The money should go toward the medical expenses," Essie said. "Their recovery is what matters. Money can be replaced, but our dear family, we must cherish and support them in every way."

"But saving up to buy the bishop's place was your dream," Harlan said. "You've worked hard for that money."

"It was our dream, Harlan. Our dream together. Yes, I want to marry you and have a home. But the money is only a tool to get a roof over our head. The bank account was never my dream. A life shared with you—that was what I've hoped and prayed for."

He winced, turning away. "I'm sorry, Essie. I've made

some mistakes. I know I've hurt you, and right now, I don't know what to do. In the past, the way forward has always been clear to me, but not so much anymore."

His words cut her to the quick.

"You don't know what you want?" she whispered. "You don't want to get married?"

"I do want to marry you, Essie. You know I do. It's just that, we can't get married this season. How can we go through with our plans when my family has such a huge debt, and Mem's planning to move us to Ohio?"

"We could get married," she said, her voice wobbly with heartbreak. "And we can work through those things as a couple. We'll figure it out together, Harlan. I know we can."

"Nay. That wouldn't be wise, would it? And you know I'm not one to jump into the pond headfirst. As they say at the factory, caution keeps people safe. Details need to be straightened out before we go down that path together."

Details. Caution. Money.

Were these things real obstacles, or was Harlan just stalling again?

Just then a bank of pewter clouds pushed together, blocking out the sun and casting a gray pall upon the garden.

"I need to get home," she said.

"Essie, wait . . ."

"A storm's coming, and Comet's waiting outside." She pushed past him, glad that she had an excuse. She was headed to the door when she remembered the cash. She reached into her shoe and removed a stack of carefully folded bills.

"Here's the other half of the money from our bank account. I left two hundred dollars in, so that the account could stay open." She still held out a hope that they'd need the account in the future. "But the rest is here." She placed the crisp, folded hundred dollar bills in his hand. "I know it won't pay all the hospital bills, but it should help."

"Essie, no. This is yours."

"*Ours*, Harlan. It's our money, and I can't think of anything better to do with it than to take care of family in need."

"But you don't have to do that. Mem and Suzie aren't your family."

His words were a thorn in her heart. "Good-bye, Harlan."

By the time Essie got home, the buggy and the horse were drenched. Poor Comet; in her fury to leave Harlan behind, she'd pushed him hard. It took her extra time to let Comet cool down from exertion, before she could dry off the horse. "You look the way I feel," Essie told the horse as she ran a towel over his flank. "Wet and upset."

Essie kept to herself through dinner. As soon as the dishes were cleared away, she set up a batch of peach jam with the ripened, juicy peaches from the cellar and sterilized her newly purchased jars. As she carved up the peaches, she had to toss away a few on account of mold. They should have been canned a week ago, but she'd been too busy. The sight of the spoiled peaches made her want to cry. But then, it wasn't peaches making her sad; she knew that.

When she'd finished with the last of the season's peaches, she scrubbed the pot and thought about heading up to bed. Her lower back was sore, though the tenderness paled in comparison to the ache in her heart.

Sleep seemed so far away from her grasp.

She decided to take advantage of the quiet house and do the plums tonight. The Damson plums were still purple, firm and perfect. Like dark, oversized grapes. She sliced them and put them on to boil, then set up the food mill, turning the bolts to affix it to the edge of the table.

Tomorrow, she planned to experiment with a cranberry apple relish, and then maybe an apple cinnamon pie filling that she could sell with the jams. If customers liked the easy pie filling, she would work on an apple cranberry filling that would look festive for the holidays. With the inventory of apples and cranberries likely lasting through December, the pie filling would take her into the New Year.

The New Year. She wanted to cry at the way her hopes for the next few months had been shattered.

Come January, she would welcome the New Year as plain old Essie Lapp, not Essie Yoder.

Because her beau was too careful. Unwilling to take chances.

Or maybe he just didn't love her enough.

Trying to swallow back her sadness, she tended to the purple-skinned plums on the stove. Plums made the perfect jam, as the sweet fruit required little sugar. The simplicity of the recipe always made her think that Gott had created plums to become a delicious jam.

She stirred the deep purple jam in the stockpot, wondering if she would ever get to marry Harlan. Her dream seemed to be disappearing like a delicate cloud on a windy day, and there was nothing she could do but stand by and watch it vanish.

Out in the great room someone was coming down the stairs. She turned to the doorway and saw Mem in her nightgown, her dark hair in a single braid down her back.

Essie turned off the first boil, put her spoon down, and turned to her mother. "Did I wake you? I couldn't sleep."

"So much on your mind, daughter." Miriam came forward and folded Essie into her arms.

For a moment Essie let herself soak up Mem's strength and love. When things went wrong, Mem was always there for her. "How did you know I needed a hug?" Essie asked, her cheek against Mem's nightgown.

"My first clue was coming down here in the middle of the night and finding you deep into canning peaches and plums." Mem patted Essie's back, a gesture so loving and reassuring that Essie thought she might melt in her mother's arms. "The kitchen smells wonderful good, but you look like you're stranded on an island in the river, all alone."

Sighing, Essie straightened to face her mem. "I don't know what to do. I'm not sure what's going to happen with Harlan, and I don't know how to reach him right now. So I decided to make some jam. Busy hands distract from problems."

"Sometimes that's all we can do . . . wait it out," Mem agreed. "It's good to have something to occupy the mind. Even if it is nearly two o'clock in the morning."

"Right now, putting up jam is one of the only things I feel sure of. And at least I'll be able to make money to help Harlan with his family's medical expenses."

"Harlan shouldn't take that on as a worry. I hear the church is planning a fund-raiser for the Yoders, and there's also a medical fund that can be used. We take care of our own."

"You know how Harlan feels about charity," Essie said. "He's always tried to turn away help. I think it's got something to do with his dat leaving. Harlan learned how to pretend things were fine when they weren't."

"This is something Harlan needs to figure out." Mem tipped Essie's chin up so that she met her daughter's gaze. "In the meantime, you must remember that you're not alone, Essie. Even when your problems seem like an impossible mountain to climb, we're here to help you. You have many people who love you."

Essie nodded, grateful that Gott had blessed her with a family who loved her when others pushed her away. "Denki, Mem."

"I love you, daughter."

Chapter Twenty-Two

Miriam put the lids on her casserole dishes and set them aside. One was ready to pop into the oven when they arrived at Lloyd and Greta's. The other would be a few dinners for Collette at her new home. Cheesy tot casserole was not one of her favorites, but the children always loved it, probably because of the crispy tater tots on top.

It was an off Sunday, a day without church, and Miriam and Alvin were preparing to go visiting. The older ones had a frolic to attend, but Miriam was trying to round up the younger ones—unsuccessfully, as the last she'd heard, Peter and Paul were down by the river, trying to catch frogs.

Miriam stepped onto the front porch and set her casserole dishes down on a table. At least the girls were ready. Lizzie sat on the porch, a bag of coloring books and crayons ready to entertain herself and the other children. Sarah Rose sat beside her on the glider as Lizzie read a picture book to her. Miriam walked to the porch railing, taking in the crisp air and autumn foliage. Magnificent colors burst in the trees that lined their lane and bordered the main road. Burnt orange and mustard yellow and a spicy deep red! Gott gave them such a beautiful palette in the fall.

The door opened behind Miriam, and out stepped Essie and Serena, both smiling into the autumn sunshine. Essie wore a new dress she'd helped Miriam sew, and the blue fabric reminded Miriam of a cross between a summer sky at twilight and the deepest, bluest part of Joyful River where it flowed under the Pine Covered Bridge. Serena wore a print skirt and a denim jacket, and her eyes were bright with anticipation.

"We both have dates with our guys," she announced, smiling at Essie. "I'm going to catch an early movie with Scout, and Essie is going frolicking with Harlan."

"We're just going to a frolic," Essie said. "Not really a date. Annie and Sam will be there, too. Grace and Megan could come along. There'll be volleyball and a bonfire."

"Sounds nice, but my sisters always have too much homework on Sundays." Serena put a hand on Sarah Rose's shoulder and brushed a few loose hairs behind her tiny ear. "Are you reading to your big sis?"

"I can't read yet," Sarah Rose said. "But I know all the words."

Everyone laughed. Indeed, Sarah Rose had memorized most of her favorite books. But something about seeing the girls together, teasing and supporting one another, made Miriam's heart sing with joy.

Especially Serena. When the girls had first arrived, Serena had seemed so willful and displaced that Miriam had worried she might run away and come to harm on her own. And yet, over the weeks, Serena had become a bright part of their family as she'd found a hobby she enjoyed and a young man who was quite dedicated to her. Most weekend nights, Serena and Scout made time to be together, either in town or hanging out at the farm, sometimes playing board games with anyone who was interested. During his last visit, Sully had met Scout, and he clearly approved of the young man. Miriam was tickled to see all the signs of love casting its seeds in her family.

The crunching of gravel on the lane revealed Scout's red pickup rolling toward the house. He hopped out and walked to them with a lift in his step and a wave. So happy he was to see Serena.

"Hey, there! Sorry I'm late. I came as soon as I got off from the firehouse, but I'm not really ready to hit the movies." There was a smudge on his cheek, and as he got close Miriam noticed a burnt smell. "There was a kitchen fire on Elm Street. Everyone's fine, but I'm sorry to say Helen Kramer's pot roast didn't survive. Anyway, I didn't get a chance to stop home and shower."

"Whooboy!" Serena sniffed at him and made a face of mock horror. "You stink to high heaven!"

"It's just a little smoke," Scout said, tugging the hem of his sweatshirt.

"Like a walking barbecue pit," Serena exclaimed.

"Like a bonfire," Lizzie said.

Serena shook her head. "Okay, change of plans. Let's catch a later movie. We'll stop at your house so you can shower, and I can chat with Bonnie. Then we'll hit the cinema."

"That works for me." Scout smiled, tipping his hat back a bit. "Let's go. I have the windows of the truck open, so it shouldn't be too bad on the way there."

Serena headed down the porch steps. "As long as it doesn't ruin my fabulous hair. It's not easy to style your hair without a blow-dryer."

"With the truck windows open, you can use nature's blow-dryer," Scout suggested.

"It just doesn't work that way," Serena said before climbing into the truck.

As they drove off, Alvin came around with the buggy, and the boys turned up from the river after Sam had gone to find them. The twins washed up quickly, and the children climbed into the buggy for dinner down the road. The plan was for the children to settle in at Greta and Lloyd's while Alvin and Miriam went on to visit with Collette Yoder, who was still a guest at the Hostetler home. Miriam had heard reports from Essie that Collette was grateful for the lodging, though worn down a bit by the lack of privacy.

"Every time I bring food for Collette, Linda comes rushing in for a helping," Essie had told Miriam. "And anytime I'm there with Harlan, Linda's daughters June and Dotty come in to steal his attention away. It makes the whole visit go sour."

"Do they know you and Harlan have been courting for years?"

"Yah, they know. I think they're trying to win him away."

"Maybe their mem is pushing them."

"Maybe. But that doesn't make it right."

As soon as they arrived at the Hostetler home, Linda sent Alvin around to the back of the house to join her husband Len in his bird watching. "It's become such a peaceful Sunday hobby for him, after a week of hard work at the shop," Linda said. "Are you a birder, Alvin?"

Miriam's eyes opened wide as she waited for her husband's answer.

"I learned how to spot a red-bellied woodpecker after one of them banged three holes in the north side of our stables," answered Alvin with a straight face.

Miriam laughed, breaking the ice, and the other women chuckled.

"Len will educate you on the birds on our property. Goldfinches, robins, nuthatches . . . we see them all."

Alvin nodded. "They're Gott's creatures." As he headed outside, Miriam sensed that he would have preferred to visit with Collette, but he respected his host, and it was more to the custom of Amish life for the men and women to spend time in their own groups.

"You look well, Collette," Miriam said with a smile. "I brought you a casserole from home. I thought you might be able to nibble on it for a few meals."

Collette gazed up from her wheelchair, a look of pleasure warming her face. "Denki."

"I'll take that." Linda wrested it from Miriam's hands and lifted the pot's lid to peek inside. "This will make a perfect supper for us, and I'm a bit peckish. I'll go light the oven."

Miriam's mouth opened in surprise as Collette watched her host disappear. "As I said, thank you."

"I didn't know you'd be taking your meals with the Hostetler family," Miriam said.

"I didn't either." Collette sighed. "I'm grateful for their

generosity, but living here, I feel like a prize hog at the mud sale auction. Always on show, and people are always traipsing through my pen here."

"Well." Miriam folded her arms and looked down at Collette. "You would certainly take the blue ribbon."

The two women stared at each other a moment and then burst into laughter. Miriam was glad for the release, as she wasn't close friends with Collette, but she was beginning to feel that they were very much on the same page.

Collette was still chuckling as she wiped away a tear. "Oh, my heavens. I do appreciate Linda and Len's kindness. I should bite my tongue and not behave like a cranky old goat."

"You don't seem cranky to me, and since we're the same age, you can't be old. Maybe we should get some fresh air," Miriam said, lowering her voice. "And get you out of your pen. Can you make it outside in your chair?"

"Yes, indeedy. I can wheel myself out to the porch, and Harlan built a small ramp that takes me down to the driveway. Let's go!"

Miriam followed, then ducked back inside to grab the butter-yellow crocheted afghan from the bed in case Collette grew cold in the waning October afternoon. Outside she settled the blanket over Collette's shoulders and then took charge of the wheelchair to ease it down the ramp and driveway. "Should we stroll a bit?"

"That would be nice," Collette agreed with a deep sigh. "There's a park not far from here. A nice river view."

"Sounds perfect." Miriam understood the need to be free of another woman's rule, just for a bit. Amish families often built a Dawdi House on the property for exactly that reason—to give the elder couple of the family control over their own space and comfort.

"What a beautiful day Gott has given us," Miriam said as she pushed Collette over a sidewalk covered in golden leaves. "So much color, everywhere you look."

"Fall is such a beautiful time of year," Collette said, "and that sun feels lovely."

"Too lovely to leave behind," Miriam said. "Essie tells me you're considering a move to Ohio to be with your brothers."

"I think it's time," Collette said. "Joyful River is a wonderful good place, and there are so many things I'll miss when I go." She stared off into the distance, wistful over the blurs of red, orange, and yellow foliage.

"Then don't go," Miriam suggested gently. "Stay here, where you have many friends and a caring church community."

"I wish the decision was that simple, but so much of it is . . . It's out of my hands. Out of my control."

Miriam pushed her along as they basked in a thoughtful silence. Was Collette talking about money or something else? Her curiosity was piqued, but it would be wrong to probe.

"Long ago I learned that when things are out of our control, we can only give them up to Gott," Collette said. "It took this accident to make me realize that I was holding on to Joyful River for selfish reasons. It's time to let go."

"I understand," Miriam said, "and I guess they have sunshine in Ohio, too."

"I reckon they do." Although Collette shared the joke,

it was clear that her decision was weighted in a heavy cloak of sadness. This wasn't a happy choice for Collette.

"But Gott does let us know what we need. My husband injured his leg two months ago in the milking barn. It's better now, nearly recovered, but at the time, he could barely walk. It taught him that he needed more hands to run the dairy. That's when Annie left the pretzel factory and the twins started helping run the cows in for milking. All this is to say, Gott gives us messages in many ways."

Collette sighed. "Sometimes it's a message that breaks the heart."

Miriam's heart ached for this kind woman who had managed to love and care for her children on her own for so many years. She could only pray that Collette would find joy again in her next home, but she wondered about how Harlan and Suzie would fare in a new place. "What about your children?" Miriam asked. "As you know, our Essie will be devastated to see Harlan go."

"Suzie will stay with me, but I'll need to leave Harlan to make his own decisions. He's a man now, a baptized member of our church. It's not my place to tell him what to do. Once he gets me to Ohio, he'll be free to choose where he wants to spend his life."

Such a heavy choice to place upon Harlan's shoulders. Miriam felt the weight of the decision Harlan would be facing. "Harlan is a good and dutiful son," Miriam said.

"He is," Collette agreed.

"It will be hard for him to make such a choice without feeling that he's betrayed his mem in some way. He already blames himself for the crash."

"I keep telling him it was not his fault."

"And yet, he feels responsible. That's the kind of man he is."

"You know my son well," Collette said. "And here I've been focused on recovery and the move, seeing only myself. I've lost sight of everyone else around me."

"You've had a lot on your plate," Miriam said. "You've been working hard in physical therapy since the accident. You're only human."

"But I can't be taking over my son's life. I'll pray on it and speak to Harlan directly."

They reached the edge of the little park where the road turned onto a small bridge over the river. The railing was low enough for Collette to be able to see the water from her chair. Miriam locked the brakes of the wheelchair and sat on a ridge of the low stone wall, her chin resting on the railing. "Joyful River," Miriam said. "It comforts me to know that this is the same river that runs along beyond the back acres of our farm . . . the same river that weaves through the lives of many folk in and out of town. I like to think of it as a ribbon that Gott created to draw his children together."

"That's a lovely thought," Collette agreed. "Before the accident, I didn't realize how closely knit our community is. I kept to myself, probably more than I should have." She shook her head. "I didn't know what I was missing."

"It's good you've found the silver lining in that cloud." Miriam rose and brushed off her dress. "We should get back. Linda will be missing you."

As they navigated the short walk back to the house, a man in Amish clothing appeared on the path behind them. When he nodded, Miriam recognized Aaron Troyer.

"It's the bishop," she said. "Walking in this same park."

"He lives nearby," Collette explained. "His farm's on the other side of the river."

He was smiling as he approached. "I was just on my way to pay you a visit, Collette. I see Miriam has you out for fresh air."

"It's a beautiful day," Collette said, "and I'm grateful for the company."

As they returned to the house, Collette and the bishop discussed the weather, the chances of a batch of hay he had mowed drying out before the rains, and Collette's bird watching from the Hostetlers' porch. There was nothing unusual about the conversation apart from the way each person's gaze was glued to the other's, as if they were laying eyes upon a glorious light for the first time in their lives.

By the time they reached the house, it had grown cold. Miriam wheeled Collette into her room and went to start a fire in the wood stove. Collette remained in the wheelchair, and the bishop paced, moving toward Collette, then striding away and turning. All the while Collette and Aaron kept the conversation going in a cheery manner.

Miriam closed the door on the stove, sat on a nearby chair, and tried to blend into the background as Bishop Aaron talked with Collette. She couldn't help but notice the shift in the mood of the room. Now that the bishop was here, the air seemed light and joyous, as if they were awaiting a celebration. Collette's cheeks were flushed, her eyes bright, and the bishop was actually smiling. Miriam hadn't seen him smile for quite some time, perhaps since his wife Dorcus had been alive. It pleased her that he was enjoying their company this much, but it was surprising, too.

Miriam blinked as the reality hit her.

Love.

Oh, thanks be to Gott for love. But had it come in the wrong place?

It was clear to her that Collette and Bishop Aaron had a deep affection for each other. She could tell by the tenderness in their eyes when their gazes met. Their carefully chosen words. The way the bishop kept his distance, pacing away from Collette and sitting a bit across the room.

Love was a wondrous gift from Gott, and Gott's gifts were meant to be cherished. But nothing could ever come of their love. These two could not be together. The bishop was a free man, encouraged to marry since the death of his wife. But Collette was still a married woman, and even though her husband had been gone many years, she was still another man's wife in the eyes of the church. A church that did not allow divorce, no matter if the husband had been gone for more than a decade. There could be no pairing for a person who had been abandoned by their husband or wife.

Feeling as if she had stumbled on a beautiful secret, Miriam kept to herself through much of the conversation. There were so many kinds of love, and she knew that Collette and the bishop would stay within the boundaries of what was acceptable for an Anabaptist leader and a church member.

Alvin appeared with Len Hostetler, and the tide shifted again as the men conversed. When Linda came in to announce that dinner would be ready soon, all the visitors declined. The bishop said he was having dinner with his eldest daughter and her family, and Miriam and Alvin had to join their family back at Lloyd and Greta's. Collette thanked them for coming and wheeled herself into the dining room.

Before Miriam and Alvin got into the buggy, they asked Bishop Aaron about plans for the fund-raiser for the Yoder medical expenses. "We heard that planning is underway," Alvin said.

"The date is set for the second Saturday of November at Miller's Auction House, so we've got the ball rolling. Molly's Home Diner will be serving barbecued chicken. A few folks have already pledged farm equipment, furniture, quilts, and what have you. We'll need someone to organize it, but we're off to a good start."

"Thanks to Gott in heaven," Miriam said. "It's wonderful good that our community comes together when someone's in need of help."

"We're looking for someone to coordinate donations if you're interested," Aaron suggested.

Alvin's eyes twinkled as he glanced at Miriam. "I think our Essie could spare the time to take that on."

"A fine idea," Miriam agreed. "And Alvie, we'll have to find something to donate. I'll knit a blanket and bake something with the girls. What do you think?"

"We might have a dairy cow we can spare." He stroked his beard, considering. "We'll find something."

"We must do our best to raise the money to cover those medical expenses," Miriam said. "Already Harlan feels the responsibility falling on his shoulders, and it's such a heavy burden for young people about to start out on their own."

Oops! The second she said the words, she knew she

had slipped. She was thinking of Harlan and Essie starting their household together, though their plans to marry were far from public yet.

Fortunately, the bishop didn't flinch. "We will do our best," he said, "and Gott will help us do the rest."

Chapter Twenty-Three

As Essie guided the horse toward the Hostetlers' driveway, she realized that her visits to Harlan's mother had become her most dreaded part of the week. Although she enjoyed Collette's company and longed to see a glimmer of love in Harlan's eyes if she was able to catch him visiting, the nuisance of facing Linda Hostetler overshadowed all the positive aspects.

It didn't help that Linda was bossy by nature. Because it was her home, she seemed to think she had the right to tell Collette what dress to wear that day, how much wood to put into the stove, and how to live her life. Collette was good-natured about taking Linda's advice, but in private she had confided irritation to Essie. "I broke my leg," Collette said under her breath, "but my brain is working just fine."

Another problem was that Collette's room at the front of the house seemed to get as much traffic as the farmer's market in Joyful River. Even when Collette closed the door, Linda popped in as regularly as the bird on a cuckoo clock. Linda's son Emmett frequently burst in, escaping from chores or playing a joke on his mother, who would find him and pull him out from under the table while she lectured him on commandments in the Bible. The little ones would toddle in and out, but at least this cheered Collette, who chatted with them or enjoyed watching them play a made-up game.

Linda and Len's teenage daughters Dotty and June were scarce, unless Harlan happened to be visiting his mem. Once he came in the door, the young women came in with a cup of tea and snacks made especially for him. Not for Collette, and certainly not for Essie. "Try some of these whoopie pies that I made," Dotty would say, claiming that she had worked on them all day in the kitchen.

"These molasses cookies are still warm," June would claim. "Fresh out of the oven." There were popcorn balls, fudge, streusel cake, and banana bread—enough goodies to open an Amish bakery, all offered to Harlan with a smile and soft words.

It made Essie sick to the stomach.

Not that she could blame June and Dotty for liking Harlan. In Essie's mind, he was the most wonderful, lovable Amish man in Joyful River. But he was her beau—a fact that Linda didn't seem to accept as she pushed her daughters at Harlan, egging them on to chat with him, even while Essie was sitting right there!

Today Essie came bearing an unusual array of gifts for Collette, whose latest bone scan had revealed that she had a calcium deficiency that might have contributed to her broken leg in the crash. *Osteopenia* was what they called it. While damage to the bone couldn't be reversed, it could be stopped with exercise, medication, and a diet of calcium-rich foods.

During her last visit Essie had studied the pamphlet the

doctor had given Collette, and back at home Mem had helped her assemble some foods loaded with calcium. In the back of the buggy she had two types of cheeses from Uncle Lloyd's farm, almonds, and a white bean casserole with extra broccoli. She prayed that the combination of diet, medication, and physical therapy would bring Collette back to good health.

It was no surprise that Linda answered when Essie knocked on the door. "Come in," she said, a sour look on her face.

"Hello, Essie," Collette said cheerfully. She stood in the center of the room, holding on to a gray-framed walker.

"Look at you! On your feet and walking," Essie exclaimed. "Good for you!"

"The physical therapist wants me to start using the walker," Collette said. "And honestly, I'm happy to be up and moving again. But they don't want me walking around without supervision."

"If you don't need me, I'll get back to my chores," Linda said.

"Essie can take over," Collette said. "Denki, Linda."

Essie showed Collette the basket of foods she'd brought, and Collette seemed delighted by each little thing. "I've never had white bean casserole. It sounds delicious."

They walked around the room, then ventured outside, Collette taking her time with the walker and taking extra caution going down the ramp Harlan had built. Although it had rained that morning, the afternoon was dry and cool. Wet leaves decorated the sidewalk, red, gold, and orange, as if a child had glued them down along the way.

When Essie saw that Collette was tiring, they turned back to go inside. "Besides, it's time for me to pick up Suzie from the pretzel factory," she told Collette. "I promised her a ride so she can have dinner with you. She misses you so."

"Harlan's just not the cook I am," Collette joked.

"What man is?" Essie added. "Though Harlan has special talents with wood. And now the factory is paying him to do his carving for customers."

"It's truly a blessing," Collette said, taking measured steps, slow and steady. "He's always enjoyed carving things out of soap or wood. Who thought he would find work doing something that unusual? Gott has blessed him."

Although Collette seemed so pleased with Harlan's success at work, her plan to leave Joyful River was going to end Harlan's job. Essie wanted to ask Collette why she planned to uproot Harlan and take him away from the things that he loved. Take him away from his satisfying job and his loving future wife.

But Collette didn't know about their wedding plans, and these days it seemed that Harlan would never tell her. It was wrong to blame Collette for trying to make an easier life for herself and her family. It was time for Essie to realize that things would not always go her way in life.

Sometimes, Gott's will was hard to understand and accept. But as Mem always said, Gott did not make mistakes.

When Essie returned with Suzie, Harlan and Collette were in front of the house, taking yet another walk.

"Mem!" Suzie jumped out of the buggy, happy to see her mother. "You are walking again!"

"Only with my walker and a helper," Collette said, now leaning heavily on the walker, her head down.

"It might be time for a break," Essie said.

"The doctor wants her on her feet," Harlan said. "So I brought her out to walk."

"Yah, but he doesn't want her to overdo it," Essie said, careful to avoid Harlan's eyes, knowing that with one look he could unravel her emotional composure. "Let's go inside. Suzie brought you a lovely surprise."

"Fresh pretzels!" Suzie said, fetching the box from the buggy. "Mr. Smitty wanted you to have them. And they're still warm."

"Such a nice treat," Collette said, starting her careful steps up the ramp to the porch.

"Let's sit, and I'll catch you up with everything that's going on at the factory." Suzie stood on the porch, waiting patiently as her mem walked to the door. "Deborah and Josie had cross words for each other, and now no one's sure if Josie is going to be a table waiter at Deborah's wedding."

"Ach, those young girls don't know how to let the small things go," said Collette as she made it into the house.

Inside her room, Harlan had a million questions for his mother. Did she want to sit in her chair or the bed? Did she need help getting into the chair? Had she gotten enough exercise? Was she taking her medicine?

Collette's usual calm remained in place as she answered her son, but Essie felt bad for her. As Collette and Suzie settled in, Essie suggested that Harlan come out to the porch and let mother and daughter catch up.

Outside a jittery Harlan paced as Essie took a seat. He wanted to make sure his mem was doing everything right for her recovery. Plenty of exercise, medication, and those foods with calcium. "Did she try any of those foods you brought?" he asked.

"She had some almonds, but I know she'll eat everything she's given," Essie said. "She's trying hard, Harlan."

"I know," he said, shaking out his hands as he paced. "I just don't want anything else to go wrong."

Just then the door opened and out popped the Hostetler girls.

"I brought some drinks," June said, putting down a tray with two pitchers. "Would you like iced tea or lemonade?"

"Iced tea," Harlan said.

"And I'd love a glass, too," Essie added before the girls could plow over her.

Dotty offered cookies, and, when she launched into a story about how she'd gotten up early to bake them, Essie found her thoughts drifting away from this porch, miles from this house.

Her visits with Harlan at the Yoder family apartment had always been so pleasant, with time for food and conversation, board games and puzzles. Now she wondered sadly if she'd ever see that apartment again. With Collette planning to move to Ohio, she suspected they'd let the lease go in the next few months.

The thought of such drastic changes made Essie want to cry. Today's Harlan seemed impatient and annoyed and so unhappy. She tried to joke with him the way they'd always done, teasing him and waiting for him to make a little joke in return. But he seemed to have lost his sense of humor.

Once, she had looked into his amber eyes and found security, hope, and a joy that sparked love in each moment. Today, those eyes held darker things: fear, annoyance, worry.

She wondered if she'd ever get her old Harlan back.

Chapter Twenty-Four

Scout held on to the popcorn and a medium Coke for them to share as Serena picked out two seats in the cinema and settled in. It was Saturday night, the best part of Serena's week, when she got to be with Scout without a worry in the world.

"I love movies now," she said, gathering some popcorn in one hand. "You appreciate stuff like this more when you don't have TV or Internet access at home."

"I like watching movies with you," Scout said. "You always see things that I miss."

"You're so sweet. You'd be more tuned in to the plot if you'd grown up watching TV the way I did."

"We never had time for it in my house," he said. "There was always something to do outside, and now I've always got work."

"Except for Saturdays," she said. For several weeks they had made Saturdays their night together, catching movies, playing mini-golf, bowling, or just hanging out. The trucking company had found a driver to replace him Saturday nights, and sometimes Fridays, too. Weekends were the fun reward for a week of hard work at school and in the woodshop, where Serena was now managing two projects at a time, applying color and new life to old, neglected pieces of furniture.

"Except for Saturday." Scout popped a piece of popcorn into his mouth. "That's our day."

The lights in the movie theater dimmed as Serena took a sip of soda. "Here we go. Hey, you should take off your hat. It's good manners."

Scout cupped a hand over the top of his head. "That's okay. I don't think people mind it."

"Take it off," she insisted. "You always have it on."

He shook his head, looking down at the popcorn. "I'm more comfortable with it on."

She let out a breath. "Come on, Scout."

"Shh. It's starting."

She shot him a stern look, but he was immune to it, pretending to watch the film. He could be a stubborn one, but she was going to keep working on him. Sooner or later, she would get him to take off his hat inside buildings.

When they left the movie theater, it was dark outside, with the earthen smell of autumn in the crisp air. Neither Serena nor Scout were hungry, but neither wanted to end their date.

"Do you think we'd be able to see the stars from the river park?" Serena asked.

"Let's check it out," Scout said.

The little park at the edge of town had a tree-lined walkway along the river and a small parking lot. Scout parked in a spot overlooking the river and distant hills, and they meandered down the path to an area with picnic tables. Under a blanket from Scout's truck, they sat on the tabletop and snuggled together. It was too overcast to do any real stargazing, so Serena updated him on her recent school assignments. "So I memorized all the countries in Africa for the geography quiz, and—oh! I started reading *To Kill a Mockingbird,* and you know what? Scout is a girl."

"Yup."

"Did you know that?"

He nodded. "The book is required reading in our house. My mom was so in love with it when she was pregnant, she was determined to name me Scout, regardless of gender."

"You gotta love Bonnie's passion for things. When she's interested in something, she jumps right in."

"It's a great quality," Scout agreed. "Reminds me of someone else I know."

She looked at him blankly, and then did a double take. "Who, me?"

"The girl who started her own furniture business because she needed a place to put her clothes. The city girl who's learning to chart the stars."

"I guess I am all those things," Serena said, smiling coyly. "You can add, the girl who stole your heart."

"That's a little corny, but very true."

"Sometimes corny is romantic," she said, shifting slightly to face him.

He tipped his hat back, which gave her a better look at his beautiful pale eyes, his smile lines, his wide smile, a broad happiness that seemed to reach from head to toe.

They were a good match in that way—two easygoing, upbeat people who tried to see the positive side of things.

"You want romantic? Maybe I should sing." He cleared his throat and started singing a song about stars. How each person had their own star, shining love on other people.

As he sang, Serena lifted her face to the sky and breathed in the glittering fields of stars. Although she had learned to find the North Star and the Big Dipper, tonight she just wanted to bask in the gems in the sky and Scout's song about love. This night, this moment full of love, was something she would always remember.

"That's one of the sweetest songs I've ever heard," she said when he finished.

"I kind of meant it as a joke." He tucked his right arm around her waist. "I don't have the best singing voice."

"But you get an A for effort."

His left hand touched her shoulder, then ran down her arm, leaving tingles in its wake. "You're getting cold. I can get my jacket from the car."

"No, stay here with me." She edged closer, resting her head on his shoulder. "You're keeping me warm."

"You sure? I think it's near forty degrees."

"I'm fine," she insisted, feeling the warmth of his body under her cheek. She loved the coziness of Scout's arms. Glancing up, she got an idea. She reached up toward his head. "Maybe I'll just borrow your hat." The second she lifted it from his head, his body went rigid, and he jerked away from her.

"No! Hey! Give me that."

"It's nice and warm." She was about to put it on her head when he grabbed for it, but she evaded his reach.

"Give it back!" he said, wildly raking through his hair, pushing it to one side.

"Just a second." She pressed the stunt, despite his irritation. "Calm down and let me get a real look at you. I don't think I've ever seen you without your hat on."

"There's a reason for that. I wear a hat to cover a scar."

"What? Wait. When did you get hurt?"

"In high school. I'd been hired to help on an Amish farm, and the horses pulling a manure spreader got spooked. I ended up with a concussion and a nasty scar."

"Oh my gosh, that's awful, but I had no idea. You never told me." She held his hat behind her back, out of reach as she studied the side of his head. In the dim light, all she saw was mussed blond hair. "I can't even see a scar."

"Because I grew my hair out to cover it. But it doesn't really . . ." He jerked away when she reached up to touch his head. "Stop it!"

"I'll be gentle."

"It doesn't hurt it just . . . looks demented. And freaky."

"It's not even noticeable."

"That's a lie." He leaned over and reached around her. "Give me the hat."

"No," she insisted, wanting to know more about this. "I want to see."

"Back off, Serena. I'm not kidding."

"I'm not either," Serena said, suddenly noticing his set jaw and flaring eyes. "Scout, come on. I just want to understand this better, and I can't believe you feel like you need to hide this from me."

"And I can't believe you could be so inconsiderate and pushy. You just . . . you have no respect!" He leaped down from the table and jogged back toward the truck.

"Wait! Scout, come on." Was he leaving her here, alone in the dark?

"Why don't you just shut up?"

Stung, she felt her jaw drop open. That was an obnoxious thing to say! She huffed out a sigh, gathered up the blanket and hat, and hopped down from the picnic table. Trudging toward the truck, she felt bad. Maybe she should have reacted with a little more sensitivity, but she hadn't known that he'd been in an accident. She'd had no idea that he always wore a hat to cover a scar. And she didn't understand why it was such a big deal to hide the scar when you could barely see it, anyway.

So it wasn't really her fault.

She'd been goofing around, curious to see him without a hat.

And he'd freaked out and stormed off. Was that fair?

A dark figure appeared on the path ahead. She squinted, watching him, taking a minute to identify Scout by the way he moved.

"Where were you?" she called to him. "I thought you left."

He paused on the path, waiting for her to catch up with him. "I went back to the truck to get a hat, since you so rudely stole mine."

"Oh, please, don't make a big deal out of this. Look, I'm sorry if I was a little pushy, but I didn't know. You could have told me. You should have."

His mouth was set in a grim frown. "It's not something that comes up in conversation. 'Hi, how's it going? And by the way, I almost got killed in a farm accident.'"

"Scout, I'm so sorry, but I didn't know. And it hurts me that you don't trust me."

"I do."

"No. You didn't trust me enough to tell me. And you won't let me see your bare head. Really?" She handed him the hat, hitched the blanket over her shoulders, and continued walking toward the parking lot. "You don't trust me. You won't let me in."

"I told you from the beginning that we should just stay friends."

She didn't have an answer for that because it was true. He'd warned her, but she'd been confident that she could overcome his hesitance.

"I knew you'd end up pushing me to a place out of my comfort zone. And here we are. You're pushing, and I have to stop you."

"Why, Scout? You know I'll understand. You know I love who you are, not how you look. I mean, wait. I do like the way you look, but that's not what matters the most."

"That's what my girlfriend Eileen said right after the accident. She promised to stay by my side, no matter what. But it didn't take long until she drifted away, along with most of my friends. Some of them were kids I'd known since grade school. They dried up. Stopped coming around and calling. Not that I can blame them. I was no fun at the time, going in and out of surgeries, missing school."

"That must have been rough," Serena said. "Especially in high school, when you can feel isolated even when you have friends."

He shrugged. "Accidents happen. I got over it."

Not completely, she thought. "You probably need to

talk about it, Scout," she said as they arrived back at the truck. "It takes time to work through something that traumatic."

"Actually, I'm talked out." He took the blanket from her, opened the passenger side door, and tossed it into the truck. "Get in, and I'll drive you home."

To Serena, it sounded like an order.

She folded her arms against the chill air. "I think we need to talk about this."

"And I said no." He squinted at her, his jaw tight. "What makes you an expert on these things? On trauma in someone else's life? What makes you think you have a right to know anything about me?"

His words were an arrow through her heart. "I thought I could help, Scout," she said quietly, her voice trembling slightly. Maybe from the cold. "I think I can."

"Well, you're wrong on that." His eyes were steely blue and cold. "Listen, this is my fault, okay? I thought . . . I'd hoped that I'd moved beyond the worst of it, that I was ready to, I don't know, start over. Turns out I was wrong. I can't be in a relationship with you. I just can't do it."

A knot formed in her throat as his words sank in.

He was breaking up with her.

And her normal inclination, to talk about things and work things out, wasn't going to fly here. She'd upset him, pushed him too far.

But she had to try. "Can't we at least talk about this?" she asked.

He held up his hand. "Please, no. I just want to take you home. And that doesn't mean we're going to talk it out on the way. I don't want to hear about how you're going to help me and tie everything up with a pretty bow. Just get in the truck."

"No, thanks." Serena slammed the passenger door of the truck and stepped back. "I'll find my own way home."

"Serena . . . come on," Scout called after her as she walked along the river path through the dark park.

She ignored him, blocking out his voice as her eyes adjusted to the darkness. If she followed the path to the end, it would put her on a street that led into the main part of town. She wasn't sure what she was going to do in town, but she would figure something out.

One thing she knew for sure, she was not getting into that truck with Scout.

Twenty minutes later, Serena spotted the lights of the drive-in burger joint and decided to stop there. During most of her walk from the park, the lights of Scout's truck had been at her back as he followed along behind her.

It made her so mad. After the awful things he'd said, after he'd dumped her, he was the last person she wanted to face.

At the edge of town, she turned toward his truck and silently pointed to the side, gesturing for him to get lost.

Light flooded over her as the truck pulled up and he leaned out the window. "Let me take you home. I feel responsible."

"Don't. Consider yourself off the hook. I'll find my own way home," she said. "And you're wasting your time following me. I'm not getting in that truck. So just go. Buh-bye."

"Serena . . . please."

She turned away and marched down the street. Let him stew in his guilt. She had enough of her own heartbreak and fury to deal with.

When she walked into the parking lot of the burger place, five cars were pulled up to bays, and at the end the young people from two cars had spilled out to talk and hang out. She recognized a few people from school. Music played over loudspeakers, and the whole scene was kind of festive. She looked behind her, but didn't see Scout's car. Good. Maybe he'd given up. The last thing she needed was Scout shadowing her while she had a chance to meet other people.

The night air was getting to her, so she ducked inside the small shop to warm up. Peeking out the window around a poster of giant French fries, she figured that Scout would move on when he didn't see her in town. The handful of inside tables was nearly empty, with only an older man reading a newspaper and a middle-aged couple eating a meal. Serena ordered a burger and hot tea, and then took a seat at a table, warming her hands on the teacup while she waited for the food.

Thinking about Scout made her want to cry. She tried to clear her head, but all the awful things Scout had said came popping back into her mind.

What makes you think you have a right to know any-thing about me?

I can't be in a relationship with you.

He had called her pushy. He had told her to shut up.

Taking away her gift of speech would be like taking away a superhero's special power.

She took a sip of tea, which helped her warm up. Her

number was called at the counter, and she was just biting into her burger when Johnny Rotten came into the shop. He was talking on a cell phone, but he seemed bored. She didn't acknowledge him as he paced and talked, giving one-word answers. Talking to his mom, she guessed. Or maybe his girlfriend.

Her cell phone buzzed, surprising her. It was a text message from Scout.

Ugh.

Are you home? If you need a ride, reach out to me.
I feel bad.

She felt bad too, but turning to him was not the answer.

She was savoring the last bite of burger when Johnny ended his call and swung around toward her. "Hey, Philly girl."

In every conversation they'd had at school, he'd never been able to get over the fact that she wasn't from here. Serena had gotten used to it, realizing that being an outsider from a city gave her a certain cachet.

"Hey, Johnny. How's it going?"

"All good. I've never seen you out this late."

"Yeah. I guess I'm turning over a new leaf."

He looked around. "Is your boyfriend in the bathroom?"

She shook her head. "It's just me."

"Flying solo? You really are stepping out." He smiled as he sat down in the seat across from her. "What's that? Are you drinking tea like my old grandma?"

She shrugged. "I was cold."

He reached inside his jacket and showed her a silver

flask. "This is what you need to warm up." He took a slug and sighed. "Whiskey. You game?"

A drink would help blur out the images of Scout in her head. She took the lid off her paper cup and pushed it toward him. "Sure."

Johnny's whiskey helped take the edge off, and before she knew it they were out in the parking lot, talking and laughing with the other guys and girls there. Serena talked to everyone—a few sips of whiskey boosted her confidence—and the conversations only reinforced her theory that people are nice to you when you're nice first. Or was that Scout's theory? She was losing track.

At some point she started wearing Johnny's leather jacket and sipping from the flask that had been warmed in the inside pocket. The sleeves of the jacket dangled over her hands, and it made her feel petite as she told stories about milking cows and Amish water balloon fights to the group. She was a hit. People were laughing hysterically.

All too soon, the music stopped, and the parking lot got dark, and Johnny told her that the burger stand was closing. He showed her a glass bottle of brandy and told her they could take the party on the road. "Giddy up!" she exclaimed.

She found herself in the passenger seat, while two of Johnny's friends climbed into the back. She wasn't sure what kind of car it was, except that it was sparkly blue, low-slung, with a spoiler on the back like a race car. And loud. The engine was almost louder than the music they played as Johnny muscled the car down the road, laughing as the tires squealed on the pavement.

It was super fun for a while, but then everyone got kind

of quiet, and Serena realized how tired she was. She leaned her head against the doorframe, and when she opened her eyes again they were on a country road, speeding along. Gazing out into the darkness broken only by their headlights, she had no idea where they were. The road had brush and trees on the side, occasionally a fence or a ditch. Like any country road in any part of Pennsylvania.

"This is your lucky night!" Johnny said, slowing his speed. "We've got a horse and buggy coming up on the road ahead. That's unusual at this time of night."

Trying to focus, Serena could just make out the reflective tape and dim lights on the approaching buggy. "I wonder why they're out so late? Maybe an emergency."

"We're going to have a little fun with the horse," Johnny said.

"What?" Her head was starting to hurt. She hoped he was driving her home. "What are you talking about?"

"Watch this." He fiddled with something near the steering wheel, and the field of light grew, then dimmed again. "The bright lights spook the horses."

"Stop that!" She shoved Johnny's shoulder, but he kept flicking the brights on. "Johnny, cut it out!"

Up ahead, the horse whinnied, and Serena felt sure she could see the panicked whites of the horse's eyes as Johnny tried to torment the poor creature. The guys in the backseat laughed, a cruel laughter. A reckless, dangerous thing to do, and Serena sat right here beside Johnny, his unwilling accomplice.

In seconds the car whipped past the horse and buggy, and Serena was craning her neck to try to make sure everyone was okay. It was hard to tell, but at least she could see that the buggy was still on the road.

She set her stare on Johnny. "Stop the car," she said. "Pull over. Now!"

"Calm down," he said.

"I'm not messing around. Stop the car, Johnny."

Seeing that she was serious, he let out a huff of breath, slowed the car, and pulled over onto the shoulder. "What's the problem, Queen Serene?"

"You are." She pushed her hair out of her face and opened the car door. The blast of cool air was almost as sobering as the attack on the poor horse. "I'm not driving with an idiot."

"Come on," Johnny said. "We were just having fun. No harm done."

"You tried to startle that horse by flashing your brights. Someone could have been hurt, or worse."

"And now you're going to lecture me?"

"I should call the police, but I'm not going to stick around with you one minute more than I have to." She stepped out of the car. "Don't you ever, *ever* scare anyone like that again."

Johnny's face was a ghostly blue in the light from the dashboard. "Whatever." He said something to the guys in the back, and the rear door opened. Johnny's friend Justin got out of the car and moved to the front seat that Serena had vacated. "Good luck getting home."

Serena stepped back as gravel sprayed under the car tires. The vehicle wiggled then caught traction on the pavement as it zoomed off into the distance, two small red lights in the darkness.

As she went to pull her cell phone from her pocket,

she realized she was still wearing Johnny's leather jacket. Well, that might have been the only good thing that happened tonight. She turned on her phone, but there was no signal. Even if she had one, who would she call, anyway? Her sisters were away from a cell tower. Her dad was miles away in Philadelphia. Even if she called the phone shack at the Lapp farm, her messages probably wouldn't be retrieved for days, since the Amish didn't live for their phones the way that English folk did.

English folk? Now even her thoughts were turning Amish.

No taxi, no Uber, no cell service. She was a long way from the party nights in Philadelphia when she had stayed out until after dawn and then tried to sneak back into the house. Right now all she wanted was to be home in bed, home at the Lapp farm.

She kicked a can at the side of the road as she walked toward what looked like the lights of a house. Walking, walking. She needed water, and a headache was forming behind her eyes, and she wanted to cry.

But she had to be strong. Keep walking, one step at a time. And eventually, she'd find her way home.

Chapter Twenty-Five

Essie was deep asleep, dreaming of finding a patch of late raspberries for canning, when someone shook her awake. Her cousin Grace leaned over her, shaking her shoulder gently.

"Grace. Is everything all right?"

"All good. Except for your boyfriend waiting down-stairs."

Her boyfriend . . . Harlan? She sat up in bed, rubbing her eyes. "I wasn't expecting him."

"You should have," Annie said from her spot at the window, her arms folded over her nightgown. "It's Saturday night, time to come courting." She put her face to the window screen and called, "She'll be right down."

"I'm trying to sleep," Lizzie complained, rolling over in bed.

Essie yawned and looked around the bedroom. "Where's Serena?"

"Still out with Scout," Grace said.

Those two never missed a Saturday night, thought Essie as she wound her hair up and put her prayer kapp on. She'd been so exhausted from canning and cooking and her frequent trips to see Collette that she hadn't heard a thing. "How is it that you two heard him and I slept through it?" she asked, keeping her voice low.

"Annie thought it was her boyfriend," Grace said.

"You did?" Essie whirled around to face her sister, who'd always been too much of a tomboy to bother with fellows. "Who?"

"Maybe Zachary Coblentz." Annie closed the window and climbed up to her top bunk. "He said something about coming by, but I didn't encourage him too much."

"Do you like spending time with him?" Essie asked.

Annie shrugged. "I guess."

Essie smiled. "Next time, give him a little hope. Maybe smile. Tell him a little something about yourself, and listen when he tells his stories. Be kind."

Grace and Annie giggled, which caused Megan to remind them all to keep it down as Essie slipped out into the hall.

Downstairs, she opened the door to Harlan, all six feet of him, broad shoulders filling the doorway. With his dark hair and amber eyes, dressed in black jacket, trousers, and hat, he cut a fine appearance. Her heart raced just at the sight of him.

"It's just like old times," she said as he stepped inside. "Except I was fast asleep."

"I know. I haven't been by on a Saturday since the accident."

"You've had things to take care of," she said. "Your mem and sister. The medical bills. Your job."

"And with all that, I've neglected the most important thing of all." He stepped forward and reached for her. "You, Essie."

Suddenly it was a dream come true, having Harlan here, so close, and in love with her once again. The air left her lungs as his fingertips grazed her arms, and then he pulled her close, his arms around her waist. His golden eyes, his handsome face, his lips were inches away and so overwhelming that she had to remind herself to breathe.

"I thought I'd lost you," she whispered. "That you'd be moving off to Ohio, leaving me behind."

"Never." He nuzzled her ear and kissed her neck, sending a wave of warmth through her body that made her knees weaken. "I would never go off without you."

"But you were being torn in two directions. You're a good son, Harlan, and you don't shirk responsibility."

"I can be a good son and stay true to the path Gott wants for me. The bishop helped me see that, and I've explained it to my mem. It's time for me to stand on my own two feet, and, Essie, I want you by my side. Please say yes. Say that you'll marry me." His words were like warm honey.

She cupped his face in her hands so that she could see the love light in his eyes. "I will. I want to be your wife."

He kissed her lightly, then again, taking her deeper into the dreamy moment. When the kiss ended, he rested his forehead against hers. "Whatever else happens, good things and bad, I've realized that the most important thing in my life is for me to be with you. I love you, Essie."

"And I love you."

"Let's get married soon. December . . . the first week?"

"But it's so soon! And most of the money we saved is gone."

"The time is now, and we know your mem has been preparing. We'll work hard to make it happen if it's Gott's will. I'm sorry about the money, but the bishop will hold that land for us, and we'll earn more eventually. You're such a hard worker, Essie."

"And you got that second job as a craftsman," she said. "We'll figure out a way to make ends meet."

"Besides, I know you love December."

"It'll be like a Christmas wedding," she said, enthralled at the idea of marrying near the celebration of Christ's birth. "But it's late for wedding season."

"I already talked to the bishop, and he's got no problem scheduling it the first week of December."

"Then a December wedding it is." She hugged Harlan close, and he lifted her off her feet and twirled her around the living room.

"You've made me the happiest man on earth!" They laughed together, enjoying the moment.

But one thing remained unresolved. Although love could move mountains, Essie knew it wouldn't be so easy. "But your mem . . ."

". . . is moving to Ohio, but I told her I'm staying here with you. Turned out she didn't really expect me to up and move, but I'm going to have to help her. I might need to take her there on a bus once she's healed enough to relocate. I'll help her get settled in if she needs me, but I won't stay long. This is my home. Here in Joyful River, with you, Essie."

He folded her into his arms again, and Essie knew she had found the place where she truly belonged. Right here, at home, in Harlan's arms.

Snuggled in Harlan's arms on the couch, Essie was awakened by noise. The kerosene lamp was still burning, and the house was quiet but for a knocking sound at the door.

"What's that?" Harlan asked with his eyes still closed.

"Someone's at the door." She extracted herself from his arms, kissed his cheek, and then went to the door.

Scout stood on the dark porch, his shoulders hunched as he rubbed his face. "I'm sorry to wake you, but I'm worried about Serena." He peered into the shadowed house. "Is she here by any chance?"

"Nay. I thought she was with you."

"She was. Then we had an argument, and she stormed off."

Essie realized his shoulders were hunched in worry. "Come in."

Harlan was on his feet now, questioning Scout. "What was it that upset her?" Harlan asked.

Essie held up a finger. "Let me get Megan," she said. "She knows her twin well." Her pulse raced as she hurried up the stairs, trying to keep her footsteps light to avoid waking everyone in the house. Although she knew it was wise to stay calm, the thought of her cousin out in the night alone scared her, and she said a silent prayer that Gott would protect Serena and keep her safe from harm.

Megan jerked awake when Essie whispered that Serena was missing, and they slipped downstairs quietly to learn the details.

"I didn't mean to upset her." Scout appeared worn-out as he faced the three of them. "It just sort of happened, and we both ended up saying things that . . . Well, we argued. I told her I'd take her home, but she got out of the truck and refused. We were at the riverfront park in town then. She was mad, and she sort of marched off."

"And once she said no to the ride, there was no changing her mind," Megan said.

"Exactly. I followed her with my truck for a while, but she pretty much told me to get lost."

"She's stubborn when she makes up her mind," Megan said, raking her dark bangs out of her eyes.

"So I parked the truck and secretly followed her on foot into town. She went into the burger place, and then ended up hanging out with some high school kids. I don't know any of them. It's been a few years since I was in high school. They were passing around some booze and smoking. I kept my eyes on her for an hour or so, figuring I'd wait it out and give her a ride, but when the burger shack closed she got into some jacked-up car with some of the high school guys."

"Who are these boys she went off with?" Essie turned to Megan. "Do you know?"

"You said it was a cool car?" Megan asked. "A Mustang in metallic blue?"

Scout snapped his fingers. "It was a Mustang."

"It's probably that Johnny guy," Megan said. "Johnny Rotten, or something like that. He talks to us at school, but he's kind of a jerk. He thinks he's Elvis incarnate, but he's really a big zero."

Essie wasn't completely following the details, but a young man named Johnny Rotten did not sound good. "Where is she now? We must get her home."

"I tried to text her when I had service," Scout said, "but she didn't answer."

"She's out there on her own." Essie felt a grave sense of responsibility as she looked toward the dark windows. "What if she needs our help?"

"Serena can take care of herself, but if she gets mad enough, there's no telling what she might do," Megan said, looking pointedly at Scout. "What did you say to make her so mad?"

"I don't want to talk about it," he said, looking down at the floor. "I'd never do anything to hurt her—never— but she was definitely mad."

"We need to go after her," Essie said. "Harlan will hitch the buggy, and—"

"No, my truck will be faster," Scout said, "and safer at this time of night. Just tell me where you want to go."

Everyone looked to Megan, who frowned, and then said, "The police station."

Chapter Twenty-Six

Although it seemed that Serena had walked for a hundred miles, she'd only been plodding along the road for an hour or so before a buggy carrying a young Amish couple had come along and spotted her. The guy called for the horse to stop, and the young woman asked her if she was all right.

The woman's kind words made Serena want to cry, but she restrained herself, figuring it might scare them off if she burst into tears and began blubbering over her problems.

"I'd really appreciate a ride into town," Serena said.

The woman invited her to climb in, and they were off, the horse trotting toward town. Up close, Serena was surprised to see that the couple was really young—like, *teenagers*. Were they on a date together? Ugh. Lately she had a way of ruining people's good times. The girl shared her blanket, tucking it over Serena's legs, and the young Amish dude remarked on the cold night, and Serena thanked them profusely for helping her out.

As the horse trotted on, she realized the Amish kids weren't the only ones she needed to thank.

Oh, thank you, God, thank you! In this clear, cold moment, Serena realized she really did believe in God, and although she would never become completely Amish, she also would never return to the life of rebellion that she'd led back in Philly. Somehow, when she hadn't really been trying to, she had carved out her own path here in Joyful River. Sure, she'd had plenty of help from Aunt Miriam and Uncle Alvie, her cousins, her sisters, and yes, yes, Scout.

Another reason to cry.

But she had learned some things about herself and was moving forward in a good way.

She'd have to hold that thought until she got to the police station. Years of upbringing as a cop's daughter had taught her that if you ever got in a fix, the police would help you. If she wanted to get home before daylight, she needed to bite the bullet and go to the police.

She dozed a bit along the way, and thanked Rosie and Eli when they dropped her off. Inside the police station, she told the officer at the desk, Officer Carlucci, that she needed help getting home. A middle-aged man with curly dark hair and a mustache, he squinted at her and snapped his fingers.

"Don't tell me, let me guess. You're Sabrina, right?"

"Serena Sullivan."

"I was close. Your sister and her crew were just here looking for you. Twins, right? But she looks different with the short hair."

"Megan was here?" The thought of her sister close by made Serena's knees feel weak.

"You need to call her cell. She's staying in cell range, driving around looking for you."

Serena clutched the desk, grateful and relieved.

"Are you okay?" Officer Carlucci leaned closer. "You can use our phone if yours is out of juice. And I've got coffee and tea if you want."

"Tea would be great." Right now her legs and hands felt too cold and numb to shiver. She tapped Megan's number and held her breath. Her sister picked up on the second ring.

"Serena. Where are you?"

"The police station."

"We'll be right there. Everyone's been freaking out about you. Are you okay?"

"I will be."

The sight of them filing into the police station made Serena cry. Tears streamed down her cheeks as she rose from the bench, and Megan rushed forward and crushed her in a hug.

"You're an idiot," Megan said.

"I know. Thanks."

"Of course."

It was that twin shorthand that communicated much in few words.

Essie hugged her next, telling her how worried they were. Harlan squeezed her hand, then said she felt like a snowman. Serena laughed through her tears.

And then she saw Scout. Were those tears in his eyes?

She swallowed over the knot in her throat. In that second she was ready to forgive him for all the mean things he'd said, ready to rush into his arms and hug him.

But the moment faded, like a soap bubble that popped in the air.

"We'd better get going," Scout said, looking at the floor. "It's late."

And that was that.

The ride home was bound to be awkward. Scout's truck couldn't fit five people in the cab, so Essie and Harlan climbed into the back and bundled into two blankets that Scout kept in his rig. Scout climbed into the driver's side, and Megan pushed Serena in first, saying, "You get the hump." Serena tried to glare at her sister, but Megan turned toward the window and faced away the whole time, her way of offering privacy.

No thank you, Serena thought, folding her arms. Scout had told her not to talk earlier in the night, and she was determined to take him up on that.

Once they hit the outskirts of town, Scout opened up. "I know I shut you down before, but we need to talk," he said without taking his eyes off the road.

"Don't talk to me. I'm so mad at you right now if you say two words my head might explode."

"I'm mad at myself, if that helps at all." His eyes were shiny and more intensely blue than Serena remembered, but he stayed focused on the road ahead. "I should have never left you alone."

"That's not why I'm mad." She groaned. "I can totally take care of myself, and you didn't leave me. I walked out on you because I was so incredibly frustrated, and now you're making it worse. You don't get it. How could you not get that I care about you and I can't stand to be pushed away. *That's* why I'm mad."

"Oh. I get that."

"I don't think you do, Scout. You're so caught up in your own pride and your own fears that you aren't aware of how people feel around you. It's rotten that people let you down when you got hurt, and now you're going to push everyone else away so that it doesn't happen again. Except that when you push people away, you're just as bad as your former friends."

He rubbed his chin, thoughtful. "Okay, I actually followed all that, and you're only half right. I know I push people away, but I'm no bully. I've had to end friendships to protect myself. There's a difference."

"If you care anything about me, you're going to continue to be my friend. You can't cut off a friend because you feel sorry for yourself over an injury."

"You're only looking at part of the picture. It's not that simple, Serena. It never is. The truth is, I was in a dark place for a long time. When I started getting better, it took every ounce of energy I had to get out of bed in the morning. To put one foot in front of the other. To leave the house. Why do you think I know the stars so well? Because for a while nighttime was the only time I ventured outside. And my job driving the milk truck at night? I liked it because I could be alone and go for days and weeks without seeing any of the customers."

"That doesn't sound like you at all," she said.

"But that's how my life was after the accident. It got so bad at school that I finished through home schooling. That cut off a world of social connections, but I was okay with that. I became a hermit. You know the type. The fool on the hill, all alone and happy to be that way."

Her throat grew tight as she tried to think of an argument, but in that moment she could only imagine Scout alone, cut off from his friends, feeling bad about himself and the world. "I'm sorry," she said.

"Look, I'm not trying to get your sympathy. I just want you to know that the 'me' you've come to know is not a full picture. I got to a point where I could get out of the house. I accepted my scars, and figured out a way to keep them hidden. The fire and rescue squad and community college pushed me to be around people and make some friends. But it was all moving slowly. And then you came along, like an undiscovered star in the sky, sparkling and twinkling. I couldn't say no to you. How could I? You just shot through the sky and lit up the night and . . . you're a really great person, Serena. A shining star. I'm just not ready to have someone like you in my life."

I think you are, she thought. *Yes, you are. You are so ready for me.*

But she couldn't say the words. She just couldn't.

Serena slept in the next day, and dragged through the afternoon, not wanting to process what had happened the night before. On Sunday night, she pulled herself together and headed out to meet the milk truck. Having spent the day in the woodshop, she'd had a lot of time to think.

One coat of jade paint had helped her see that things could be fixed. Wrongs could sometimes be righted. People could be forgiven for their mistakes.

The wax coating over a lavender end table reminded her that people (and wax surfaces) could be more resilient than anyone thought. Scout would bounce back from his vulnerable moment, and she had already shaken off the bad turn she'd taken, going off with Johnny Oh-so-Rotten.

By the time she finished up in the woodshop, she felt like she'd progressed in life and with her furniture. Faith restored, she picked up the lantern and went into the house to wash up.

"You may want to get that green paint off your face," Megan said as she passed her in the hall. She was already in her pajamas and headed off to bed.

"Yeah, it's not the sort of paint that guys go for," Serena agreed.

"Are you meeting Scout?" Megan asked.

"I'm meeting the milk truck."

Megan nodded. "Good luck."

Serena made her way into the bathroom, where there was a small, scratched mirror that cousin Sam used for shaving. Mirrors weren't a thing for the Amish because they thought mirrors contributed to vanity. Now when Serena wanted to pluck her eyebrows or apply makeup, she had to turn on the selfie screen of her cell phone to make sure she was hitting her mark.

By the time she'd washed up, the milk truck was already pulled up at the door of the milking barn. Serena practiced what she was going to say as she walked across the lawn. But when she approached the truck she came face-to-face with an older driver with glasses and a big belly. "Good evening, miss. Everything okay?"

"I was looking for Scout Tanner. He's our regular driver."

He nodded. "Nice guy. Yeah, the boss asked me to take over his nighttime pickups this week."

"All week?" Serena tried to swallow, but the knot in her throat made it difficult. Scout must really hate her if he'd give up his paycheck for the week.

"Yeah, it might turn into more of a long-term thing. The boss asked if I was available. I just take things one day at a time. Too much planning makes me feel trapped."

"I get that," she said, trying to keep it casual and hold on to her dignity. "I'm going to head inside. You take care."

"Have a good night."

She walked in metered steps, gravel crunching under her sneakers, until she was sure he was involved setting up the pump. Then, she took off. Her vision was blurred by tears, but she headed toward the dim lantern light in the front room, and ran like crazy.

Inside, the house was dark and quiet—too quiet. She couldn't take it. She couldn't handle this alone.

Up in the girls' bedroom, the room was still but for the soft whisper of breathing. Serena collapsed on her bunk and buried her face in her hands. The sudden movement of the bed alerted her. When she looked up, Megan had hopped down from the top bunk.

"What happened?" she whispered.

"Scout's not there. The substitute driver said Scout won't be here all this week, at least."

Megan sat beside her on the bottom bunk. "What are you going to do?"

"I don't know." Serena pushed off her shoes and wriggled out of her jeans. "What can I do if I can't reach him?" With her sweatshirt still on, she turned away, stretched out and pulled the quilt over her. "I'm going to hibernate in here for the next twenty years. Maybe then Scout will talk to me."

A moment later, Serena felt the bed wiggle as Megan squeezed under the quilt and snuggled in behind her. "If you're hibernating, I'm coming along."

Chapter Twenty-Seven

Miriam had learned of Saturday night's shenanigans from a few sources, but she had yet to hear about it from Serena. All day Sunday Miriam had kept her distance, giving Serena room to think. On Monday when the girls were home from school and Mammi was visiting for the day, Miriam decided to draw the girls into a cookie baking session.

"This is a very old recipe for refrigerator cookies," Miriam explained as Grace, Lizzie, Serena, and Essie tied aprons on. Megan was upstairs buried in her studies, which Miriam appreciated. Sarah Rose sat at the table with her grandmother, stacking and unstacking plastic measuring cups in the way of children making a game out of mundane things. "We can actually make the batter and then put it in the freezer until just before the auction, when we'll bake them fresh and sell them in the tent."

"Can't we bake some now?" Lizzie asked. "Just a couple? Please, please, please?"

"We'll see. Hands washed?" When everyone nodded, Miriam pointed her recipe card at Lizzie. "We need a cup of chopped dates. Since they're so sticky you need to take your time cutting them. Serena will help you with that. Grace, we need a cup of coarsely chopped walnuts. Essie, you can cream the vegetable shortening, butter, and sugars together in a large bowl. And I'll measure out the rest."

"I love seeing everyone bake together," Mammi said as everyone set to work. From her spot at the table, she helped cut down the dates with a small knife.

"Many hands make quick work," Essie said as she broke down a stick of butter with a long wooden spoon. "Collette says this is one of the things she misses about not being in her own house. Linda doesn't truly welcome her in the kitchen."

"That's understandable," Mammi said. "They say there can only be one real Amish cook in a kitchen." She looked at Miriam. "And we know who the boss is."

Everyone chuckled as Miriam grinned. "If I had a rolling pin handy, I could wave it," she teased. "It was good to see Collette back at church for the first time yesterday. She seemed overjoyed to be back among friends. So smart of Harlan to build that portable ramp for her so she could ride in the horse trailer." Knowing his mother was suffering a bit of cabin fever from lack of mobility, Harlan had employed his carpentry skill to build a portable ramp that allowed Collette's wheelchair to roll up into a trailer. Alvie had been happy to loan the Yoders a horse trailer that could be towed behind a buggy. Of course, the horse trailer made for a bumpy ride, but it gave Collette a chance to travel short distances without engaging an expensive wheelchair van.

"Harlan was happy to do it, but Linda had bad things

to say about that, too." Essie kept her eyes down on the bowl as she spoke. "She thinks Collette should have kept herself at home until she could climb into a buggy. Linda says it's not the proper way to travel. And the Ordnung says the sick can stay home from church. Those are the rules. She's very big on the rules."

"As believers, we must follow the Ordnung," Mammi said. "But I look to the bishop to explain how we should live. Of course, we look to the Bible for heavenly matters. If judgment must be passed here, it's up to our church leaders."

And not the likes of Linda Hostetler, Miriam thought. Of course, Mammi wouldn't say that, as it was close to sounding like gossip, which her mother-in-law always sought to avoid. But it was a shame how living with Linda had put Collette under constant criticism. "It was most generous of the Hostetlers to take Collette in when she needed help," Miriam said. "I only wish there was a one-level home she could go to where she could be the head of her own kitchen. I know Harlan was looking at other rentals for her, but there was nothing in her price range."

"It's also been hard on Suzie," Essie said as she whipped the contents of the bowl. "She misses her mem, but it's hard for her to get over to see her every day."

"The answer is simple," Mammi said, looking up from the amber dates. "The Yoders should move into the Dawdi House out back. It's one level. Very compact. And there are enough bedrooms for Suzie and Harlan to join her."

Miriam looked from her mother-in-law to Essie, who had stopped stirring, her face alight with wonder. "It would be a perfect place for the Yoders," Miriam said.

"But it's your place, Esther. We thought you might return there someday."

Esther waved her hand, dismissing the notion. "I'm happy where I am now. Truth be told, there are so many memories of my Mervin at the Dawdi House. It makes me sad to be there without him. But the house shouldn't sit empty. Offer it to the Yoders. It would do my heart good to help them through their time of need."

"So the Yoders would be our neighbors?" Lizzie asked.

"I like Suzie," said Sarah Rose.

Essie's eyes were bright, her mouth open in a wide O of disbelief. Miriam hadn't seen her oldest daughter this happy in quite some time.

"That's a very generous offer, Esther," Miriam said. "We should let Collette know."

"I'm going to check out the Dawdi House now." Essie pushed the bowl aside and untied her apron. "It will need a cleaning, but I can do that."

"Can I go, too?" Grace asked. "The walnuts are chopped, and I've never been inside this Dawdi place."

"I want to see it." Lizzie pulled her apron over her head. "I'll help clean."

"Me too!" Sarah Rose slid off her chair.

"Good grief, our bakers are all running away," Mammi said.

"I'll stay," Serena said quietly as the others left the room. "I want to see how the dough comes together."

Miriam smiled. "It's simple from here." She had Serena break four eggs into the shortening and sugar mixture, watching patiently as bits of shell went in.

"Are you trying to add extra crunch to the recipe?" Mammi teased.

"That would be gross," Serena admitted.

"It's not a problem," Miriam said, showing Serena how to extract the shell chips with the edge of a spoon. "Now you stir in the eggs and vanilla." She talked Serena through the recipe, adding the flour and spice, the dates and nuts, and then shaping the cookie dough into two-inch logs wrapped in wax paper. "Now that we have our cookie dough in logs, it's ready to slice when we take it out of the freezer."

"That's an awesome recipe." Serena smiled. "Are we doing another batch?"

"I thought of doing a second one, substituting toasted almonds and candied cherries for the walnuts and dates. Should we do it before we clean the bowl?"

"Sure." Serena started measuring out the shortening. "And I guess this is as good a time as any to tell you about what happened Saturday night."

"I would like to hear your story," Miriam said gently. Serena was eighteen years old, beyond accounting to her on many fronts. But that didn't change Miriam's love and sense of responsibility for her niece.

"I'm sorry if you were disturbed when I didn't come home." Serena poked at the butter and shortening with a spoon. "I know Scout came here, knocking on the door."

"I did hear a bit of commotion," Miriam said.

"Gott gives mothers an extra set of ears," Mammi added.

"But I stayed in bed. I knew that someone would wake me if I was needed."

"So . . ." Serena hesitated. "The truth is, Scout and I got

in an argument, and it was worse than I ever expected."
Her voice wobbled as she added, "He broke up with me."

"I'm sorry to hear that." Miriam kept her eyes on the
cherries she was dicing, trying to let Serena unravel her
story in her own time.

"I was mad at him, really upset and angry. I wouldn't
let him give me a ride home, and I ran into some kids from
high school at the burger place. I drank some whiskey,
and ended up going off in a car with Johnny and his
friends. He's this guy I met at school. I guess I figured
that he'd give me a ride home, but he turned out to be
really rotten. So I stormed out of his car and ended up
walking alone. And then these nice Amish kids gave me a
ride, and I got help from the police, and those guys came
to pick me up."

"Are you all right?" Miriam asked.

She nodded. "No one hurt me, except for Scout
breaking up with me, but that's to be expected. I just . . .
I miss him so much, and he won't even let me talk to
him." She railed at the contents of the bowl until Miriam
stopped her.

"That's some strong stirring there. I think we're ready
to add the eggs and vanilla."

"So Mammi," Serena said. "Do you have any Amish
tricks for winning back a guy you love?"

Esther's eyes opened wide, as if the question thrilled
her. "Whenever you need help, the best trick in the book
is prayer to God Almighty."

"Yeah, I've been trying that."

"Don't give up," said Miriam. "And what's this about
Scout? Can't you talk to him when he picks up the milk?"

"He's off the route." Serena frowned. "He hates me that much."

"Or he loves you that much," Mammi said. "It's possible that he can't bear to see you, or else his resolve will crack."

"Maybe you should pay him a visit," Miriam said. "A surprise. I could take you to his house tomorrow after school when I go into town."

"I can call his mom, Bonnie, and pretend we're coming by to pick up furniture," Serena said.

Miriam nodded. "At least, he should talk to you."

"Thanks." Serena sighed. "I know you're probably disappointed with me, but trust me, I'm more disappointed with myself. I was just so mad, and in this wild split second, it felt like everything was just going to slip back to where I was back in Philadelphia, hanging out and drinking and partying and just trying to kill the pain. So I started drinking, and now I feel so guilty about it. And so embarrassed. Staying out all night doesn't bring me pleasure anymore. I've changed since I got here."

"You have," Miriam agreed. "When you first pulled up here with your father, I thought we might end up dealing with some runaway teens." She smiled. "You proved me wrong, and flourished beyond my expectations."

'That's so sweet of you to notice." Serena came around the butcher-block counter and gave her a hug. "So many good things have happened here. I just . . . I'm so disappointed about Scout. My heart is breaking."

"Oh, dear girl." Miriam patted her shoulder. "It's always hard for me to see my children suffer. Same goes for you and your sisters. You've been here only a few weeks, barely months, and I know your pain as if you were my own."

Serena let out her breath in a huge sigh. "That makes me feel a little better, though I don't know why." She stepped back from Miriam and looked down at the large mixing bowl. "We'd better finish this batch off before I start crying in the cookies!"

Chapter Twenty-Eight

After a night spent cleaning and scrubbing the Dawdi House from floor to ceiling, Essie should have been exhausted. Instead, she felt exhilarated. Humming a song, she didn't care about the gray skies overhead or the weariness that tugged at her. Her grandmother had given her a solution to a gnawing problem, and her heart was full of gratitude and joy as she turned Comet onto the narrow street by the park and pulled up in front of the Hostetler home.

Collette sat alone on the porch, bundled in a shawl and reading from a paperback novel. She seemed surprised to see the rig towed by Essie's buggy.

Equally surprised, Linda popped out the door, hands on her hips, seemingly annoyed by the intrusion. "What are you doing towing that horse trailer, Essie?"

"Are we going for a ride?" Collette asked, pushing up from the chair handles to hold on to her walker.

"I've come to take you home."

"To Ohio?" Linda asked. "It's too far to travel in a horse trailer and buggy. You'll never make it."

Of course, Essie knew that. She would be glad to be

free of Linda's gloom and doom for a bit. "We're not going that far," Essie said. "Mem and Mammi and I have made a place for you and Harlan and Suzie in our Dawdi House. That is, if you want it."

Collette gasped. "That sounds wonderful good!" She stepped the walker closer to Essie and added under her breath, "God bless you."

The three women went inside, and Essie helped Collette gather her things. Linda watched over them with her arms crossed, as if Collette's departure was an annoyance to her. Essie had to accept the fact that she might never understand Linda Hostetler. It was a relief when Linda left the room.

"So here's my plan. If you really want to go to Ohio, Harlan and I will figure out a way to get you there, as soon as you finish your physical therapy sessions. For now, I'm taking you to the Dawdi House at my parents' farm. It's been empty for a few years, since Mammi moved in with my Uncle Lloyd and Aunt Greta. The house is one story, so you should be able to manage getting around on your own. And our family will leave you alone as much or as little as you like."

"Such a blessing that would be." Collette pressed her fingertips to her lips. "And it's big enough for Suzie to join me?"

"It's three small bedrooms. Large enough for Suzie and Harlan to move in." Essie fixed her gaze on Collette. "And me, after Harlan and I get married."

Collette's dark eyes glimmered as she pressed her fingertips to Essie's cheek. "Soon to be my daughter-in-law. Dear Essie, I always knew you were the one for my son."

Essie covered Collette's hand with hers, sinking onto

the bed with relief at the long journey it had been to arrive at this point.

"I'm so happy for you and Harlan. Have you told your parents?"

"They know." Funny how Mem had seemed to know all along. When Essie had started selling jam, Miriam had commented that it would be a perfect business to run out of her home after she was married with children. Her mem had always known what was in Essie's heart.

Collette cocked her head to one side. "Is it still a secret, or can we talk about it freely? I've expected this wonderful development, but kept it quiet, of course. Joyous though it is, it's not my news to reveal."

Was that why Collette had never brought up the subject? All this time Essie had worried that Collette had kept silent on it because she didn't really approve of Harlan's marrying her. All those worries for naught! It was another example of how Essie would have been wise to put her trust in Gott for things to go right.

"You can tell folks about it. The bans are being published, and we're getting invitations printed."

"May Gott bless your marriage and join your hearts together for a lifetime of love."

Essie did most of the packing, while Collette gave instructions. "Over on the hook"—Collette nodded—"that black shawl is mine. The kapp, too."

"Don't forget your books," Linda said, returning with a paper sack of paperbacks, which she dumped at Essie's feet.

"Should I leave some for you?" Collette offered. "Pick some out."

"You can take them all." Linda turned away, muttering

under her breath, "I'm not in the mood to read, and I'm sick of looking at them."

"All right then," Collette said, keeping an even tone. Essie just kept packing, thinking what a relief it would be to have Collette out of here.

In no time, Essie had loaded Collette's belongings into the buggy. She opened the doors to the trailer and moved the wooden platform in place. She checked to make sure it was stable, and then went behind Collette's wheelchair.

"Here we go," Essie said, feeling a light flutter of joy in her heart.

"Good-bye, Linda," Collette called as Essie pushed her up the slight incline into the trailer. "Thanks for the hospitality!"

In the weeks that followed, Essie split her time between planning the wedding and coordinating the Yoder Medical Fund Auction. While Collette was still on a sure path to recovery, and Suzie had healed but for the scarred area on her cheek, which had gotten infected, the move to the Dawdi House had brought the family joy in their reunification. The little house, with its compact kitchen and single-story living space, had proved to be quite easy for Collette to navigate on her own.

"With every sunrise," Collette had said recently, "I thank Gott for a new day in a new home with my family." With Suzie's assistance, Collette was able to cook for her family, and already they'd sent two batches of fresh-baked cookies over to share with the Lapps. On wash day, Miriam and Essie were happy to include the Yoders' laundry, though Collette assured them it would not be for long.

When it came to the wedding planning, Essie was pleased to have Collette close by. With more than a hundred invitations to send out, Essie's burden was eased when Collette offered to address envelopes in her exquisite penmanship. Essie had cherished the evenings when she and Harlan and Collette had sat round the small table in the Dawdi House. Essie and Harlan stuffed and stamped envelopes, while Collette copied addresses onto them.

"This brings me back to memories of planning my wedding to Jed," Collette said. The new color in her cheeks made her seem ten years younger. "We were so in love, our heads in the clouds. It must have driven my mem crazy, but she got me through. A callus formed on my finger, a lump beside my fingernail, from all the writing I had to do. But that was so long ago." She looked to the ceiling, counting. "Your father and I were young. I was just eighteen. What did I know about life?" She shook her head.

"You knew enough to trust in Gott," Harlan said.

Essie asked Collette about her wedding to Jed Yoder, and Collette remembered the colors her bridal party had worn, along with the many pounds of chicken that had been prepared and served by family members. "Have you chosen your newehockers?" Collette asked.

"Yah. My friends Sadie and Laura will be in the wedding, as well as my sister Annie." Essie explained that she would have liked her three English cousins to be included, as she had grown close to them in the months that they'd been living here. But at least the English relatives would be allowed to attend the wedding.

"They seem like nice girls," Collette said.

"They are," Harlan agreed, warming Essie's heart.

"It turns out that cousin Megan is good on the sewing machine, particularly at pumping the treadle. She's helping me sew my dress, as well as dresses for the newehockers." Essie had chosen a deep royal-purple fabric for her wedding dress, which she would later use as a church dress. The attendants' dresses would be sewn from forest-green cloth, and the female cousins and friends who would work as servers were being asked to wear burgundy red, with an overall look that would celebrate the Christmas season of Christ's birth.

Mem was helping Essie with the rest of the wedding planning. They had rented two tents, the bench wagon, and the wedding cook wagon and cooler. A large order of chickens would arrive days before the wedding.

Meanwhile Essie's friends Sadie and Laura had been helping her coordinate the auction vendors and donations. At first Essie had thought Sadie's beau Mark would be a helpful resource since his dat owned the auction house where Mark was an Amish auctioneer. But in her dealings with Mark, Essie had grown disturbed by the way he treated Sadie.

Just yesterday, when Sadie and Essie had visited the auction house, the exchange with Mark had been unpleasant.

"You want a discount on the auction house fee just because the money goes to the Yoders?" Mark had railed at Sadie as Essie stayed a discreet distance away. "We're in business to make a profit, Sadie," he'd said.

"I know that, Mark, but it's for charity, for medical expenses." Sadie's green eyes had flashed upon Essie with a look of distress before she turned back to Mark. "Please.

Can't you help? Maybe you can donate your fees as an auctioneer for the day?"

"Is this how much you value my work?" Mark had demanded. "Dat and I conduct auctions in two languages. Do you know the value of an auctioneer who can speak both English and German, rapidly?"

"I do value your work," Sadie had said, head down and gazing at the ground. "I'm sorry, Mark. I'm just trying to help a family in need."

"Well, you want to think twice before you try to harm the business of my family because you want to do a good deed."

After that Sadie had apologized again, and Essie had tried to sweep her out of the auction house as quickly as possible. Their other errands in town had gone so well, as they'd convinced the baker and even Hostetler's harness shop to make donations to the auction. Essie hated to end the day on a sour note.

"Come with me to Smitty's Pretzel Factory," Essie had said once they were in the buggy. "We'll offer Suzie a ride home, and I'll buy you a buttery hot pretzel."

Sadie nodded. "You're a good friend," she'd said, then let out a sob.

"Ach, I think I know why you're crying, Schazti," Essie said, using a Pennsylvania Dutch term of endearment. "Mark needs to treat you better."

"I love him," Sadie had cried, leaning back into the privacy of the buggy. "I do love him, but I always do the wrong thing around him."

"From my view you did nothing wrong. It's our way as Amish to help our neighbors and treat everyone with kindness. Mark is the one who's not following the golden rule."

"But it's his family business," Sadie had lamented. "I was wrong to ask him a favor."

Essie didn't agree, but she didn't want to push her friend. "Don't be so hard on yourself," she said. "Maybe if the bishop talks with him, Mark will come around before the auction. But for now, shall we get those pretzels?"

Sadie nodded, trying to dry her eyes. "I can't let my friends at work see me crying." She had worked at Smitty's since she'd finished at the Amish schoolhouse, and the place had become like a second home to her.

"You have a few minutes to pull yourself together," Essie said as they went on their way. But the incident had stayed on Essie's mind, and she decided that Sadie would not be asked to deal with Mark again on auction business. Best to leave the two of them without tensions that might pull them apart.

Chapter Twenty-Nine

Life with a broken heart wasn't easy.

Serena had learned that cookies were still sweet and the stars were still amazing gems in the night sky, but somehow the joy those things had once brought her was diminished by her loss. Occasionally she was able to distract herself in the woodshop or at school or goofing around with her younger Amish cousins. But most of the time Serena missed Scout with a physical ache, like a bad cramp. The past weeks without him seemed like ten years, and she was beginning to wonder if she would need to leave Joyful River behind to clear her mind of him. Since the thought of leaving her new home only intensified her grief, she tried to shake that idea off.

Of course, everyone around her was trying to help. Megan let her talk about Scout and the foibles of relationships. Essie dragged her into the auction planning, sending Serena to solicit support from the English shopkeepers in town. Serena had to admit, she was pretty good at it. If the furniture thing didn't work out, sales might be her thing. Grace was full of practical advice, and Aunt Miriam always made Serena feel good about herself by expecting the best from her. It was a quality that reminded Serena of her mother: that vision of her best qualities, the expectation of positive things. In Serena's darkest moments, Aunt Miriam brought random rays of light.

As planned during their cookie baking session, Aunt Miriam had driven her to Scout's house, an appointment made under the guise of acquiring another piece of furniture from Scout's mother. They'd gotten a mile or so from the house when rain began to pour from the sky, dancing on the street and slanting through the air. Aunt Miriam had showed Serena how to put the plastic sheets down over the buggy's side openings, but water dripped inside, forming a puddle on the floor.

Aunt Miriam had moved her feet from the water in good humor. "We're so fortunate it's just rain. In a few months, snow will be coming down, and that would make for a challenging ride being pulled by good old Comet."

At Scout's house Serena had gone to the door and rung the bell as Aunt Miriam waited in the buggy. Serena smoothed back her hair and shook out her hands, a bundle of nerves at the prospect of seeing Scout.

But Bonnie had answered the door and told her Scout was at the firehouse. "Sorry to disappoint you, honey, but he made it clear that he didn't want to be here when you came around."

Another stab through the heart.

Serena had braced herself to keep breathing as she followed Bonnie to the garage. The space was still crowded with furniture, but now there was at least a narrow space to walk through to the back.

They had considered the possibilities and Serena had

chosen a console table, along with a low dresser that she would donate to the auction.

"I'll throw in the dresser for free, since it's for charity," Bonnie said. "My advice on that is to keep it as simple as possible if you want to appeal to the Amish. Color is okay, but no patterns or fancy knobs."

"Good advice," Serena said. "Thanks." She had hoisted the console table, and then put it back down again. "Before I go, I just have to ask. Did Scout tell you what happened?"

"He did."

"Can you help me understand? Or maybe you can help me get a message to him. I really need to talk to him."

"I'm sorry." Bonnie had tilted her head to the side, her eyes sad. "Let's keep this as strictly business. I think you're a remarkable young woman, Serena. Creative and energetic, with a good head on your shoulders. But I can't tell my son how to live his life." She winked. "Much as I'd like to try. He's got to figure his own path."

Serena had nodded as if she understood. In truth, she felt more lost than ever.

"Now, can I help you load this into your buggy? It looks like we have a little break in the rain."

"I think we can handle it." Aunt Miriam was suddenly beside Serena, taking one end of the skinny table.

Serena had lifted the other end of the table and they had carried it easily to the back of the buggy. The dresser was a little heavier, but Aunt Miriam made it seem light as a feather. As they were loading the rain had begun again, and Serena had been relieved to have an excuse to wave good-bye to Bonnie and duck into the buggy.

"That didn't go well," Serena said.

"She's trying to protect her son," Aunt Miriam said. "It's difficult when each person is trying to solve their part of the puzzle, but the puzzle pieces just don't fit."

"Well, thanks for helping me. Even though none of my puzzle pieces fit quite right."

Miriam had chuckled as rain tapped on the roof of the buggy.

"I'm serious. Scout told me I'm pushy, and I know that's true. I've made a lot of mistakes, and now they're all catching up with me."

"Dear Serena, love covers a multitude of sins. I know *that's* true because it's in the Bible."

Serena had followed a raindrop as it wriggled down the plastic window. "Then it looks like I'm going to need a lot of love."

Day after day, Serena pushed herself to keep busy and lose herself in activities that gave her a temporary break from thinking about Scout. As autumn leaves swirled in the air and rested in thick, crunchy blankets along the lane, she felt the new season as a passageway. Leaves and flowers withered and died in the fall, but then, come springtime, blossoms and foliage would be reborn in splashes of color and sweet fragrance.

Life went on. And though she dearly missed Scout, she couldn't give up on love. As Aunt Miriam told her, there were so many kinds of love in God's world. Serena was blessed to have the love of a wonderful Amish and English family.

One afternoon in late October, Serena was riding the boxy yellow school bus home with her sisters when they were stopped in traffic and smoke. Since only a dozen or so kids rode the bus out to their area, most people scattered and took their own seats. Now a group of kids gathered at the windows on Serena's side of the bus.

"It's a fire," someone said.

Serena had thought someone was burning leaves, but as the bus crept up in the traffic, she could see that the billowing black smoke was coming from a burning barn.

"Guys, look at this," Serena said, catching the attention of her sisters, who were tapping away on their cell phones while they were still in range of service.

Grace crossed the aisle of the bus and squeezed in beside Serena, and Megan put her phone down to stare out the window.

"Ooh. Looks bad," Grace said.

Two large fire trucks and a smaller red vehicle were there, and firefighters on the ladder truck pumped water onto the charred frame of the barn. The roofline still outlined the wall, but the second story seemed to have collapsed to the ground.

As the bus moved up and stopped again, Serena studied each firefighter in search of Scout. It was hard to identify them, as they wore the same black helmets and khaki jackets with stripes of neon-yellow reflective tape. But she would know his distinctive swagger and broad shoulders anywhere. She watched the guys near the trucks, the guys on the ladder, the guys handling the giant hose, but none of them seemed to be Scout.

Well, she could be grateful that he was safe.

"That's an Amish farm," said one of the kids on the bus. A sophomore named Dustin with curly dark hair and glasses that magnified his eyes. "It belongs to the Graber family. My brother has done some work for them during harvest season."

The Grabers . . . Serena wondered if Aunt Miriam knew them. She couldn't take her eyes off the scene as the bus moved slowly. Where was Scout? He would have been summoned to a fire this extensive. The image of the blackened barn stuck in her mind as traffic thinned and the bus finally picked up speed.

She was talking about the fire with Grace when her phone buzzed. She grabbed it quickly, knowing they would be out of range once they passed the hills ahead.

She was surprised to see Bonnie Tanner's number.

"Hi, Bonnie."

"Serena, I'm so glad I could reach you." Bonnie's voice was high pitched, strained. "Listen, Scout's been injured, and he's asking for you. Can you come to Lancaster Hope Hospital?"

Panic fluttered in Serena's chest. "I . . . Of course. Is he okay?"

"I'm on my way, so I don't have all the facts. The doctors say he's being treated for smoke inhalation and a shoulder injury."

"He was at the fire!" Serena pressed a hand to her mouth. "We just passed the fire scene. The whole top of the barn collapsed."

"Please, will you come to the hospital? I promised him I'd reach out to you."

"I'll figure out a ride."

"Call me when you're close, and I'll come find you in the ER."

* * *

Within a half hour Serena was on her way to the hospital, sandwiched in the buggy between Essie and Megan, who had insisted on coming along for moral support. Aunt Miriam had hitched up a second buggy upon hearing of the fire on the property of her friend, Rose Graber. "At a time like this, everyone needs help," Miriam had said.

Tension filled the buggy, but Serena couldn't let herself be gripped by fear. She had the support of her sister and her cousin, and her faith in God. She kept taking deep breaths to calm her racing pulse.

As they approached the hospital she sent Bonnie a text, and the older woman met her at the emergency room entrance.

"Thank you for coming!" Bonnie greeted Serena with open arms and folded her into a hug. "He's okay. The doctors think he'll be okay, but it was so close."

"What happened?"

"The fire was in the hayloft. They're still investigating it, but two boys have admitted to playing with firecrackers. Once a fire sparked, the hay bales fueled the fire quickly. One of the little boys escaped, but a second one was stranded up in the loft. The firefighters put the ladder up, and Scout climbed in. He got the little boy to the man on the ladder, but before Scout could get out, the hayloft collapsed. He was pulled from the embers after they freed him from a heavy beam that fell and hit his shoulder."

Essie clapped her hands together in a prayerful gesture. "Thank Gott they got him out."

"It sounds like he's a hero," Megan said.

Serena could only shake her head, mesmerized by Bonnie's account.

"It's a miracle he survived this," Bonnie said. "Scout

has always kept it a secret, but the farm accident left him with a metal plate in his skull. It took him more than a year to come back from head trauma, but he was left with a very vulnerable part in his skull. If that beam had landed a few inches toward his head, he might not be here now."

"A miracle," Serena whispered, tears in her eyes. *Oh, thank you, God. I may not have Scout in my life, but I couldn't bear it if he weren't in this world. Thank you!*

They were still standing in the lobby, blocking part of the entrance. Seeming to snap back to the present, Bonnie motioned them to come into the waiting room. She put a hand on Serena's shoulder. "Scout asked me to bring you in as soon as you got here. They have him on oxygen right now, but he can talk. Do you think you can handle seeing him?"

Serena nodded.

Megan squeezed her hand. "We'll wait right here," she said, and Essie nodded.

After watching her mother die, Serena hated the smells and sounds of a hospital. The beeping monitors and shiny tile floors. The antiseptic odor. The feeling of being one small, unremarkable bee in a buzzing hive of activity. She tamped down her discomfort and followed Scout's mother to his room, pausing in the doorway.

The beeping monitors and screens were there, with tubes attached to the young man resting in the hospital bed. A clear plastic mask covered much of his face. His chest was bare, one shoulder wrapped in white bandages and resting in a sling. Red blisters rose along one side of his neck, and his hair had been buzzed off on the sides, revealing the beginnings of the red scar he had always tried to hide.

You don't know me. He'd once told her that, and now, standing here, she wondered if she'd always been projecting the man she wanted on Scout Tanner.

He opened his eyes, blue as a summer sky, and the entire room changed. He pulled the mask down below his chin, and once again, she knew him.

"Scout." She came to the edge of the bed, wanting to touch him but wary.

He lifted his right hand, and, even with the clip on his index finger, he took her hand. "I'm glad you're here. I needed to see you."

She squeezed his hand, energized by a jolt of relief. "How are you feeling?"

"I've been better, but I'd rather be here with burns and torn ligaments than not be here at all."

She nodded. "I'm glad you're here. You changed your hair."

He laughed, rolling his head to the side until the laughter turned into a coarse cough. "I have undergone a style change. Some of my hair got singed, so I told them to go for it and buzz the sides. Now you can see the real me. The good, the bad, and the wounded."

"I like it. Well, not that you got wounded." She leaned in for a better look. On closer scrutiny she could see the slightly altered shape of his skull in the spot where the red scar disappeared under the blond hair they'd left on top. Yes, there was a scar there, but nothing that noticeable. "Brings out your cheekbones."

"I figured you'd see the positives."

"You know, I brought you a gift, but I guess you won't need it anymore." She reached into the pocket of her jacket and pulled out a baseball cap with the Phillies logo on it.

"Nice. I'm not sure if I'm going to stick with the hat thing."

"Why deprive the world of beauty?" she asked.

"Thanks. But I didn't ask you to come here to ply me with compliments. I wanted to apologize for cutting you off. That was wrong, I know that now. I snapped. I pushed everyone away. I'm afraid I hurt you the most because you're the one I care about the most."

Had he just said "care," as in the present tense? She bit her lower lip to keep her emotions in check.

"I don't really remember the accident on the tractor," he said. "That was a long time ago, and my memory suffered from it. But this incident today . . . It's clear as a bell. I remember it vividly, the smells of smoke and charred wood, the sounds of wood cracking and the little boy who was calling for help. Ezra Graber. The kid got out okay, and me, just minor injuries. But it could have happened differently. A few seconds one way or the other, and I wouldn't be here."

"I'm so glad it happened the way it did," she said.

"Me too. But I have to tell you, in that split second when I felt the floor let loose beneath me, I thought of you."

Her throat went dry. "Me?"

He nodded. "I've been so miserable since we ended things, and I thought, if I have to go now, you're my one regret. That I didn't try harder for you. That I didn't shake off the hermit thing and be the man you deserve."

Tears filled her eyes, and she dashed them away, not wanting to lose sight of him.

"I hope you can forgive me," he said.

"I do."

"I don't know if you've started seeing someone else. If you are—"

"I'm not," she said. "I haven't been able to get over you. I love you, Scout."

"I love you, too." He reached for her, and she leaned over him for a light, sweet kiss that restored the joy Serena found in life.

"Wow." His blue eyes sparkled as he brought her hand to his chest. "This is my lucky day."

They looked at each other and laughed. They were still laughing when his mom returned with the nurse, who checked his vitals and looked at the monitor.

"Sorry to disturb you," Bonnie said, "but the waiting room is full of people who want to thank you, Scout. That little Amish boy, Ezra, has a big family, and apparently they're all here."

"It's like a fan club," said the nurse.

Serena smiled. "And I bet Aunt Miriam brought my Amish family, too. And Megan and Essie came with me, so they'll want to see you."

He closed his eyes and let out a breath. "Is it too late to ask for that hat?"

She held the hat out to him. "Anytime."

He paused, and then shook his head. "Nah. I'm going for it."

The nurse pushed a chair over beside the bed so that Serena could sit near Scout, and Bonnie looked back at her son. "Should I go get your fans?"

He pumped the fist of his uninjured arm in the air. "Bring it on."

Chapter Thirty

Auction day!

Essie had been down in the kitchen before sunrise, starting coffee, loading wood into the potbelly stove, and starting a pound of bacon sizzling for the family breakfast. While she was cooking, the day dawned cold and bright, with the mercury only in the forties. Standing at the kitchen sink, looking at the orange and purple glow on the horizon beyond the slightly frosted window, Essie suspected it would warm up to a more comfortable mid-fifties, just like yesterday.

Soon Mem came into the kitchen to take over, pulling out a dozen eggs. Essie poured a mug of coffee, pulled a shawl over her shoulders, and carried the steaming liquid out the back door and down the path that had become exceedingly familiar in the past few weeks. Winding around the vegetable garden, she went to the back of the Dawdi House and tapped on the window.

The green shade moved up, and Harlan's smiling face filled the window. He unlatched it, swung the glass open, and leaned out to kiss her. The touch of his lips stole her breath away, and she gravitated toward the warmth coming from his body. He wore a long-sleeved cotton jersey shirt for sleeping, and his eyelids still had that hooded, sleepy look that made her heart melt. How she loved seeing him first thing in the morning. Soon she would wake up beside him instead of having to steal out in the cold.

He took a sip from the mug and grunted. "Essie . . ." His amber eyes reminded her of warm honey. "That's the most delicious cup of coffee I've ever tasted."

She smiled. "Denki, but you say that every morning."

"Because it's true."

"Are they getting ready to go?"

"They're up. I'm sure they're ironing their Sunday clothes."

"Well, your mem is the guest of honor."

"She is. Will you come along in our buggy?"

"I will, as long as you're not late. I want to make sure the parking attendants are in place to take care of horses and buggies."

"The Millers hold auctions all year long. I think they can manage the buggy parking."

"You're right. I just want everything to go smoothly."

"Then we'll get there early to ease your mind." He kissed her again and started closing the window. "And when you come tomorrow, I wouldn't mind a little bacon."

She tossed one end of her shawl over her shoulder and shook her head. "For that, you'll have to wait until we're wed."

His laughter was still booming in the morning air when she rounded the garden.

* * *

"What? Wait!" Serena gestured to the line of traffic in front of Scout's truck. "All these people are waiting to get into the parking lot at the auction house?"

"Yes, they are."

"This is huge. It's definitely going to be a success."

"I hope so. Medical bills can really put a family in debt, and I'd like to help the Yoders."

"I've never been to an auction before," Serena admitted. "So they're popular around here?"

"They are. Probably the biggest auction of the year is the annual mud sale held in the early spring to benefit the local volunteer fire department. They call it the mud sale because the ground is usually wet and mucky that time of year."

"So why don't they do it in the summer?"

"They like to hold it in March, after the harvest and before spring planting, so that more local farmers can attend. It helps fund equipment and gear for us firefighters. But charity auctions pop up throughout the year," Scout explained. "What time is your dad supposed to be here?" he asked as he found a parking spot a few blocks away.

"He said around lunchtime, so we should keep an eye out for him." Sully had promised to drive out for the auction, and then stay for dinner at the Lapp farm.

In the distance a sea of people, Amish and English, mingled on the grounds of the auction house. The crowd was a blur punctuated by the bright colors of Amish dresses in green, blue, scarlet, peach, mint, and purple. Among the festive attendees Serena saw countless straw hats, black jackets, baseball caps, and white prayer kapps as people milled around two raised platforms, each one sporting an Amish auctioneer and a few assistants. Conversation bubbled up here and there as people checked out merchandise and ran into friends.

"What are they auctioning over there?" Serena asked, pointing to a distant stage.

"That will be quilts and specialty items. The dresser you donated will probably get auctioned on that stage. The bleachers inside are usually for people bidding on livestock and horses. And over there, in that ring, they'll be doing farm equipment."

"It's such a big operation, and so well attended."

"Yeah. Folks in these parts love a good auction." Scout glanced toward the tent. "They've got food inside. Do you want something?"

"You're hungry?" Serena said.

"I could go for some roasted chicken. And then a whoopie pie for the finish."

"Sounds great!"

Inside the tent, they encountered Rose Graber, who was working at the bake sale. She ran out from behind the stand to clap Scout on the back, and she made sure everyone who passed by knew that he had saved her Ezra from a devastating fire. Men and women walking by thanked Scout, mentioning that they'd seen his photo in the newspaper. Serena stood off to the side, watching with a smile as Scout received the recognition he deserved. She knew that his celebrity would eventually fade, but right now she appreciated him having time in the spotlight, which seemed to reinforce the new Scout. After this, he couldn't go back to being a hermit.

Rose made sure that Scout got a box of whoopie pies.

After that they feasted on grilled chicken and mashed potatoes, and then strolled around some more. Serena was amused by the rapid babble of the auctioneers, calling out numbers in their sing-songy voices. Some called the auction in two languages, which she found amazing, though one language was hard enough to understand when it went that quickly.

Serena and Scout ventured into the horse tent, where tall, silky brown horses waited in a pen to be auctioned. "They're so beautiful," Serena said. "Each one is tagged with a number."

"That's to keep track of them," Scout explained.

"I know, but it would be so much better if they had their names on the tag. You know, Misty or Thunder sounds so much better than horse number 2396."

"True."

They were leaving the horse tent when they ran into Serena's father. "Dad! You made it."

"Hey, honey, I've been looking for you. Your sisters steered me over in this direction."

She hugged him, working around the large pastry box in his arms. "Wow, Dad. Taking a few cookies home? Or are you eating those all today?"

"I'm taking them back to the guys at the police station. I'll score major points with homemade cookies." Sully extended a hand to Scout. "I hear you're a hero, Scout. How're you doing?"

They shook hands. "Doing well, sir."

Serena patted Scout's shoulder. "Yeah, Dad, this is my guy."

"My daughter tells me great things about you," Sully

said. "And that was a spectacular save in the fire. It's fortunate you were able to get those kids out in time."

"I thank God for that every day," Scout said, and Serena smiled up at him, knowing it was true. She linked her fingers through his, so grateful to be by his side.

"I saw your furniture on display over by the quilts," Sully told Serena. "You did great work, honey. I'm really pleased that you've taken the initiative to start your own business."

"Starting small, and I had some help along the way," she said.

"But you're producing something people need and want, in such a creative way. I'm proud of you."

"Thanks, Dad." Praise was not what she usually heard from her father. It used to be that she was the one lectured for getting in trouble. Well, some things had changed.

"So listen, honey. My detective buddy made some inquiries about the man you asked about. Your friend's father?"

"Harlan's father." Serena nodded. She had asked her dad to look into Jed Yoder and see if there was a possibility that he would meet with Harlan. "Did you find him?"

"I did. Harlan's lead about that county in Maryland was helpful, but I'm afraid there's some sad news."

"Oh, no. Wait! Don't tell me." Serena hadn't been expecting Dad's research to backfire. "Let me get Harlan here. He should hear everything from you firsthand."

"I'll go get him," Scout offered.

Serena moved close to her father as Scout headed off. "So? What do you think of Scout? He's amazing, right?"

Sully rubbed his daughter's shoulder. "Does he make you happy?"

"All the time. He's smart and engaging and incredibly self-deprecating. All the qualities I don't have."

"And he makes you happy?"

She nodded. "Absolutely."

"Then he's amazing."

Essie and Harlan stood in the crowd of bidders, watching Mark Miller call the bids on farm equipment. Much as Essie didn't want to like the young man who was so hard on her good friend, she had to admit he was truly gifted as an auctioneer. He was charming, fast-talking, and handsome, for sure, and the way he bounced back and forth, calling the bids in English, then in German, and then in English again was truly remarkable. Seeing Mark in action, Essie began to understand why Sadie was drawn to him.

And in the auction house, where Mark ran the show, Sadie was thrilled to be his girl. She watched him intently and joked with the other girls about not being able to keep up with such a fast-talking beau. Essie wanted Sadie to find her happily ever after with Mark. But Essie had also noticed Mark flirting with other girls a few times when Sadie's back was turned. Such a difficult situation.

Before Essie could fret too much over her friend, she was pulled away from that auction ring by Scout, who had someone she needed to talk with. "Harlan needs to come, too," Scout said. It turned out to be Uncle Sully, who was talking with Serena and Mem. Sully seemed to tighten up a bit when he saw Harlan. Essie listened as Uncle Sully explained that Serena had given him the little she knew about Harlan's dat, and Uncle Sully had used his police connections to get information about Jed Yoder.

"My intention was to find him so that you two could set up a meeting," Sully told Harlan. "But now that we've gotten some information, I'm afraid that won't be possible. Your father passed away, Harlan. I'm sorry."

Harlan hitched his thumbs on his suspenders, taking in the news. He squinted in the distance, as if trying to swallow a bitter pill. "Did you learn anything else about him?"

"We did. The information you had about Somerset County, Maryland, turned out to be a solid lead. He rented a trailer down there. Attended a Mennonite church when he first moved down there, but other than that, he wasn't very active in Maryland. No job, no social life. A neighbor said Jed found it difficult to get out of the house. Seems he might have suffered from depression."

Harlan nodded. "He did suffer some bad spells. I don't remember much, but Mem said he was sad much of the time."

"I wish I had better news for you," said Uncle Sully.

Harlan gave a hard nod. "I'm grateful you found the truth. Thank you. I need to tell my mem and sister. They need to hear it." He turned to Essie, tenderness in his amber eyes, a pain she wished she could soothe.

She could offer the comfort of her arms, and, like a salve applied every night, over time, that would be enough. Enough comfort and love.

Miriam said a silent prayer for Jed Yoder as Harlan and Essie went to find Harlan's family. Such a sad moment for the family. Death was always hard to understand. But

Harlan and Suzie had lived without a father for so many years; the brunt of the news would be somewhat removed for them.

Miriam watched as Harlan searched out Collette. When she lost him in the crowd, Miriam stepped up onto an empty stage behind her and spotted him again. Harlan located his mother sitting beside Suzie at the baked goods booth. Collette bowed her head when the news broke over her. Then she turned to her daughter, who seemed to have many questions.

Harlan left them to comfort each other and, head held high, he moved across the tent, to a group of Amish men. The bishop was extracted from the huddled conversation by Harlan. Concern was plain on the bishop's face as Harlan leaned in to tell him something. After a pause, Aaron patted the young man on the shoulder, consolingly.

So now he knew.

Her eyes were still on the bishop as he scanned the auction tent, searching until his gaze locked on Collette, who was talking with her daughter. Such a play of emotions on the bishop's face as he stared at Collette: relief, restraint, tenderness.

Life would change for Collette Yoder. She was now free to marry, and Miriam knew the perfect match for her. Miriam recalled that feeling of shock she'd felt weeks ago when she'd recognized the love between Aaron and Collette. She smiled at her silliness, thinking that love had come at the wrong place and time. She was the one who'd been wrong. To everything, there was a season, and Gott did not make mistakes.

The crowd parted, and Alvie appeared just below the stage, a curious smile on his face as he looked up at his wife. "Are you set to auction off the next item?" he asked, teasing her.

"I'm just keeping an eye on things," she said, reaching out to him. He helped her down from the stage. "What are you up to, looking like the cat that got the cream?" she asked.

"I just witnessed that Scout Tanner is very famous in Joyful River right now. I was just given a free whoopie pie simply because I'm Serena's uncle."

"And where is this whoopie pie?"

He touched his flat belly. "It was delicious."

Miriam nodded. "It was a wonderful thing that Scout could save Rose's boy. And I'm grateful Scout and Serena were able to find a way back to each other. But mostly, I thank Gott that she's found her way in the world. She's learning the importance of love and family. All three of the English girls are learning important lessons. Do you notice how they've been getting along? Even supporting one another."

"Your sister would be quite satisfied," Alvin said.

"She would, may she rest in peace."

"So . . . one niece is on the right path. That leaves two to go."

Miriam chuckled. Her husband always had a way of reminding her that men and women saw the world through a different lens. "Alvie, they're girls. We're not breaking horses."

"I know that." He touched the brim of his hat. "Horses would be so much easier."

Epilogue

Tomorrow was the day.

Amid the commotion and noise of setting up the large barn that would house tomorrow's reception, Essie Lapp lifted her head from her task of laying out spoons and took in a breath of gratitude. The sight of so many women buzzing around tables decked in Christmassy tablecloths, preparing the room for the festive celebration of her own wedding, overwhelmed Essie with joy.

Her dreams were coming true. Tomorrow morning she and Harlan would marry and begin their lives as husband and wife. Friends and family had been planning and preparing for weeks. Mem had managed to get the main rooms of the house painted for the ceremony, and relatives had come from other Amish communities as far away as Michigan to attend the wedding.

Early this morning the buggy barn had been cleared out for the occasion. Webs and dust had been knocked from the exposed beams in the ceiling, the floors swept and mopped, so that the helpers who pitched in to work on the wedding could set up seating for nearly three hundred. They had unloaded long tables from the wedding wagon and set them up in seven rows so that each table would seat forty. Then the long tables had been covered with tablecloths, alternating green and red for each table. Essie had chosen the colors for the Christmas season, and the cloths matched the dresses of her attendants.

Now the tables were being set, and the women working in the room were like a patchwork quilt of her life. Mem was off in the corner, showing some of her cousins how they should set up the Eck, the special table for the bridal party. At one end of the Eck, Harlan's mem and sister sat folding white paper napkins. Essie's Aunt Greta pushed a rolling cart of china plates as Annie sat each plate on the table, facedown and perfectly spaced. They were followed by small teams comprised of her friends Sadie and Laura, and her English and Amish cousins, who placed silverware and water glasses on the table. Mammi moved along the table, straightening forks and smoothing creases in the tablecloth so that everything was neat as a pin. With so many people working together, they'd have 280 place settings neatly set in no time.

Of course, with dozens of women in the room, the chatter throughout the barn rivaled the birdsong in the riverbank trees on a summer morning. It was a scene that warmed Essie's heart.

"Doesn't it look great?" asked Serena as she unloaded one of the last coffee cups from a tray her twin Megan was holding.

"It looks very inviting," Essie agreed. "Thank you for helping."

"It's not every day you get to set up a party for three hundred people," Megan said.

Three hundred . . . how the guest list had grown!

"Are you nervous?" asked Grace, who was taking a break from setting out knives. "I mean, will you be with all these people watching you tomorrow?"

"I've been too busy to get nervous," Essie said. "Which is a good thing. You know I'm shy in front of strangers, but there'll be no strangers here. Everyone who's coming is either a friend or family."

"People who love you," Serena said, her face puckering briefly with emotion. "Aw. We love you, too, Essie, and we're so happy for you." She shoved the empty tray in her sister's arms so that she could lean over and give Essie a hug.

"She's not married yet," Grace said. "Save some of that for tomorrow."

"She'll be getting plenty of well wishes tomorrow," Annie called from one of the rolling carts. "Better get your moment while you can."

As they chatted Lizzie popped in the door and hurried toward them, the cold seeping from her coat. "Dat sent me," she said breathlessly. "Harlan is here, and he wants to talk to Essie."

"Ooh," Serena said. "The groom is in the house."

"And Dat wants Annie to come help with the evening milking."

"I'll be right there," Annie said as Lizzie took Essie's hand.

"Come," Lizzie said. "I promised Harlan I wouldn't come back without you."

Essie smiled at the young women gathered around her. "Come to the house when you're finished setting up . . . everyone. Aunt Greta and Mammi brought sandwiches and soup for supper."

Lizzie took Essie's hand and led her out the door. A

blustery December wind rippled the skirt of her dress and her apron as Essie stepped out of the buggy barn. Beside her, Lizzie let out a whoop, and Essie put an arm around her sister and held her close as they hurried down the path to the house.

"Don't go blowing away from me before the wedding," Essie teased.

"I won't! I don't want to miss a minute of it," Lizzie said. "Mem keeps calling it secret vows. If it's a secret, how come everyone can watch?"

"*Sacred* vows," Essie corrected. "That means it's blessed by Gott."

"That's what she's been saying?" Lizzie rolled her eyes. "That changes everything."

They skirted around the wedding wagon, the RV where helpers were using one of the six ovens to bake bread and make other preparations for tomorrow's wedding. Lizzie led Essie to the house, where the door and shades were open and the inside lights seemed bright against the gathering dusk. The first floor was a hub of activity as men carried furniture out to the storage shed and worked on dismantling the temporary wall between the kitchen and the living room. The space was being cleared so that they could hold the wedding ceremony here, and then move the celebration to the buggy barn for the dinner.

Although there were at least a dozen men moving furniture, Essie spotted Harlan immediately; the heart had its way of finding its match. He was hoisting one end of the sofa, carrying it out with her cousin Isaac Lapp. Isaac was a good friend of her brother Sam, one of a handful of young men in Sam's buddy bunch, most of whom were still not baptized or married.

"There you are!" Harlan called, smiling the moment he laid eyes on Essie. "I have something for you. Give me a minute to get this out to the shed."

"I got it." Sam edged close to Harlan and took his end of the couch. "We don't want the groom to strain himself the night before the wedding."

"I'd carry two couches on my back if they'd let me," Harlan joked, and the guys around them chuckled.

As Harlan motioned Essie and Lizzie over to the shelves in the living room, Essie noticed how relaxed he seemed. A good, healthy pink had returned to his skin tone, and the lines of worry had dissolved from his face. The strains of the past few months seemed behind them now, and she was ever so hopeful for their future together.

"Here's your quarter for fetching your sister," he said, handing Lizzie a silver coin.

"Denki." She beamed up at him. "It's going in my piggy bank." Lizzie was always saving up for some book or art supplies. She touched Essie's arm. "Wait 'til you see what he made for you!"

Harlan took something else from the shelf and presented it to Essie. It was a chunk of wood smoothed and finished to a rich sheen, with a carving on one side. "Another bookend."

Essie's breath caught in her throat as she accepted the well-crafted wooden sculpture. "And now my books can stand on their own. The set is complete." Just as Harlan would complete her life as her husband.

The gift hit an emotional cord within her. The thoughtful simplicity of it, the meaning of it, made her throat tighten up. She hadn't expected this, but here, on the eve of her wedding, she was being reminded of the big step she was about to take, and the goodness of the man she'd fallen in love with.

"What's the matter?" Lizzie asked. "Don't you like it?"

"I like it so very much." Essie's fingers smoothed over the engraving in the smooth oval—a sheaf of wheat. "It's solid and delicate at the same time."

"Just like you," Harlan said. "The wheat stands for love and charity. That's you, Essie. You have such a big heart."

She waved the notion off as her eyes misted with tears. "You make it so easy to love you."

"Good grief," Lizzie said. "This is getting too corny for a kid like me."

Harlan's laugh was deep and rich as he touched Lizzie's shoulder. "You'd best get used to it."

Essie ran her hand over the carving once more, and then handed it to her younger sister. "Will you take this upstairs for me? Put it in a safe place, maybe on the dresser."

Lizzie nodded, accepting the important task with reverence.

Once Lizzie turned away, Harlan grabbed Essie's hand, and they stole out the door and around the side of the porch, away from the hustle and bustle of the setup. Cold swirled around them, but they found a spot in a nook sheltered from the wind, and Harlan's hands rubbed some heat into Essie's arms and shoulders.

"Essie . . ." The warmth of his smile reached his amber eyes. It was the special way he looked at her, the light in his eyes that told her time and again that she was the woman he truly loved.

Glancing up at him, she felt her knees soften like warm candle wax. "Will it always be this way when you're near?"

she whispered. "My heart is thumping like a rabbit, and my legs feel weak."

One of his dark brows lifted. "Your legs might turn to jelly, but you're the strongest woman I know. You held me up when the world seemed to be falling around me. The buggy accident. My mem wanting to leave. Me thinking I had to go with her." He shook his head. "Through it all, you were there, my rock."

"Gott was there," she said.

"And you, Essie. You work in humble ways, but your love and support hold up so many folks. Not just me. I see how you take care of your brothers and sisters and cousins. My mem, and yours, too. Your mem keeps saying she doesn't know what she'll do without you at home."

"My mem . . ." The thought of her dear mother choked Essie up all over again. Her parents had raised her in a home of love and faith, and now it was time for Harlan and her to make such a home of their own. "Did you tell my mem she's not losing a daughter but gaining a son?"

When he smiled, the shifting light of dusk caught his handsome face. "Your family has always welcomed me with open arms, and that's been important to me. Growing up with just Mem and Suzie, I've always wanted the noise and love of a big family."

"Now you'll have the loud and loving Lapps," Essie said.

"And you." He moved closer, and she rested her hands on his shoulders, thinking of how right this was, to be warmed by Harlan's embrace. This was where she belonged. "I can't wait to be married to you, Essie. Tomorrow can't come soon enough."

She nodded slowly, all the while basking in the light of

his amber eyes. "Just the two of us, on our own. No more waiting for youth events or Saturday night so that we can be together. And with Gott's blessings, we'll soon start a family of our own."

A new light sparked in his eyes. "Children would make me the happiest man on earth. And you'll be such a good mother. Loving and caring. And a good cook, too."

"And now, my family is yours. And our children . . ."

"Will have their mother's beautiful smile and strong heart, Gott willing."

"And their father's golden eyes and talent for wood-working."

"And a loving Amish home," he said.

"A home bursting with love." It was the last thing she said before rising onto her toes, pressing into his warm embrace, and losing herself in his kiss.